Love is Forever

By

Melissa A. Ross

Merry Christm[as]

To Jen

Thanks for your support
and belief in me.

M. Ross

12/23/02

ISBN: 1-4033-1667-8 (Ebook)
ISBN: 1-4033-1668-6 (Softcover)
ISBN: 1-4033-1669-4 (Hardcover)

Library of Congress Control Number: 2002091208

This book is printed on acid free paper.

Printed in the United States of America
Bloomington, IN

1stBooks - rev. 04/25/02

Prologue

Bristol, Louisiana

1970

Ms. Melinda smiled into the light as she saw the face of her beloved husband Javier. Oh to walk into his arms once again after nearly 40 years. Tears of joy slid down her cheeks as she rejoiced at their being reunited. Yes she could hear him calling her name a little louder now, reaching out to grasp his hand she cries out as he moves away, just barely out of reach. It almost seemed as if he was trying to tell her to turn around. But that is impossible why would he not want her to join him? She is puzzled as he motions frantically for her to go back. Just as she calls out to him for an explanation, she is awakened by her daughter.

"Mother, wake up, you're dreaming", said Camille.

"NO, no", cried a distraught Ms. Melinda, "Don't want to come back." Then turning to the sound of her daughter's voice she said sadly, "I could almost touch him."

Tears spilled from Camille's eyes as she looked down on her mother's pain filled face. Crooning softly she tried to calm her mother's despair as she encouraged her to speak of the old times. Talking about old times was the only thing that seemed to ease her mother these days. Many thought that perhaps she wasn't lucent but Camille knew different. For although she'd lived for over a century, Ms. Melinda's mind was still sharp as a tack. She knew that her time here was nearly over, soon and very soon she'd be united with many of her loved ones, her beloved husband, her father, brother, and oh her dear departed mother. She waited as Camille called in all of her relatives. Many had begun to gather at the house as word had gone out that old Ms. Melinda was moving on to a building not made by the hands of man. Young and old gathered and filled the small room with the large cast iron bed as they listened to Ms. Melinda, their mother, grandmother, great-grandmother and yes to some great great-grandmother, tell of the love, joy, and sorrows of times passed..., smiling she began to speak softly of what had once been.

Love is Forever

Sitting here surrounded by family,

I feel something missing within my heart.

Their love for me is incredibly comforting,

but something is drawing me away.

I feel my heart letting go,

Moving to another plain.

Then I see him,

My memories drift back to another time.

When my life felt so perfect,

and my heart so complete.

I remember the look in your eyes,

I have never felt so loved or alive.

As my time is now at an end,

Know that I go not into the unknown;

But into the arms of my beloved,

Whom, I 've waited and eternity to behold.

Don't cry for me, my loved one, this I beg,…,

Know that we're together again

In Heaven is where we now dwell;

For Love you see, is Eternal

Love is Forever,…,

Author: Araina Rigmaiden

Chapter One

Bristol, La

1889

"Good Morning Ms. Melinda", called Mr. Grayson.

Mr. Grayson's General Store was the only one of its kind in the small town of Bristol, Louisiana. Bristol was a small town nestled thirty miles to the south of Opelousas in the heart of Acadiana.

At the edge of town, lived a few of the areas wealthiest families. One such family was the Savoies.

The Savoie family had come over from Canada as so many other persecuted Cajuns. Their most famous and well-known ancestor was none other than Jean Francois Savoie who along with his wife and sons escaped starvation and execution by sailing to Louisiana and carving out a living by working the trade route. The Savoie's as had many of the families in this small town had sent it's sons to fight in the illustrious Civil War, Yes, they fought along with their neighbors to preserve their way of life. They owned most of the land

1

surrounding the small settlement and most of the citizens there had once served on the old plantation. The Big house, as it was called, still stood as a testament to the wealth once possessed by the Savoies. Many a children were born to the Masters of the Big House, many of who now owned property in and around Bristol.

Ms. Melinda was rumored to be a part of the Savoie family but no one knew for sure if this claim was true or not. Melinda was a petite woman with rich auburn hair, a small button nose, blue-gray eyes, and skin the color of golden honey. Some speculated that she was a Creole or mulatto from Hispaniola. Whatever her race none could deny that she was a beautiful, vibrant young woman. She was also the town's only seamstress, which made her a very valuable commodity. It was hard work for one so young, but it afforded her a pretty decent living. It was important to Melinda to be able to provide for herself honestly. She had no family to speak of, and wanted to be respected in town as an honest, hard working woman.

Acknowledging Mr. Grayson's greeting, Melinda spoke in that soft cultured tone that revealed to all that she was not just your ordinary mulatto. "Why Good morning to you also Mr. Grayson, How is your wife, Ms. Amalie doing today?

Beaming, Mr. Grayson replies, "Oh she's right as rain." "What can I help you with today Melinda?"

After removing her bonnet and gloves, Melinda moves over to the new fabric that had just arrived a few days ago and states, "I am in need of some of your fine cloth for several ball gowns ordered for Saturday's big dance."

Nodding Mr. Grayson moved over to show her several new bolts of damask that had just arrived from Paris. Proudly he proclaimed to Melinda, "You're in luck, Feast your eyes on these." "Aren't they the most beautiful cloths you've ever seen?" Ooing and Ahhing Melinda selected several of the bolts of fabrics and bought matching thread and buttons appropriate for each gown. Leaving the store she reflected just how friendly and kind the Grayson's always were to her. Shivering she noticed, Mrs. Thibodeau, the Church pianist, crossing the street to pay Mr. Grayson a visit.

Melissa A. Ross

Melinda hurried down the street to avoid an unpleasant confrontation. It seemed to her that Mrs. Thibodeau went out of her way to be mean and spiteful. Casting away the dreary thoughts Melinda headed home to get an early start on the gowns ordered by several of her clients.

Later while examining the fabrics and deciding which fabrics would look best on which customer, Melinda allowed her thoughts to wander back to the encounter she'd had with William.

William Bell, the Domengeaux's butler, had cornered her earlier and asked her for a date. While waiting for Mrs. Caroline to appear for her measurements, William had entered the study and asked her to keep company with him on Saturday night. "It's so good ta see ya agin, Ms. Melinda, he'd said."

"I wuz wondin if'n you'd like ta go for a stroll one Saturday or maybe ha' me over fur dinner one evening."

After recovering from her shock, Melinda managed to accept his invitation, "Sure William, I'd love to go for a stroll this Saturday, maybe Grover's park around three."

4

Looking disappointed William pointed out that he really had Saturday night in mind as opposed to afternoon. "Well I wuz thinkin mo bout the night, hee hee hee."

Angered by what she was sure was just another way to get intimate with her, Melinda kindly stated that she didn't go out at night with men on the first date. Leveling him with a look that would have withered anyone else she said, "You are welcome to take me out in public but not in the privacy of my home, I don't know you that well yet." Offended by her refusal William admonished her for being a high yellow fancy missus and exits the room just as Mrs. Caroline enters.

Flustered Melinda very quickly took her measurements and left the grand estate. Mrs. Domengeaux shook her head at Melinda's strange behavior and said to no one in particular, "I'll never understand these people, one minute they're respectful and in their places. The next they're walking round here like they own the place."

Making her way home, Melinda stops to watch as some passersby leave Mrs. Olson's place. She is struck by the handsomeness of one of the young men. He was swarthy skinned with hair as black as midnight. He had muscles like a Greek God and she could see a dimple in the most unusual place.

She listened as the two men walked along and spoke in Spanish. She'd known it was Spanish because there were some Spanish Grocers down the road in Canktown.

Let's see now what was the family name, oh yeah Romero. She wondered if these people were somehow related to the Romero's of Canktown, I mean after all not many people even knew that Bristol existed, let alone came through town and stayed for a spell.

That evening Melinda stayed up longer than usual to finish the work on several gowns she was making for the annual Country Ball.

As she finished sewing on the small pearl buttons down the back of Beatrice Savoie's dress, Melinda's mind once again strayed to thoughts of her mother. Mary Harmon had come to Bristol in the year 1844 as a servant from some island or another; her mother, Melinda's grandmother had died on the journey, and so she had been sold to Mr. Gestave Savoie as a companion for his children.

Melinda's mother had grown up alongside the Savoie children, Jean Pierre, Marie Antoinette, Daphne Nicolette, and Joseph Charles.

As she grew into womanhood she became a constant companion to Mrs. Camille Savoie, the mistress of the household.

Mary, watched as one by one the Savoie children grew to adulthood and prepared to leave the plantation. The eldest son, Jean Pierre, went off to a higher learning academy up north.

Both of the Savoie daughters married into influential families and the younger son Joseph Charles was also on the verge of becoming a man of the world.

One day Jean Pierre returned from the Academy and pursued her relentlessly. At first she'd been afraid of being sent away, but after he had assured her time and time again of his love, she finally gave in and fell deeply in love with her owner's eldest son.

When the news came down that the slaves had all been freed by Mr. Lincoln's Proclamation; the two had secretly celebrated with their newly born son, Jean Charles.

Within a year Mary was once again pregnant with their second child. However, things had changed dramatically. Jean's father, Mr. Gestave, had found out about the relationship and determined to put an end to it. Relentlessly he threatened to write his son out of his will.

Finally he let it be known, that before he'd sit back and watch Jean Pierre destroy everything the family had worked for, he'd kill the little negra.

Jean Pierre made plans to send his son into the safety of the north. He convinced Mary to let their infant son travel to friends in Pennsylvania and remain there until it was safe to go and get him. They made a pact to never speak of him for fear that his father would reek out vengeance. Eventually his threats had taken a toll on the relationship and Mary, for fear of losing her life and that of her unborn baby, had given in to the demands of Mr. Savoie and left Bristol.

True to his word Mr. Savoie provided a monthly stipend for them to live on for staying away. Mary's only regret had been not informing Jean Pierre of the birth of their beautiful daughter, Melinda, created out of the love they'd shared.

Mary and Melinda lived away until Old Mr. Gestave Savoie passed on to the other side. Mary had simply told Melinda that they were returning to the place she once knew as home.

The two had been home only about six weeks when Melinda had begun to notice the stares and heard the snide remarks linking her to the Savoies who lived up at the Big house. She asked her mother about the remarks but Mary always changed the subject quickly.

Melinda eventually learned of her father and his family from one of the citizens of Bristol, but never came forth to divulge the information to her Mother.

She and her mother lived in a small home located on family property until Mary Harmon had become ill and died. Melinda now lived alone in the small house, and used her seamstress abilities as a means of supporting herself.

Chapter Two

The next morning Melinda was awakened by sounds of horses and wagons passing through town. Opening the curtain and peeking out she saw several men with building materials at the end of the road. Curiosity certainly peeked her interest since no one had mentioned a new family coming to town.

Rising she went out back to retrieve water from the well so she could wash up before dressing and setting out to visit friends. After her usual breakfast of coffee and toast Melinda set out to visit Old Nell.

Nellie, one of the oldest living citizens of Bristol, lived on the north side of town along with most of the other black families. Old Nell was one of the few in town who accepted Melinda for the fine young lady she was. Old Nell never called her high yellow or made snide remarks about her.

Instead Old Nell treated her with gentleness, and often told her stories of the old days. Melinda loved to hear about the past, especially the stories about her father. Old Nell had been the only one who had enough courage to talk about him as certainly no one else had, not even her mother, God rest her soul.

Melinda still missed her mother who'd died this past winter of consumption of the lungs. Doc Miller had said that there was nothing he could do to save her. Tears filled her eyes as she remembered again those final moments with her mother. Since that awful time Old Nell had sort of taken her under her wing, giving her advice when she needed it, and just listening when she needed someone to talk to, even giving her comfort when she needed a shoulder to cry on.

Thinking of just how good Old Nell and her family treated her brought a genuine smile to Melinda's heart shaped face. She certainly wasn't so readily accepted by the rest of the town. Her mixed heritage caused quite a problem in a town of little more than 250 citizens. The whites felt that she was too black, and the blacks felt that she was too white. Sure the women of the town saw her as an exceptional seamstress, but they didn't exactly invite her to afternoon tea. Life had not been easy for this young woman, but she never gave up the hope of one day having a husband and family of her own.

As she reached her destination she called out a greeting, "Yoo hoo, Ms. Nell, It's me Melinda Harmon."

Coming out to greet her, Old Nell came out onto the porch wiping her hands on her apron and called out, "Cum on in chile I wuz jus giting dese greens clean fa da menfolk."

Placing a kiss on her cheek, Melinda followed closely on her heels and walked to the kitchen of the small sharp shooter home. After asking about everyone's health Melinda then shared with Old Nell the information of a new family moving into town.

"Hey there's a new family coming into town, I saw their building materials on the wagons as I walked here this morning." "That so, who dey be?" asked Old Nell.

"I haven't the slightest clue as to who they are, and neither does anyone else for that matter."

"Humph, wunder if'n its that bankin fella peoples been saying wuz gon come", asked Old Nell.

Laughing Melinda states, "I really don't know, after all I don't understand why anyone in his right mind would think a Bank would survive here."

12

"I know what cha mean chile, who in dey right mind gon let a stranger hole dey money", asked a laughing Nellie.

"I don know a better place than right here", she further states as she pats her large bosom.

After helping Old Nell shell peas and clean greens the two women moved to the porch with each holding a glass of lemonade.

Wiping her face with a delicately embroidered handkerchief Melinda said, "I'll be glad to see winter come this year, this by far is the hottest summer I've ever known.

Cackling Old Nell remarks, "I seen hotta." "Dis ain't nuttin compared to da summa yo Pa got yo Ma pregnant wit you." "Yes sir indeed dat wuz one hot summa." "Ole man Gestave wuz madda than a bee whats lost his honey."

Always eager for tales of her father and mother Melinda urged her on. She listened as Old Nell described how the young son of the most influential family in the area fell in love with a young Negro servant. She told of how the two had met in secret and fallen in love, much to the family's dismay. She recalled how the other blacks working at the big house had feared for Mary's life once Ole Man Gestave found out about the relationship.

Old Nell spoke of how the two fell in love and vowed never to separate. "Boy he threatened yo papa and mama sumptin fierce."

"Only thang worked wuz when he said he'd kill her." "They both knowed he'd a done it to, he wuz the meanest old hypocrite I ever knowed, ole man Gestave."

"Well let's go check on the cobbler honey", stated Old Nell once again coming back to the present.

After spending the rest of the afternoon reminiscing Melinda kissed Nellie's cheek and promised to return for another visit soon.

Determined to find out who the new family was Melinda decided to drop by the Grayson's again. If anyone knew who he or she was by now, certainly Mr. Grayson did.

Looking up from a catalog Mr. Grayson spots Melinda and calls out a greeting.

"Hello Melinda, how are you this fine day?"

Smiling she answers, "Oh fine Mr. Grayson, I've been out visiting friends."

"Good, good, you young people need to get out and socialize every now and then."

As another wagon went by with supplies Melinda suddenly asked, "Who's the new family moving into town?"

"Don't rightly know Ms. Melinda, No one does for that matter."

"You mean no one's come by to introduce themselves as the owner of all those materials yet?"

"Nope, fact is I don't think any of them even speak English, they're Spaniards you know", quipped Mr. Grayson.

Truly interested now, Melinda asks, "Yes I overheard them speaking to one another and wondered if they were any relation to the Romero grocers in Canktown"?

"You know you just may have something there. I also know they're staying over at the Olson place."

Chuckling Melinda says, "Well if that's the case we'll all soon know just who they are."

The two laughed together until they were wiping away tears from the corners of their eyes. It was a well-known fact that Mrs. Olson and her dearest friend Abigail Owens were the town gossips, and as the saying went around town, neither of two could hold water.

Augustos Javier de Soto watched the beautiful young woman leave the General store, with a deep longing to get to know her better. At first he'd been too busy with the unloading of the supplies to notice anything, but he'd caught a glimpse of lilac just out of the corner of his eye. He'd looked up just in time to see the lovely vision as she picked up the hem of her long skirts to sidestep a small mud puddle. He watched her walk to almost the end of the street and turn into the drive of a small property. Javier determined to get to know her before the end of the week. She was by far the best- looking thing he'd seen since arriving here a couple of evenings ago.

The de Soto family had settled in Louisiana way back around 1563, in the town of New Orleans, and was one of the few wealthy Spanish families still remaining after Napoleon claimed Louisiana in 1803 and then sold it to the United States.

WHITE STAR LINE

TICKET # 365226

Passenger Ticket per Steamship: R.M.S. *Titanic*

SAILING FROM: Queenstown   DATE 10/April 1912

PASSENGER NAME: Miss Hanora Hegarty

AGE: 18   FROM: County Cork, Ireland

ACCOMPANIED BY: Jeremiah Burke (cousin)

CLASS: 1ST ☐   2ND ☐   3RD ☒   CABIN # Unknown

TRAVELING TO: Charlestown, Massachusetts

REASON: Nora was traveling to America to join an order of nuns.

PASSENGER FACT: When Nora's aunt went to Queenstown to purchase tickets for a transatlantic trip, the ticket clerk suggested she wait a few more weeks in order to sail on *Titanic*'s maiden voyage.

136

WHITE STAR LINE

BOARDING PASS

PERMISSION GRANTED TO COME ABOARD
WHITE STAR LINE'S
R.M.S.
TITANIC

ISMAY, IMRIE & CO.,
34, LEADENHALL STREET, LONDON,
AND
10, WATER STREET, LIVERPOOL

They owned some 40,000 acres of land that spread throughout the southeastern section of the state. The family also owned several ships that some said brought in slaves by the droves at one time, but mostly they were known for their indigo crops grown on the banks of the Mississippi.

Javier, as he liked to be called, was the oldest son of Senor and Senora Juan Valdez de Soto and had been sent to ensure the building of their new home.

The de Soto sons were on all of the eager mama's lists, as eligible bachelors but so far no one had been able to snare one of the gorgeous devils.

The young men had become quite adept at dodging eager mama's who wanted their beautiful daughters to be connected with this most influential family. Javier more than his three younger brothers hated the constant scheming by both the eager mamas and his mother to marry him off.

He learned to never be around, and to stay out of sight when he was in residence at the family home. Of course being nearly 6 feet tall with shoulder length black hair, black eyes with long sooty lashes, a stern chin with a dimple smack in the middle of it, and having a body that looked as if the muscles had been carved by a sculptor, didn't help matters any.

Javier called out instructions to the workers even as he made a mental note to find a way to introduce himself to the lovely senorita in the lilac dress.

Still daydreaming about the beautiful young lady, Javier suddenly heard his name being called by his, co-worker and cousin, Jose Alvarez de Soto.

Jose's eyes followed the direction of Javier's as he spoke of her beauty, "She is muy bonita, no Javier?

Curtly Javier answers, "Si, let us get back to work. The house must be completed before big storm season."

Javier and Jose returned to the building of his parent's home and neither spoke another word about the mysterious beauty. Javier worked all day alongside his employees until his muscles ached from head to foot.

When the daylight began to fade, he called the workday to an end and everyone headed back towards the boarding house on Mouton road.

Mrs. Olson couldn't have been happier about her good fortune of having so many people stay on at the boardinghouse at once.

She worked all day to ready the house for their return. The wealthy young man, Mr. de Soto, had paid her in advance for three months, she'd actually gasped aloud at the sight of so much money.

Finally near sundown, she looked up and noticed that the men were returning, and scrambled to finish making up the last of the beds on the third floor.

Still flustered from her exertions, Mrs. Olson had just made it to the landing when Mr. de Soto entered the house along with several of his employees. "Hello, Senora Olson how was your day?

Blushing like a young school miss she bats her lashes, pats her hair and states rather matter of factly, that her day had been just wonderful.

"Oh, I've done a little of this and a little of that, nothing over taxing I can assure you."

"That's good to hear Senora, a woman of your charms should not be working so hard."

"Oh, Mr. de Soto do you compliment all of the ladies this way"?

"Only those beautiful and talented alike Senora Olson."

"Oh away with you now you young devil, I must get dinner ready." Chuckling Javier removed himself to the bedroom he shared with his cousin Jose. Looking up as the door opened Jose laughed and teased Javier for his apparent attraction to their lovely host.

"Well glad to see you could tear yourself away from the lovely dragon, Senora Olson", said a chuckling Jose.

Javier, who had until this very moment been able to suppress his own laughter lost all control, and went down in a fit of laughter atop his bed.

"Surely dragon is too kind for her, primo", chimed in Javier.

Imitating his cousin, Jose, holds an invisible hand to his mouth and says, "I have never seen more beautiful curtains Senora, did you make them yourself?"

Having had enough of his teasing Javier defended his actions by claiming he was only flattering her to ensure that they would receive adequate service while staying at the boardinghouse.

Deciding that he wasn't quite through teasing his cousin, Jose suddenly brings up the young lady that his cousin seemed so interested in earlier.

"Did you happen to find out the name of the lovely vision in lilac, primo?" Thrown by the change in subject Javier suddenly found himself without and answer and discovered that he was none too happy about it. Gruffly he answered "No and I hope that you remember that we are not here to ruin young innocents."

Before Jose could reply his cousin went on to say, "You and every man here was sent to do a job, I expect all to act with respect towards the good citizens of Bristol."

As Jose made his way to the door and he said, "Sure thing Senor de Soto, I will personally see to it that no one bothers the lovely Ms. Melinda Harmon."

Javier swung towards the door to reply but Jose had already disappeared down the hall. All alone Javier said the name out loud a few times and practiced rolling the name off of his tongue until it felt like silken strings.

As he let the name roll off his tongue, "Melinda", he began to recall her rosy lips and the slight slant to her beautiful eyes. Taking a deep breath he resolved to forget about this young lady and go to the saloon tonight to cure what was ailing him. He would find some lovely vision of confection and lose himself in the pleasures she would provide.

Sitting alone at the bar Javier awaits for some of his men to arrive. He'd learned early in Orleans that one never drank alone.

It was common knowledge that Bourbon Street wasn't the safest place to be, and that went double for someone feeling the effects of too much drink. It had taken only one attack by hoodlums to teach Javier this valuable lesson, and he made it a point to always learn from past experiences.

Javier had been attacked as he left the Astoria on Bourbon Street, one night after drinking way too much rum. The ruffians had broken three of his ribs, and had beaten him within an inch of his life before taking his purse. He had lain in the alley all night in agonizing pain, laboring for each breath, and had nearly given in to the blackness that kept threatening to engulf him. His cousin Jose had been the one to find him after returning to the family home on Canal Street and being informed that Javier had never returned. Jose had gotten worried because Javier had left the bar and assured them all that he was returning to the mansion.

It had taken him months to recover from the broken ribs, but it was a lesson he would never forget. Soon Jose entered the saloon with three other de Soto employees and they made their way to the bar where their friend was seated.

Javier tried to find someone to attract his fancy but kept seeing the beautiful face of Melinda Harmon. He decided to drink himself into oblivion, and so, along with his friends and co-workers, took turns buying the next ten rounds of homemade rum.

Javier and Jose winced as they tried to adjust their eyes to the light as they exited Mary Carmichael's place. Neither man was exactly sure just how they'd gotten there but both were too embarrassed to admit it.

Melissa A. Ross

Rubbing his eyes and speaking in an almost whisper Jose asks what the daily work order encompassed. "Well primo what is planned for today?"

Swaying slightly Javier shakes his head gently as if to clear it of cobwebs and simply points in the direction of the boardinghouse. Jose gave a slight nod of understanding and began to walk gingerly towards Ms. Olson's place.

Upon spying the two young men approaching the house Ms. Olson rushes to greet them calling loudly, "Good Morning gentlemen breakfast is already on the table in the kitchen and awaiting your pleasure."

Gritting their teeth and clutching their stomachs both men declined the invitation. "No thanks Senora Olson", they chimed in unison and headed up towards their second floor room.

Watching them disappear Mrs. Olson shook her head and smiled knowingly, guessing that they'd spent the night up at the saloon and Mary Carmichael's place. Clucking she simply patted her hair in place and headed towards the kitchen to serve breakfast to the others employed by the de Soto family.

Chapter Three

Melinda set out early that morning for the general store. She was completely out of flour, sugar, and a few other small things.

She dressed carefully paying special attention to her hair. She pinned up the curly auburn mass into a French roll leaving a few wisps to decorate her face and nape.

She decided to go by Old Nell's place first and so headed off to the northern end of town.

By now everyone in town knew whom the house belonged to, it seemed that it was the only thing the townspeople had talked about for the last three weeks. Melinda was no exception to the rule and often found herself daydreaming about the young handsome Mr. de Soto. She imagined a young beautiful wife with a baby awaiting his return, and felt the longings of having a family of her own one-day.

Javier looked up the exact moment she headed in his direction. Without thinking he made his way towards her to introduce himself.

"Hola, hello, Senorita Harmon."

Blinking back astonishment and disbelieving that she'd heard him call her name Melinda froze to the spot.

Taking her hand he placed a light kiss on it's back and asked, "Hola, hello senorita, I am Javier de Soto, how are you on this fine day?"

Tied tongued Melinda manages to stumble over an appropriate response. "Good Morning Mr. de Soto, I'm just fine thank you for asking."

Javier notices that she doesn't take her hand away and smiled his most heartwarming smile before letting it drop back to her side.

"Tell me senorita, would you like to have dinner with me tonight?"

Taken completely by surprise Melinda searches her memory for a moment and then replies that she would love to have dinner with him. "I'd love to have dinner with you Mr. De Soto."

Trying to bring her breathing under control, she fought to calm her racing heart, while flashing him with one of her blinding, dimpled smiles.

Mesmerized by her beauty Javier didn't hear his name being called by Jose, and only did when he noticed that he no longer had Melinda's undivided attention.

Turning his head to see what had taken her gaze away from him, he cursed under his breath and sought an explanation for the interruption.

"Mierda, Que Pasa Jose?" Grinning Jose walked towards them and began extending his hand to Melinda in greeting.

With all the flourish of Don Juan, Jose introduced himself. "Buenos Dias Senorita Harmon, I am Jose Alvarez de Soto, cousin to Javier."

Smiling brightly Melinda placed her hand into his and returned his greeting. "Hello Mr. de Soto nice to meet you. I hope you said Good morning but I'm not sure."

"Perdoneme, I forget that not everyone speaks my wonderful language, I said Good Morning (Buenos Dias)."

With her hand still inside of Jose's Melinda tried out the greeting trying to imitate the sounds as he had done. "Oh, Buena's Deeas Mr. de Soto."

27

Laughing he shrugged and said that she was forgiven for butchering the language because she was more beautiful than the Sunshine. Placing his hand over his heart, he declared, "I forgive your pronunciation only because you are more beautiful than the sun."

Melinda stumbled over her next response but couldn't be heard because at that exact moment a loud clash was heard coming from the direction of the building site. Both men turned in unison and ran towards the house leaving Melinda standing alone in the street.

Javier and Jose reached the crash site at the exact moment. Jose began issuing orders to the rest of the workers while Javier began speaking with the injured man.

Speaking rapidly in his native tongue Javier asks the man if he could hear him and where was he hurt. "Senor Gonzales, me puedes oir, donde le duele?"

Weakly Angel answers that he hurts everywhere and his head feels like its broken in two. "Me duele todo, mi cabeza parace que se va a partir en dos."

Trying to calm him Javier whispers to him to just lie still and that the doctor is on the way. "A cuestese mi amigo, el doctor esta en camino."

Making his way through the crowd Dr. Miller pushed several people out of the way and announced to everyone to make room and give the man some air. "Pardon, pardon, make room, let him breathe for God's sake."

Reaching the injured man's side, he began to question him of where he felt pain. "What happened to you youngun, tell old Doc where it hurts ya"?

"Everythin Senor, my head is giving me great pain right now and my leg feels like it's on fire."

Using his hands to do a thorough examination Dr. Miller clucked his tongue and informs Javier that Angel has a broken leg. "Well it looks to me as if he's got a broken leg and a concussion.

"He'll need to be watched for signs of blacking out and nausea."

"Yes doctor we're staying at the boardinghouse and we'll make sure that someone is with him at all times."

After making this statement Javier instructed some of the men to move Angel gently to Mrs. Olson's place.

"How much do I owe you Dr. Miller?"

"Well I won't collect til afta I'm no longer needed. You'll be seeing much of me in the coming week." Shaking his hand firmly Javier thanks him for coming once again and then walked back towards the construction site.

Melinda who'd been watching from the sidelines decided to leave the area and allow Mr. de Soto to get back to work, after all he'd clearly forgotten that she was anywhere on this planet.

Adjusting her matching lemon colored bonnet Melinda heads off in the direction of Old Nell's. She stopped to pick a bouquet of wild flowers and watched as a hummingbird floated from one honeysuckle vine to the next.

Losing herself to the beauty of her surroundings she hardly even noticed that she was nearly at her destination. Old Nell looked up and saw Melinda walking towards her with a strange look upon her face and got alarmed. "Chile you ok", asked Old Nell. Coming back to the present Melinda ran into Nell's gesturing arms nearly knocking the wind from her. "Oh Ms. Nell he's the most wonderful man in the world."

"Who you carrin on bout chile, what man"?

"Oh Ms. Nell why Mr. De Soto of course."

"You carrin on bout the man billdin dat house"?

"Yes ma'am he invited me to dinner Ms. Nell, can you believe it"?

Turning serious eyes towards Melinda, Old Nell takes her chin into her gnarled hand and issues a warning about the dangers of the mixing of the races. "Na you be careful girl you hear me ain't safe for a yung black woman to be seeing no white man."

"But he's Spanish Ms. Nell and after all it's only dinner."

"Na you lissen ta me gal, if'n he ain't colored you gots ta be careful." Sighing heavily Melinda listens as Old Nell reminds her of all the things that were not safe about keeping company with a man of another race, and reminds her of what her mother suffered.

After listening as Old Nell went on and on for what seemed like an hour or more Melinda finally won a reprieve by promising not to be alone in his company.

31

Melissa A. Ross

Suddenly Old Nell's son Wilson burst through the clearing to inform them of the accident that just happened in town.

He retold the story of what happened on the construction site and Melinda thought it best to keep silent since Wilson didn't mention seeing her there. After all of Ms. Nell's questions were answered about the accident, Wilson moved on to inform the neighbors of the latest news.

Melinda slowly made her way back towards town feeling a little dejected after all the dire warnings Old Nell had given her.

Now she wasn't so sure that she'd like to go to dinner at all. What did he really want? Did he think that she was one of those women who accepted gentlemen callers in their homes at night? Did he think that she was looking for a keeper? The questions went round and round until she had a splitting headache. Wearily she made her way back home without even bothering to go on to the general store, which had been her destination as she set out that morning. "I'll just get some of that sewing done and go later", she muttered to herself.

After returning she removed all of the layers of her apparel and decided to lie down to take a short nap.

"They were at the pond on a blanket and he was kissing her. She was in his arms reclining against the old Magnolia tree that her grandpa Ennis had planted. Javier was telling her how much he loved her and that he could never live without her. After another lingering kiss he asked her to be his wife. Suddenly another face appears, that of Sheriff Comeaux and with him several others with rifles. They were all yelling that it was against the law for anybody to marry a negra except another negra. Javier began fighting them off as they dragged her away, but some to them held him down while others beat him with their fist and booted feet. Believing they would kill him she began to screaming and clawing at them."

Melinda sat up in bed looking around at her surroundings and realized that she must have been doing all the screaming. Gripping her robe she left the bedchamber and went outside to gather water from the well to wash her face. Shaking mightily she could hardly pump fresh water into the small tin bucket but finally managed to fill it half way. She attributed the nightmare to all the gloomy stories Old

Melissa A. Ross

Nell was always telling. After much thought she decided that no harm could possibly come from having dinner with someone and started getting dressed for dinner.

Chapter Four

Javier looked up as Melinda entered the boardinghouse and sucked in his breath at the vision of loveliness she presented.

She was dressed in the softest hue of pink he'd ever seen. She looked like a porcelain doll complete with matching bonnet and gloves. Her neckline was in the newest style, square with lace trimmings. The waist was pinched in and the skirt was wide, non-hooped, free flowing, with lace trimmings slightly above the hem.

He rose to meet her as she drew nearer to the table he'd selected and found himself holding his breath with every step she took in his direction. He felt himself grow tense as he noticed that so many of the boardinghouse's patrons were also staring at her opened mouth and round eyed. He could understand why the gentlemen were staring so openly with lust dripping from their very pores but the women?

As he moved forward to take her hand and lead her to their table, he overheard one of the patrons remark on the purpose of Melinda's presence in the eatery. "I thought negras weren't allowed to eat with decent folk, must be here just meeting a potential customer."

"Knew it wouldn't be long before she joined the rest of them mulattos like her, selling themselves to the highest bidder." Javier turned to glare at the old dragon and noticed that it was none other than Mrs. Thibodeau and Mrs. Owens passing judgment on Melinda.

Ever so politely he reprimanded both ladies about jumping to conclusions without first knowing the facts. He made sure that his remarks were heard by nearly all of the patrons as he greeted Melinda as if she were the queen of Spain herself. Bowing he gripped her hand and says, "Ms. Harmon you humble me with your presence, thank you for accepting my invitation to dinner."

"The pleasure is all mine Mr. De Soto thank you for inviting me", Melinda replied as she seated herself in the chair he held out for her. Conversation began to buzz round and round the establishment until it swelled to a crescendo.

Melinda was so uncomfortable with all the attention that her hands began to shake and sweat began to bead up on her dainty brow.

He noticed how she darted glances left and right as if in fear of getting physically attacked.

Javier, noticing her discomfort offered to forgo dinner there and maybe have dinner at her home if she'd be more at ease.

"I am sorry about this Ms. Harmon, but if you'd like we could have dinner at your home, we could share the cooking."

Taken by surprise at the offer Melinda wrestled with the thought of being alone with this handsome stranger. She kept hearing the warning Old Nell had given her about being alone with this man. No matter how hard she tried she couldn't however resist his beautiful smile and charm. "If you don't mind my cooking Mr. De Soto I'd love to cook dinner for you."

Melinda and Javier strolled arm in arm down the road to her humble home, the closer they got the tenser she became. Javier noticed her reaction and tried to soothe her.

"If you'd rather we pack a picnic and go out to the lake, it would be fine with me." "Really? She asked in awe. Chuckling softly he declares, "I simply want to spend time getting to know you, I doubt I'll be able to concentrate on eating much anyway."

Blushing to the roots of her hair Melinda suggested that they stop off at her home to get a blanket and then go to the general store for a few items they might need.

"Sounds like an excellent idea to me senorita", agreed Javier.

Once inside the general store Melinda found herself suddenly shy but couldn't figure out why she was so giddy.

Mr. Grayson greeted them with a look of query on his face but kept silent so as not to pry. Melinda was the one to be forth coming with the information. "Hello, Mr. Grayson we're headed out to the lake for a picnic dinner."

"Sounds right nice Melinda", he replied and gave a slight nod in Javier's direction. To put him at ease Javier whispered when Melinda was out of ear shot that he would be perfect gentlemen and treat her like delicate china.

"Don't worry Senor Grayson, I won't do anything to hurt her. I will be the gentlemen mi papa taught me to be."

Clearing his throat Mr. Grayson leveled him with a steely gaze and said, "Just'n you make sure you treat her like the lady she is." Careful not to let Melinda pick up on the hostile feelings floating in the air Javier took her by the arm and led her out the door. Smiling brightly he placed her arm through his and let her hand rest at his elbow. Together they walked slowly in the direction of the lake.

Spreading the blanket for the two of them to seat themselves Javier strikes up a conversation with Melinda about her family. "So how many sisters and brothers do you have senorita"?

Not knowing how to answer the question Melinda dodged it by promising to answer all questions after they ate.

Puzzled at her response Javier opened the basket and took out the chunks of ham they'd picked up at Melinda's house. After he laid out all the goodies he sat back against the old oak tree and watched her eat.

Chewing on a strawberry out of the basket, his imagination began to run away with him. *He was licking the strawberry juice from her fingers. He took them one by one into the warmth of his mouth and suckled away all traces of the sweet nectar. She moaned softly and began to lean forward brushing her lips lightly against his...*

"Mr. de Soto are you ok"?

Coming back to the present Javier abruptly stood and walked closer to the water's edge. "Yes I'm fine, I was just daydreaming about being out on the lake on my sailing vessel."

"You own a ship"?

"Yes, it is a small vessel that the family uses to go on sailing trips to the islands."

"I'd love to go out sailing someday."

Glad that the evidence of what he'd been daydreaming about was now gone Javier decided to walk back towards where Melinda was seated. Lounging against the tree trunk he again asks about her family. "Now tell me about your familia senorita."

"I don't have a family, I mean not really. My mother passed away last year, and I have no sisters or brothers."

"And tu papa, where is he"? This time it was her turn to stand and walk towards the Lake.

With her mouth suddenly gone dry and her palms sweaty, she tried to come up with a suitable answer. Beginning to fidget she nearly tore the lace off of her bonnet.

40

Taking the wrinkled item from her hands Javier tries to calm her fears. "If it upsets you so much to talk about him mi corazon, we can talk about my family."

"Could we really", asked a now smiling Melinda.

"On one condition, you sit back down beside me and relax."

Taking her seat once again Melinda took two calming breaths and asked, "How many brothers and sisters do you have"?

"I have three brothers and two sisters, I am the eldest. There is Roberto, Graciela, Juan, Julio, and Maria Antonia.

My family came over from Spain long ago and now we own many, many acres of land, which we use for planting. Mi Abuela's familia, my grandmother's family, came here nearly three hundred and fifty years ago for the King of Spain.

My oldest relative to come over to this land was Don Hernando de Soto."

"Wow how nice to know your family history. I must be honest with you Mr. de Soto."

"Javier", he interjected.

Groping for the right words she stood once again and turned to face the water. How could she tell this man who could trace his roots back to a king, that she had no father. How could she tell this wealthy heir that she was and illegitimate daughter of a sewing woman and a plantation owner's son?

"Mr. de Soto, I mean Javier there is something you should know about me."

Alarmed at her despondent tone, Javier stands and turns her to face him. Taking her hands he says, "What is it sweetheart"?

With her eyes downcast Melinda tells him of her parentage. "My mother was a servant for the Savoie family and my father was a favored son of the Savoie family. He doesn't acknowledge me in any way. My mother came over from Haiti when she was just a child and began working for the Savoies when she met and fell in love with Jean Pierre Savoie, my father. Down in these parts marriage between the races is against the law and his father forced him to abandon us by threatening to have my mother killed, he even sent us away before my father knew that I was born. I moved back here with my mother only a year ago when Old Mr. Gestave died. I know that my mother told him about me when we returned but until this day he has chosen not to know me." By the time she'd made the last declaration he could hardly hear her. Tears were streaming down her beautiful face and his heart crumpled at the sight of her.

Javier took her into his arms then, and kissed away the tears staining her beautiful face. He kissed her brows, her closed eyes, her nose and finally her irresistible lips. Melinda who'd never been kissed by a man let alone one as handsome and experienced as this was lost instantly to the sensations coursing through her body.

His hands came up to cup her cheeks and to tilt her head back. He coaxed her lips apart and kissed her into near mindlessness. Taking his cue Melinda began to move her tongue in the same patterns as his without realizing that she was throwing heat on the fire.

Crushing her closer to him Javier trailed kisses down her slender neck down to the tops of her breasts. Moaning deeply in her throat Melinda wound her arms around Javier's neck to get even closer to the source of all this newly found pleasure.

Javier knew that if he didn't stop this now he'd take her here on the banks of the lake. Swearing he broke the kiss and struggled to calm his breathing.

"Dios mio, we must stop now Melinda or we will make the same mistakes as tu mama and tu papa, eh"? Mortified at her behavior Melinda tried to flee but was caught by Javier.

"What is it Melinda, where are you going? Did I do something to offend you, if so I apologize truly."

"No, no it's not you, it's just that I've never done anything like this before, I acted like a lady of the, evening."

"Shh, sweetheart listen to me there is nothing wrong with what we just did. I am surprised that you've never been kissed like this, it speaks all the more as to your integrity."

Taking her hand he led her back towards the blanket and said, "Lets finish our meal and then we go back ok." In no time at all he had her laughing at his silly antics.

He was so pleased at the how their picnic was going, he felt as if he'd known her all of his life.

Javier wasn't always comfortable around single young ladies and made it a point usually to avoid them at all cost. He couldn't for the life of him phantom why he wanted to spend so much time in this young lady's company.

Packing up all the remnants of their lantern lighted meal he helped her fold the blanket and headed towards town.

Chapter Five

Today was the day that he was going to ask her to travel to New Orleans with him to meet his parents. He was sure that after avoiding the marriage market for so long and declaring that he would not marry until he was old and gray that his parents would be overjoyed at the prospect of him finally settling down.

Sure she was not a belle of the society but no one could deny that she was a cultured lady, beautiful inside and out. Taking longer than usual to dress Javier let his memories of the last couple of months wash over him with pleasure.

He remembered their first kiss at the lake, their trip down to Opelousas for the Yam festival, their daily walks in Grover's Park, and their evenings spent talking into the wee hours of the morning with only a few stolen kisses here and there.

He marveled at how long he'd been able to remain a real gentlemen with the young innocent. Not once had he taken advantage of their time spent alone in each other's company.

Javier, the connoisseur of young beautiful women, had not once sought another woman in the last 9 months, and now that he thought about it, he realized that he was satisfied to simply spend time with Melinda.

Walking towards the home he was building for his parents, Javier noticed that several of the townspeople avoided making eye contact with him and didn't even bother speaking. Deciding that they were all simply stewing about his relationship with Melinda he continued on to the site.

Upon reaching his destination he set right to work giving orders for the last minute details. Working until lunchtime the crew decided to move on to Mrs. Olson's place, while Javier decided to stop off at Melinda's place.

Javier arrived just in time to see what looked to be his parent's carriage parked beside the small home. Blinking rapidly he looked towards the carriage again because surely he had to be wrong, what could his parents possibly being doing here? They certainly wouldn't be at Melinda's even if they were in town, after all they didn't even know about her.

Taking another look he discovered that he was not mistaken the first time, for surely before his very eyes was Eduardo, the driver of the carriage, sitting under the huge magnolia tree.

Panicking now Javier ran to the back of the house around to the kitchen and entered just as he overheard his father saying, "You must understand that we have to look out for our son's welfare. He must marry someone who is his equal in society."

"I am sure that the two of you have had lots of fun but you must understand that this cannot be allowed to continue", his mother added. "You see my son Augustus", at Melinda's puzzled look, his mother explained, "Ah yes he prefers Javier, he is scheduled to marry soon. We hate to be the ones to break the news to you but he will be leaving in a short while and won't have time to say goodbye."

Next he heard his father state that she would be compensated for her time spent as companion to his son. "We will ensure that your time spent with Augustus, will not have been wasted time. We are prepared to pay you handsomely if you agree to our demands."

"And just what demands are those Papi", asked and infuriated Javier as he walked into the room. Turning to face her son his mother gasped aloud and nearly fainted on the spot, his father however was much more prepared for the situation.

"Well my son, how long have you been standing there"?

"Long enough Papa, to overhear everything."

Walking towards Melinda he beckoned her to come to him, and he kept a steady gaze on her until she reached his side. Placing his arm protectively around her shoulders he once again made eye contact with his parents and stated his intentions towards Melinda.

"Madre and Padre, I am now a grown man and able to make my own decisions." "I have decided that Melinda is whom I will spend the rest of my life with."

Without waiting for their approvals or objections he gets down on one knee, takes her hand and asks, "Melinda will you do me the honor of becoming my wife"?

Looking down at him through a blur of tears, Melinda shocked everyone with her response. "No Javier I cannot marry you. Now will all of you please leave my home at once."

Unable to accept or believe what he'd just heard Javier rises and demands an explanation. "Melinda surely you don't mean this, what is the matter"? With her heart breaking into a million pieces Melinda simply repeats her request; "Please leave my home all of you." Walking to the door she opens it and looks outward. Senor and Senora de Soto walked past her and awaited their son just outside the door.

Stopping just in front of her Javier asked again, "Melinda why will you not marry me"?

Refusing to look at him she managed to say in a barely audible voice, "Goodbye Javier and may you have a wonderful life, we have had a good time but this is as far as it goes. I am not ready to marry anyone yet. I hope you understand."

"Come my son let us do as she wishes", he dimly heard his mother say. "No, I will not leave until she gives me an explanation", said Javier. Summoning every ounce of courage she could find, Melinda straightened her spine and spoke the lie without blinking an eye. "You were only a diversion to pass the summer, I have no intentions of becoming any man's possession Mr. De Soto. I am sorry if this upsets you but it is the truth. Now all of you please leave my home." Moving slowly past her, he dared to glance back at the young woman who'd stolen his heart these last nine months. He thought he saw a tear fall from her eye, but surely he must have been mistaken after all she had just broken his heart not the other way around.

Leaving his parents to follow in their carriage, Javier went straight back to the boardinghouse. He packed a few belongings and saddled his horse. Before anyone could stop him he rode out of town at breakneck speed letting the tears fly away on the wind.

Javier rode on and on only stopping once to change horses on the long ride to New Orleans where he'd already made up his mind to find a ship at dock. He would sail to his family's native Spain and begin anew, after all there was nothing left here for him anyway. He also resolved on the long ride from Bristol to New Orleans that he'd never let anyone hurt him this way again, and cursed himself for forgetting that women only really served one purpose.

With this last thought uppermost in his thoughts he steered his horse towards New Orleans, leaving the dust of Bristol under his feet.

Slowly Melinda slid down the wall to the floor and wept until there were no more tears. She wept for what could have been if only the world were a different place, where there were no rules separating the races. She wept for all the hopes and dreams she'd had to become the wife of someone who really and truly loved her. She wept for the future that was now gone. Finally she wept at the look of devastation she'd glimpsed upon her beloved's face.

Oh if only she'd listened to Old Nell who had warned about seeing someone as rich and powerful as Javier. Crying aloud she wondered aloud why she was destined to live a lonely cold life. "Why God, why, all I wanted was someone to finally love me." Burying her head in her hands she cried great heart wrenching sobs until she fell asleep where she lay.

Chapter Six

"Land Ho", went the cry as Javier opened his eyes in the dark hull of the ship, bound for Spain. He had wandered down to the docks the same night he'd arrived, and found a ship leaving port the following morning. He'd gone to his parent's ancestral home on Canal Street and packed several trunks with his possessions.

Javier made sure to sleep in one of the hotels that night because the last thing he needed was to come across one of his wayward brothers.

Lifting his head he swayed with the ship as the evidence of too much drink announced its presence. Last night he'd gambled and drank until the wee hours of the morning, hoping to wipe out all thoughts of Melinda Harmon.

His heart pulled when he thought of her and the love he believed they had once shared. Yes he was sure that it had been love they'd shared until that fateful day when his parents had shown up on her doorstop.

It had been 3 months since he'd left New Orleans but the pain had not lessened as time went by. There were times when he thought he'd go insane from wanting her, at other times he hated her for what she'd denied them. Hated his parents for convincing her that they didn't belong together.

Placing his feet gently on the floor, Javier walked over to the basin and poured water over his head. Making his way up to the deck he inquired after his companion of last evening and laughed outright when told of his condition. To Javier's amusement it seemed that El Capitan, Antonio de la Cruz was at this very minute using the chamber pot for something other than to relieve himself. So, El Capitan was not used to the mildness of <u>Taffia</u>, the homemade rum brew he'd brought on board. Chuckling all the way to the deck Javier decided that today may not be such a dreary one after all.

They took several small boats from the ship to land and Javier went first in search for an establishment where he could get a good strong drink and a bath.

Reflecting on the events that had taken place the last few months he recalled that he'd been to Cuba, Haiti, and now he was in St.

Lucia. Next they would head to the Canary Islands and then finally to Spain.

Soon he'd be arriving in Cadiz the birthplace of his great great, great- grandfather Don Juan Alfonso de Soto. Cadiz was an important seaport for Spain and his family had served the kings of Spain since the 1400's. Many a male relative had sailed out of this port on more than one treasure hunt. Some had found treasures here in these very islands where he now stood, while others had ventured to the new world and made their way to New Orleans.

Javier stopped to ask directions to the bordello, after all he might as well take care of first things first.

Sitting knee deep in the bathing tub Javier groaned as the beautiful young lady washed the filth of the ship from his body. Her hands worked a magic spell on him as they messaged the very areas she'd just washed with the sponge. He leaned back so she could wash his hair next. Handing him a large fluffy towel she busied herself with tidying the room as he dried himself off.

"Truly your hands are magical senorita, I haven't felt this clean or relaxed in months", drawled Javier.

Blushing the young servant replied, "Oh no magic Suh, I's jus a good washer."

"Yes a good washer." Handing her a silver coin he thanks her again and dismisses her. "Gracias once again senorita, that will be all for now."

Curtsying the young lady stashes the coin in her bodice and leaves the room thanking him profusely. "Oh thank you kindly suh, and don fret none, one of de boys gon cum see bout that tub."

Strolling down the stairs Javier seeks out the owner of this establishment, Madame Mamie Larousseau. Spotting her in the meeting room with several beautiful young ladies Javier clears his throat and waits to be acknowledged. Looking in the direction of the sound Mamie rises and walks over to the handsome patron.

"Well Mr. De Soto what is your pleasure this evening"?

Shrugging Javier pours on the charm and says, "Well now Madame Larousseau, the way I see it you'd fit quite well into the plans that I have made for this evening."

Laughing coyly she replies, "That can also be arranged Senor, for the right price of course." It wasn't often that she dallied with the customers but when one as handsome as this one came along she couldn't very well lose out on this golden opportunity.

"Well then let us get the discussion underway Madame."

Licking her chops at the prospect of spending and evening with this virile young sailor she sashayed towards her own private sitting area.

"I am not to be disturbed this evening", she informed her butler and turned her attention back to what was at hand.

Javier settled back against the pillows as Mamie fed him strawberries and cream. Sucking the juice from her delicate fingers he sets the bowl on the table.

He picked up his goblet only to discover that it was empty. He reached for the bottle but discovered that it to was drained. Shrugging he decided that he probably didn't need anymore of the dangerous brew anyway.

He began unbuttoning the back of her dress and trailing kisses down the sensitive soft skin of her neck where it joined with her delicate shoulder. Sliding her dress off her exquisite shoulders he rained kisses over them expertly until she was quivering in anticipation. Turning she began to pull his shirt from his waistband and moved to unfasten the buttons as she returned his kisses. When they were both without a stitch Javier lowered her to the mattress and lost himself in all her wondrous knowledge of pleasuring a man.

Waking, Javier at first was unsure of where he was. He no longer felt the gentle swaying of the ship's hold. No, he was in a bed, but whose bed? Lying still for a moment he searched his mind for a memory of last night's activities and found himself smiling as he remembered Madame Larousseau and her expertise.

Rolling over he ran his hand along her thigh and planted tantalizing kisses on her neck and ear.

Turning over, Mamie wrapped her arms around his neck locking him in place and returned his kiss. Against his lips she stated, "This one is on the house Senor de Soto."

Chapter Seven

Gone was the carefree smiling chatterbox once known as Melinda Harmon. Instead one now saw a quiet, withdrawn, lonely young woman. Mr. Grayson bristled as she entered the store and cursed the de Soto's for ever coming to their town.

"Mornin Miss Melinda what can I do for you today"?

Melinda smiled but it didn't quite reach her eyes. They remained cold and void of any emotion as she returned the greeting. "Morning Mr. Grayson, I'm fine, just here for a few supplies."

Hearing voices Mrs. Grayson comes into the shop and envelops Melinda in one of her heartwarming hugs. "Oh Melinda what could possibly bring you out in all this horrid rain?" Looking as though she had no idea what Mrs. Grayson was saying, Melinda shrugged and said, "I simply needed a few cooking items Ma'am." "Well we'll get you whatever you need come this way", she added when Melinda said no more.

Melinda paid for her goods and walked back towards home. She looked around and was surprised to see so much water about. It must have rained sometime during the night but for the life of her she hadn't even noticed the rain when she struck out for the General Store this morning.

Clucking Mrs. Grayson shakes her head as she comments on Melinda's state of well being. "I worry so about her Charles, it as if there's only a shell of whom she used to be living there now."

"It tears me up to see the change in her, Amalie, tears me up", agrees Mr. Grayson. Crying softly Mrs. Grayson walks into her husband's outstretched arms as he tries to soothe her with words of reassurance.

"Shh, now you stop all this I'm sure she'll be alright real soon." Dabbing at her eyes Mrs. Grayson sniffs and shakes her head in agreement. "I'm sure you're right dear, I'll go make us some coffee and bring out some tea cakes."

It had been over a year since Javier had walked out of her life, but Melinda had never truly recovered. She'd changed so much in this last year; she didn't even visit Ms. Nell anymore. Melinda didn't visit anyone anymore, she simply did her sewing and that was all. She didn't even take care with her appearance anymore. No longer did she stand before the mirror in her room and fuss with her hair or the fit of one of her gowns. In fact she had given most of her elaborate gowns to Suzanna, another young mulatto who worked at the Savoie plantation.

Melinda was nearly home when she saw the shiny black carriage round the corner and head in her direction. Not willing to stand there and find out which one of the illustrious de Soto's was arriving this time, she cut through the park and entered her small property from the back entrance near the pond.

Melinda fought the tears threatening to spill forth and had to bring her fist to her mouth to keep from crying out in despair. After all this time she was amazed that she still felt so much pain over the failed relationship she'd had with Javier.

Melinda had known that they came from two different worlds and was aware just what could happen to a mixed couple living in the south. God knows she'd lived many a year yearning for the father she'd never known. While she was loath to subject her child to those same conditions, she had still hoped and prayed for her own family, with Javier.

The day his parents had shown up, all of her suspicions had been confirmed about them and how they'd accept her into their family. When his father had said that he would do whatever it took to put a stop to the relationship she knew that he would, just as her own grandfather had done. She'd refused to marry the man of her dreams that day and in her mind's eye, her life had ended right there in the doorway. She was dimly aware that she no longer felt anything but numbness. Gone was the easy laughter she once knew and in its place was a heavy burden of pain that never lifted from her heart. Shrugging she entered the kitchen and began making the bread dough, and mumbled, "Guess I'm just one of those people, meant to be alone." After working into the wee hours of the morning on a wedding ensemble for one of her patrons Melinda finally crawled into bed. Snuggling deeply under the covers she said her nightly prayers and fell asleep almost immediately. That night she dreamed of Jaiver.

Benito, the de Soto's butler raced down the steps of the mansion to meet the conveyance in the drive. Opening the door to the carriage he watched Senors Juan and Julio the handsome de Soto twins exit the carriage. All of the family had been summoned to the Bristol residence for the annual Christmas Ball given by their mother.

The two young men smiled to each other as they lighted from the carriage and asked the whereabouts of their brother Roberto. After being given the information they were seeking the young men headed off to their father's study to join their father and brother. Knocking they waited for the call to enter and straightened their lapels while they waited. "Entrar", came the summons, and they both entered with a sober expression. This would be another Christmas where their mother cried because Javier had chosen to leave and hadn't taken the time to contact them in over a year. Their father would sit silently and soon his sisters would join in the crying until they would need to be escorted from the room.

After this their father would rant on and on about ungrateful children who had no respect for their parents wishes. Later they would welcome the quests and dance until two or three in the morning. The eager momma's would also give chase with their single daughters and before the night ended they would be committed to nearly ten engagements apiece.

Entering the study both men acknowledged their brother's presence with a nod and proceeded to greet their father with a kiss on both cheeks and a slap on the back. "Hola Padre, Berto", said Juan and moved to pour himself a snifter of brandy. "Que Pasa Papi, Roberto", said Julio and accepted a glass of rum punch from one of the servants and took a seat.

"You two will be on your best behavior tonight. Your mother has invited all the good citizens of Bristol and some of our good friends are also coming from New Orleans and the surrounding parishes, I don't want any trouble out of you two", their father informed them.

"Papa, there is no need to worry, we will be perfect gentlemen tonight", said Julio.

Chiming in his reassurances Juan said, "Si Papa, we will be on perfect behavior tonight."

"Don't worry Papa all will be well, I will keep an eye on these two for you", added Roberto.

Before Senor de Soto could answer a knock sounded at the door and the butler announced that dinner was now served in the family dining room. All four men walked slowly from the study to join the ladies for dinner.

Juan and Julio were both determined not to let dinner digress into a fit of wailing, began speaking of all the new exciting things happening around Louisiana.

"And did you hear that Senor Oscar de Leon will be the new constable in Bernard Parish", asked Julio.

"Well I hadn't heard this bit of news, when will it take place", asked an interested Don de Soto.

"He'll be sworn in at the beginning of the year, and I couldn't be happier about myself", chimed in Juan. Roberto surprised everyone by his next statement. By saying he'd found the girl of his dreams and wished to marry her.

"Madre, Padre, I have found the woman of my dreams and wish to marry." Rushing on he gives them no time t object by saying, "She is from a good family and has accepted my proposal."

Placing her hand on her heart Donna de Soto asks, "My son who is this girl"?

Swallowing the lump in his throat Roberto states that she is the daughter of Bristol's most influential family. "Her name is Beatrice Savoie, and she will be attending the ball tonight with her parents."

"I see", was all, his mother said. Roberto looked to his father for some clue as to how they were digesting this information. His father's face was simply blank which made Roberto all the more nervous.

Placing her napkin beside her plate his mother excused herself and left the room without another word. His father then stood and went after his mother, which left the remaining four children to stare in wonder at each other. His sister Graciella was the first to recover from the shock and offered congratulations to her brother.

"Congratulations mi hermano, she is quite lovely no doubt."

"Gracias, Gracie, and yes she is very beautiful."

Rising from the table Julio stood and proposed a toast to his brothers' upcoming nuptials. "May I propose a toast to the soon to be groom and his future bride."

"Thank you Julio, I have a feeling I will need your support in the moments to come."

"I wonder why madre left that way, she surely should have no objections to your marrying someone like Senorita Savoie", said his sister Maria Antonia.

"Maybe the shock of one of us finally bending to her wishes was just too much for her", answered Juan. The siblings sat round the table and offered toast after toast to the upcoming nuptials of their brother, while their parents spoke quietly in Senor de Soto's study. Gathering his wife in his arms Senor de Soto says, "Maria you must calm yourself, no one knows that she and this Melinda girl are from the same family."

"Oh Juan do you think we did the right thing, I wonder sometimes if we didn't destroy two lives."

"Do not second guess what we did, Maria, in time Augustos will come to see this."

Crying she said, "I am not so sure that this will be the case, we have not heard from him in almost two years.'

"Shhh, mi corazon, he will come around", her husband reassured her.

"Now dry your eyes and let's go back to dinner and reassure our son that we stand beside his choice."

"But we have not even met her, how could he keep this a secret for so long"?

"Whatever his reasons I am sure that he feels justified."

Worried she asked, "Is it possible that he knows about what we did to Augustos"?

"No, no one knows except us and Augustos, and he has not bothered to contact us in nearly two years as you said."

"Oh Juan I will never forget the look on my son's face that day, never", she wailed.

Setting her away from him he said firmly, "We did what was right for the both of them, Maria."

"Now dry your eyes and lets go out there and congratulate our son."

"You are right Juan, you always are", she said as she dried her eyes and pinched her cheeks. When she was satisfied that she again appeared ready to entertain they left the study arm in arm and headed towards the Dining Room. Senor de Soto pulled out the chair and his wife sat down and took his own seat at the head of the table. Raising his glass for silence he then offered a toast to his son and his future bride. "May I offer a toast of congratulations to you my son, I am sure that you have made a wise decision." Tapping their glasses lightly, everyone responded with a hearty here, here. Noticeably everyone breathed a sigh of relief, but none more than Roberto. Soon they were all chattering gaily as they finished their meal and prepared to meet their guests.

Greeting their guests the de Soto family presented a united front as smiles were once again on every face. As the Savoie family arrived Roberto left his father and mother's side to embrace Beatrice. After acknowledging her father and mother he brought her hand to his lips and said, "Good Evening my love."

"And good evening to you Senor de Soto", answered Beatrice in her husky southern belle cultured voice.

Placing her hand on his sleeve he then led her to his parents for and introduction.

He could feel her trembling slightly as he said, "Mama, Papa, may I present to you Beatrice Savoie and her mother and father Mr. and Mrs. Jean Pierre Savoie." Beatrice curtsied to his parents and then was quite astonished as his mother enfolded her in a heart -warming embrace to welcome her into their home. Everyone including her parents gave a sigh of relief that at least for the moment their daughter seemed to be accepted by these wealthy newcomers.

The music was just about to begin when Roberto raised his hand for silence and declared his attentions towards Beatrice. "Everyone may I have your attention please"?

Moving to stand in front of his beloved he went down on one knee, took her hand in his and asked as he looked into her beautiful eyes, "Beatrice would you do me the honor of becoming my wife"?

Overcome with emotion Beatrice simply shook her head yes as the tears ran unchecked down her face.

Clapping broke out around the room as Roberto stood and took her in his arms to place a chaste kiss upon her closed mouth.

Mr. Savoie was the first to offer congratulations to his daughter as he kissed her on the cheek. "Congratulations my dear and may you find true happiness with this man."

Next her mother embraced her and they cried happy tears together. "Oh Bea may your life be filled with joy."

Still crying Beatrice replied, "Thank you Mamman and Papa."

Senor and Senora de Soto came next and wished them well. Following suit each of his brothers and sisters did the same. If anyone wondered where the eldest son was and why he wasn't present no one mentioned it.

Holding up his hand once again Roberto invited all the quests to join them in their first dance as a newly engaged couple. Round and round he twirled Beatrice on the dance floor as their neighbors looked on. All present were enveloped in the gaiety of the evening and danced until three in the morning.

A short distance away alone in her small home, Melinda dreamed of what could have been if only their relationship had lasted. She saw herself smiling up into his beautiful face and him bending down to bestow a kiss upon her lips.

Totally engrossed in the pleasant dream, she rolled to her side taking her pillow with her in an embrace. The only time she was truly at peace, was when she slumbered, there she could slip into dreamland and escape from life's brutal realities.

Chapter Eight

It had been three and a half years since he'd left Louisiana and over that time, life had not been an easy one for Javier. He had struggled to make it on his own without any help from his parents. He'd worked as a deckhand, enduring the backbreaking work until slowly but surely he now captained his own vessel. Javier had decided that it was not good for one to be dependent upon the good graces of another's whims because then, they controlled your every move. Over the past three years he'd learned to be self-sufficient and use his resources to his benefit. Here he stood today as a free man so to speak, one which controlled his own destiny. Javier had made his fortune in the shipping industry and solely owned the ship on which he was now standing. He stood at the helm and watched as the ship glided into Guantanamo Bay. He was transporting goods to the Cuban Island and would then head on to the port of Neuva Iberia to pick up more sugar and cotton and deliver them to Spain.

Preparing to leave the ship he gave orders to those under his command, reminding them that they only had two days in port.

"Remember we pull out in two days for Neuva Iberia, no trouble with the citizens, is that clear."

Mummers of ascent made their rounds and soon the men were climbing down to dry land. Javier watched as they disappeared towards the city and made a mental note to speak with his second in command to instruct him to leave any whom did not return before departure time.

They had been in Neuva Iberia for a day and a half when he first saw her. She was working as a cleaning girl for the bordello. She had momentarily taken his breath away; at first glance he would have sworn that she was Melinda. Looking at her intensely he noticed however that her hair, was brown, not auburn, and her mouth was a little fuller, but it was her eyes that had told him the truth, they were not almond shaped and were brown not blue with gold flecks inside. Making his way towards the young lady he asked, "Excuse me senorita, but may I ask your name"?

Looking up from the mop pail, Suzanna blinked and said, "Excuse me suh"?

Laughing at the expression on her face he reiterated, "I asked you your name, senorita."

Straightening she pushed a lock of curly brown hair from her face to reply, "The name is Suzanna suh."

Extending his hand Javier replied, "Nice to meet you Suzanna, my name is Javier."

Smiling she shook his hand and asked, "What ken I do for ya Mr. Javier"?

"Would you care to have dinner with me tonight"?

"Suh you askin me to have supper with you"? "Suh I's jus a cleanin girl, I don keep company with the gentlemen callers."

"All I'm asking for is dinner, nothing else", he replied.

"Well suh I don know what ta say, I's never been asked for jus dinner afore."

Chuckling now he said, "Just say yes senorita."

"Ok suh, yes, I be ready round six, you come around da back to da kitchen door and I'll meet cha dere."

"Six o'clock it is, he said as he lifted her hand to his lips and placed a gentle kiss on the back.

Shocked to the roots of her hair Suzanna stared opened mouthed as he turned and winked at her as he walked away.

Once out in the afternoon heat Javier wondered to himself just what in the dickens he was doing. He could have kicked himself for even speaking to the young lady. What in the world had he been thinking to invite her to dinner? Had he simply done it because she'd caught his fancy or was it because she bore such a striking resemblance to Melinda Harmon? No he refused to believe that it had anything to do with Melinda, he'd closed the book on that chapter in his life 3 years ago when he'd left for Spain. He convinced himself that he'd asked her because she'd stirred something back to life in him, it had been so long since he'd felt excitement about spending time with a young lady, he'd started to believe that he could no longer feel emotion.

He returned to the ship to oversee the loading of the goods and went down to rest until dinner.

Suzanna turned round and round in front of the mirror and smiled to herself at the image she presented. Gone was the bedraggled harpy and in her place stood a beautiful vivacious young woman. She'd swept her hair up into a French roll and put on her best Sunday dress, it had been made by her dear friend Melinda Harmon, who some said was really her sister because they shared a father. Melinda had given her the dress as a going away present when she'd decided to leave Bristol and make a life for herself elsewhere. Oh, that reminded her, she owed Melinda a letter. She made up her mind to sit down tonight and write to her friend and also send one for her mother. In Melinda's letter she would ask her to deliver the letter to her mother and to read it to her as well if it wasn't too much trouble.

As she looked at herself standing in the mirror, a vision in the Lilac dress with matching handbag and gloves she decided to place a sprig of dried babies breath in her hair just to make things more complete. Noticing that it was nearly six o'clock she rushed down the stairs towards the kitchen to meet the handsome new stranger.

Javier looked up at the precise moment she came out the door and was momentarily transported back to another place and time when he'd met another young lady dressed just as this one was today. Giving himself a mental shake he greeted Suzanna and apologized for staring. "Do forgive me for staring senorita but for just a moment you reminded me of someone else."

"You don't have to apologize suh, people say that all the time, guess I jus got one of dem faces."

"Oh and what a very beautiful face you have indeed, shall we find a place to eat"?

Placing her hand on the bend of his arm she says, "Thank you kindly suh, and yes, let's go to dinner now." After their third glass of wine Javier suggested they walk to the docks so that she could see his ship. He paid the bill and took the bottle with him as they left the restaurant giggling like children. Suzanna couldn't believe how much of a gentleman he was being towards her. Most of the men of his class would have tried to seduce her before they even made it around the corner.

She stole a glance at him as he led her towards his ship and once again noted just how handsome he was.

Once on the ship Javier took her for a tour on deck, the hold, and finally to his cabin. He followed her in and pulled out a chair for her to sit. Nervous as a cat on a hot tin roof, Suzanna accepted her fifth glass of wine and tried to calm her racing heart. She'd made up mind to give herself up totally to this man if things led that far. She was tired of life as a cleaning woman and was grateful for the gloves that covered her reddened rough hands. Life as a cleaning woman was certainly taking a toll on her and now she was determined to start living life as the other half lived. Watching the candlelight dance around her features Javier sat back and studied her more closely. Although he'd gone to dinner with her tonight with all intentions of it ending there, he was finding it hard not to take her in his arms and dispense with all of his honorable intentions.

Clearing his throat he said, "I want to thank you for sharing dinner with me tonight and would like to do it again before I leave, if that's alright with you Suzanna."

"Yes I'd love to see you again Mr. Javier", said a smiling and slightly tipsy Suzanna.

Noticing the barely audible slur Javier rose and placed an odd looking disc into what looked to be some sort of small music machine. To get a better look Suzanna rose and went over to inspect this strange new machine. "What is that suh"? She asked.

"It is called a gramophone, and it plays the music on this round disk."

Clapping with delight Suzanna asked, "You mean dat dere be the music"?

"Yes this is the music." After cranking the handle he asks, "May I have this dance senorita"?

Stepping into his arms she and let him twirl her around the cabin. She was glad now for the time she'd spent watching the dancing at the Savoie Mansion. She simply imitated what she'd seen Miss Beatrice do on countless nights as the family had entertained guests.

Lost in the music she floated on the air as he twirled her round and round. When the music stopped he immediately set it up to play again and continued to enjoy every moment of the time he spent in the company of this enchanting young woman. After twirling round and round Suzanna began to feel slightly lightheaded and let a bubble of laughter escape before she could stop it.

"Ah so you're enjoying your evening I take it", said an equally giddy Javier.

"Immensely suh, and are you enjoying yourself as well", she asked in a hopeful voice.

"I can not say when I've had a more enjoyable evening madam, thank you once again."

Staring at his lips Suzanna found herself leaning just a little closer and before she knew what was happening Javier was kissing her soundly. Suzanna kissed him back with an equal amount of eagerness and wound her arms around his neck to press even closer to the heat he was generating.

Javier trailed kisses down her neck to the square neckline of her dress and pressed kiss after kiss to the tops of her exposed flesh. Moaning Suzanna ran her hands through his hair and lost herself to the magic his mouth was creating.

So lost was she that she didn't even notice that he'd unbuttoned the back of her gown. At the burst of cool air on her bare back and shoulders Suzanna gasped and stepped away momentarily. Holding his breath he waited for her to make the next move.

Holding her dress up with her hands she levels him with a sexy smile and slowly lets the dress fall to the floor. Javier catches his breath at the sight standing before him; unlike ladies in his class she wore no underclothes with wire, only a flimsy white shift.

"Are you sure Suzanna, because if I walk over to where you stand, there will be no turning back."

To answer his question Suzanna surprised them both by extending her hands to him in welcome. Walking into her arms Javier lifts her and places her on his bunk.

For the first time in a long time Javier lost himself in the wondrous feelings washing over him. He spent the night worshipping her body in every way imaginable and reveled in the emotions that played across her face at each new sensation. Finding out that she had been a virgin weighed heavily on his conscience, but it couldn't be helped now. He was glad that he'd thought to leave provisions for her while he was away.

Javier watched as Suzanna stood on the docks waving goodbye. He felt a small tug on his heart as the ship pulled away. Although he'd spent a glorious week with her, he could never truly love her. He did however suspect, she fancied herself into thinking she was falling in love with him.

He'd found her a place and paid the landlord in advance for her upkeep until he would return. Would she still be here when he returned in another three or four months? Well just in case he'd instructed the landlord to give her what was left of the rent if she decided to move on.

He'd also left her over 1,000 dollars underneath her pillow in a small beaded bag. He was sure she'd find it when she returned, and she'd probably wonder if he weren't coming back. Turning away he instructed his second in command to take the wheel for a couple of hours.

Sadness, a deep gut wrenching sadness washed over him as he recalled his actions of the past week. And again he wondered for the hundredth time if he'd not done Miss Suzanna a grave disservice.

Chapter Nine

Today was the day that Melinda had made up her mind to start living again. She was no longer going to be slave to her past memories. She dressed in her finest satin striped gray suit and took a last look at the picture she presented in the mirror. Deciding that she looked as good as she would ever look. Picking up her small handbag she left the house and walked towards the Savoie Mansion.

She was determined to get some answers from this man who was her father. She wanted to know everything, starting with had he ever loved her mother or was she just a product of raw lust.

Poising to knock Melinda is surprised as the butler opens the door and says, "Yall's posed to go round back gal."

Bristling with anger Melinda retorted, "I'm not here as a servant Isaac, I am here to see Mr. Savoie on a personal matter.

Pushing him aside she walked into the front entrance and ran right into just the person she came to see.

Catching her he gave her a little shake and said, "Gal why you coming through the front door, yall are supposed to call at the back entrance."

Bringing herself to her full height Melinda responded by saying, "Hello, I'm Melinda Harmon, and I'm here to see you sir."

Staring at her open mouthed he recovered in time to suggest that they go to his study. "Right this way child." Before closing the door he instructed Isaac that he was not to be disturbed.

Seated across from her father Melinda asked, "Did my mother ever mean anything to you at all Mr. Savoie"?

Uncomfortable Mr. Savoie shifted his weight and answered, "I don't think this is an appropriate discussion for us to be having at this time young lady."

Forcing herself to remain calm Melinda said mildly, "Whether you deem it as appropriate or not Mr. Savoie, I've come here for some answers."

Before he could inquire further the door to the study swung open and in walked Beatrice, Roberto, his wife, and his mother, the matriarch of the family, Camille Savoie.

Stopping short, Beatrice was the first to notice that her father was not alone. She looked from one to another and asked, "Papa is everything alright, We could come back if you are busy?" All sorts of thoughts ran through Jean Pierre's mind at that moment. All the years of making sure that his family had been protected from the scandal that was sure to brew if he'd acknowledged Melinda in any way. All his scheming was about to come to nothing right here, right now.

Standing Melinda turned around to greet the members of the Savoie clan and nearly fell over where she stood when her eyes lit upon Roberto. Just for a moment she thought that she was standing before Javier but then realized that she'd heard of the marriage between the son named Roberto and Beatrice.

All eyes quickly turned to his mother as she clutched her chest and fell to the floor. Mrs. Camille hadn't believed her eyes when the young lady had risen and turned to face them. There before her eyes was herself in her younger years but in a darker shade. Lifting his mother in his arms Jean Pierre gently placed her on the sofa in his study and called for the smelling salts.

Mrs. Savoie however was galvanized into action and turned eyes full of hatred upon Melinda saying, "What do you want here gal"?

Numbly Melinda responded, "I simply wanted some answers, I didn't come here to stir trouble."

Tartly Mrs. Savoie said, "Well, you have, are you happy now"?

Roberto watched all of this with open curiosity and asked Beatrice for an explanation. "What is going on here, who is that young lady"?

Beatrice who'd known all along about the family secrets stated non-matter of factly, "I do believe dear husband that this is one of my father's secret love children."

Walking towards the bewildered looking young woman Beatrice says, "Hello, I was wondering if it was all true, the stories I've heard, now I know that the old servants were not just spinning tales." "Melinda, this is my husband Roberto de Soto", she said as she pointed to Roberto.

Shocked at her behavior her mother said hotly, "Beatrice you and your husband may wait in the drawing room for us, we'll be right out, as soon as this unsavory business is handled."

"Mother I am not a child anymore and besides I already know about her, I have for some time now, and since I am still a part of this family I would like to stay."

Coming around Mrs. Camille asks, "Oh son, tell me I didn't see a ghost."

"No, Mamman you didn't, what you saw is flesh and blood."

"Oh dear God", she mutters as she sits up. Looking at Melinda she says, "Who are you young lady and what do you want." As her son and his wife object strenuously she holds up her hand for silence and awaits Melinda's answer.

Taking a deep breath Melinda said slowly, "Mrs. Savoie, my name is ·Melinda Harmon." Before she could finish the old woman interrupted with, "Harmon you say"?

"Yes Ma'am I said Harmon, it was my mother's name."

Motioning towards Melinda she says, "Come closer child, let me have a better look at you."

Obeying Melinda absently put one foot in front to the other until she found herself standing in front of the old woman. In a whisper the old lady said softly, "So you're Mary's child."

"Yes ma'am I am Mary Harmon's daughter." With a far away look in her eyes Mrs. Camille said, "I always wondered what happened to Mary, she was a good and kind woman." Turning accusing eyes towards her son she states before walking out of the room, "Jean Pierre, you will take care of this won't you"?

Reassuring her he answers, "Yes mother I will." Turning to his wife he spoke rapidly saying, "Please escort her to her sleeping quarters my dear, I will be done here shortly."

Not wanting to leave, reluctantly Mrs. Savoie led the older woman out of the room and upstairs to lie down.

Clearing his throat Roberto said, "I think we need to leave these two alone Beatrice." Thinking it would be wise to do as her husband suggested Beatrice turns to leave but says, "I'm glad this is now out in the open, I'll be stopping by soon Ms. Harmon." Turning sympathetic eyes to her father she places a kiss on his cheek and whispers, "All will be fine Papa, just sit and give her the answers she needs."

Grateful for her wisdom he closed the door after them and instructed Melinda to take her seat once again.

Sitting at home later that evening Melinda reflected over all that happened at the Savoie place earlier. She'd sat and listened as her father, Jean Pierre Savoie, had told her of the love he'd felt for her mother. She also cried along with him as he told her of the ugly truth of the horrible lengths his father, her grandfather, Gestave Savoie had gone to separate them. Wiping away the errant tear that ran down her cheek she said, "Oh Mama he really did love you."

Thinking that she was well and truly over her own bad experience with love, Melinda was unprepared for the torrent of tears that overtook her at that moment. Maybe it was seeing Roberto who looked so much like Javier, or maybe it was finally knowing, that she was not just a product of out of control lust. Either way whatever it was she couldn't stop the tears as they gave way to heart wrenching sobs.

Finally able to staunch the flow of tears, she got up, washed her face and prepared a small salad for dinner. Tomorrow she would jump back into life and live as she was meant to live. No more would she be an empty shell, simply existing while others lived, loved, and enjoyed being alive. Tomorrow she would go to visit Old Nell and others she hadn't bothered to acknowledge in nearly 4 years.

Chapter Ten

Javier lifted Suzanna in his arms and kissed her heartily. Laughing she said breathlessly, "Welcome back Javier." Setting her down gently he deepens the kiss and only stops when he hears all the whistles and catcalls of his crew. Issuing last minute orders he took her hand and led her towards her suite of rooms at the Inn.

"I can hardly wait to get you alone", she teased.

"That goes for the both of us, it's been so long since we were last together.

Growling deeply at what she left unsaid, Javier picked up the pace until they were nearly running down Main Street.

Closing the door with his foot Javier took Suzanna into his arms and kissed her as if his very life depended upon it. He kissed her deeply until both of them were panting heavily.

He began removing her clothes with the same enthusiasm until she stayed his hands and said," slow down Javier we have all night to do this, if you aren't careful you'll owe me another gown."

"I'll buy you more gowns that you can wear in this lifetime, just let me love you sweetheart." Burying his head in the valley of her exposed flesh he took away any response she may have given him.

Stretching languidly like a cat Suzanna awoke to Javier trailing kisses over her face and neck. Giggling like a schoolgirl she lifted his head and said, "Mmmm I'd like to wake up like this every morning. "I haven't started yet and already you're purring like a kitten", he teased. Purring deeply in her throat she rakes her nails lightly over his back and teases, "GRRRRRR."

Walking through town Javier and Suzanna stopped at several shops and purchased several items, including a near transparent red negligée. "Let's stop for lunch now and afterwards we can go to the Opera house", suggested Javier.

"Your wish is my command", she answered in that sexy husky tone that drove him wild.

"Keep that up and we'll only make it back to the room."

"You may just have something there my love", she adds with a smile. Javier stops and kisses her soundly right in the middle of town for everyone to see. Breathless now he says, "Come let us return to the Inn, we'll have lunch in our suite, and follow up with dessert." Watching her eyes cross in anticipation he asked, "What would you like for dessert corazon"?

At the end of the week Javier once again stood at the helm of his ship and watched as Suzanna waved goodbye from the dock. He watched her until she was as small as a pinhead and only then did he give over control of the vessel to his second in command. Going below he vowed to end this relationship before things got out of hand. He could see the look of love in her eyes when they were alone together. Once or twice she'd almost said the words I love you, he was sure of it. Javier knew that on the next trip he'd speak with her and tell her that it was over, besides he made it a point to never spend time with the same woman more than twice. He'd make sure that she was well taken care of but their relationship was over.

Suzanna hung her head over the side of the bed and emptied her stomach's contents once again for the fourth morning in a row. When there was nothing left but dry heaves she walked over to the basin and rinsed her mouth. Washing her face she sits down until the dizziness passes, and tries to figure out just what could be wrong with her. She wasn't aware of any sickness that could cause such symptoms. She had no fever, only dizziness every now and then and this horrible vomiting in the mornings.

Searching her mind's eye she went over every illness that came to mind that included symptoms such as these and froze as her mind lit on...

"Oh No it can't be", she wailed. Counting back she began trying to remember the last time she'd seen her courses and realized that it had been nearly two months. Crying into her hands she realized that she'd not seen her courses since Javier had left on his way to drop supplies off in Hispaniola. She had to figure out what to do, she knew without a shadow of a doubt that he wanted no children, after all what good was a sick, fat mistress.

She would have laughed at her circumstances if they weren't so dire, but what could she do? Making up her mind she decided first to go see Dr. Jefferson to confirm her suspicions and then she'd decide what to do.

Walking along the docks to Main Street, Javier's heart grew heavier and heavier at what he must do. He realized now that he'd put off coming back for this exact reason. He should have been back three months ago but purposely had taken on another shipment that kept him away two extra months. He hung his head now as he realized the dilemma he'd probably placed Suzanna in, and hurried to tie up all loose ends so that he could journey back to Nueva Iberia.

He'd neglected to send a note to the Inn telling her when he would be arriving so that he would have time to gather his thoughts and build up the courage to deal with the problem at hand.

Taking a deep breath he lifted his hand to knock and waited for her to answer. He nearly swallowed his tongue when someone else answered the door. Standing before him was his brother Roberto. Anger was the first thing he felt, here he stood at his mistress' door and who answers but his younger brother.

Roberto was the first to recover saying, "Well, well, well, if it isn't the prodigal son returned to his father's homeland."

Javier answered by letting his fist fly into Roberto's beautiful face knocking him to the floor. At the sound of someone fighting Beatrice ran into the foyer only to scream at the sight before her. Turning at the sound of the ear-splitting scream Javier stood in shock at seeing her.

Standing before him was a strawberry blond, blue eyed, creamy skinned version of Suzanna, no, Melinda. Lost in his musings he was unaware that his brother had recovered from his surprise attack and was gearing up to return the favor.

Turning to apologize to his brother for what must seem like madness, and seek and explanation, he caught the punch thrown by his brother on the side of the head in the temple. Crumbling to the floor Javier is enveloped into a cloud of blackness.

"Oh No Berto, I think you've killed him", shouted a horrified Beatrice.

"He's not dead yet, my love. Bring me the pitcher of water."

Scrambling to do as he husband asked Bea said, "Berto who is that man, and why did he attack you"?

"Why this is the famous Augustos Javier de Soto, my love, the heir of the de Soto family fortune. This I regret to inform you is my older brother."

Speechless Beatrice watched as her husband emptied the pitcher of cold water into his brother's face. Sputtering Javier sat up and shook his head to clear it of all the cobwebs.

"Get up and explain yourself, and make it good, hermano."

Javier knew that his brother was asking for an explanation of more than just what had happened here, but first he needed some answers of his own.

"I'll give you all the answers you need, but first I need to find the landlord, there are some things I need to know first." Turning to Beatrice he says, "Pardon me ma'am for my lack of manners, I am Javier de Soto, brother of Roberto."

"It is a pleasure to meet you brother", she said while extending her hand in welcome.

"Brother", he asked, turning questioning eyes to Roberto.

Smiling for the first time since his brother's surprise visit, Roberto moves to stand next to Beatrice and says, "Yes, brother, Beatrice and I were married soon after you left."

Credulous Javier extended congratulations to the couple and asked, "How long have you been here in this room"?

Beginning to understand Roberto said with a grin, "Has the little birdie flown the coup Javier"?

"Just answer the question hermano", Javier said quietly.

Chuckling Roberto says, "We've been here for a couple of days, you will have to seek your answers elsewhere." Sighing Javier once again turned to Beatrice and welcomed her into the family. He also briefly apologized for not being present at the wedding. Turning to his brother he states, "I really am sorry for not being there Berto, but there are many things we must discuss later." "Would the two of you meet me for dinner tonight, there are things we need to speak about?"

After taking a few minutes to ponder the question Roberto agreed to meet him for dinner and added, "Yes we'll meet you later on Bordeau Street, and Javier, I hope you find what you're looking for."

"Gracias, hermano. Until later, venga un dia." Turning to Beatrice he places a brotherly kiss upon her cheek and said, "Bienvinidos a la familia, hermana."

Later that evening Javier sat across from his brother and sister in law and wondered again just who this beautiful young woman was. He knew that there had to be a connection between her and Melinda and if he admitted it deep down all along he knew that Suzanna was somehow connected to Melinda as well.

Taking a sip of his wine he asked politely, "Well my brother where did you find this beautiful saint, and how did you get her to marry one such as you."

Casting a steamy glance at Beatrice, Roberto supplies, "I assure you dear brother that this lady is no saint, although I have it on good authority that she is often heard calling on God."

Blushing profusely, Beatrice kicks Roberto under the table. Still blushing she says playfully, "So glad to know that someone else understands my trials."

Giving a bark of laughter Javier said, "Then we are in agreement about this one eh."

Steering the conversation back to Roberto he asks again, "Where did you meet this paragon of perfection hermano"?

It was Beatrice who spoke up then to provide Javier with what he was seeking.

"We met in the sleepy little town of Bristol, do you know the place brother"?

Turning white as a sheet Javier says, "Yes, yes I do."

Eager now to find out what was going on Roberto urged Javier to tell him why he'd left after building his parent's home there five years ago.

"Yes my dear he knows the place in fact he was in charge in the building of the home my parents frequent there from time to time. "You said there was something you wanted to talk about tonight hermano."

"Yes I wanted to speak with you about why I left, if anyone would understand my actions certainly it would be you." "May I ask you one more question mademoiselle"?

· "Sure what is it you'd like to know Javier"?

"What was your family name before marrying my brother"?

Not knowing why it should matter Roberto interjects that he doesn't see what that has to do with Javier's leaving.

Beginning to understand Beatrice says simply, "My maiden name was Savoie. Are you the one who broke poor Melinda's heart"?

Feeling as if he'd been punched in the gut, Javier clenched his stomach and said, "I need to get some air, perdoneme." Stumbling out into the night air he gulps breaths of air until his breathing returns to some semblance of normalcy.

Running to catch his brother, Roberto paid the bill quickly and escorted his wife out into the night. Spotting him at the corner he rushed over and suggested they all return to the Inn.

The three of them set up all night talking of the heartbreaking details that had kept Javier away for so long. Roberto was beyond furious over his parent's actions and determined to confront them when he returned in a couple of days to the family home in New Orleans. Javier told them of his years away building his own fortune and sadly of the toll it had taken on him to leave everyone he knew, especially Melinda.

He even told them of his relationship with Suzanna, which brought forth a gasp from Beatrice. While she'd suspected that there were other children born illegitimately to her father she wasn't quite prepared to find out this way. The three talked until the wee hours of the morning. Javier felt as if a huge weight had been lifted off of his shoulders when he finally stood to leave.

After he left, Beatrice placed her head against Roberto's chest and cried her heart out for all the pain and despair that had touched so many young lives. She cried for the pain they'd been made to suffer all because of the hatred one race bore against another.

Had she really lived here all her life and not given a second thought to the struggles of those around. She realized that she hadn't really cared what went on around her so long as she was happy and had all of the comforts afforded to one of her class.

Sobbing loudly she says, "Oh Berto, Is it right that we are so happy, while so many others suffer unbearable injustices"?

"Shhh my love, all will work out for Javier and the one he loves."

"Honestly, do you really think so Berto", she asked sniffing loudly.

Kissing the top of her head he states, "Yes if I know my brother, he will find a way to be with the one he loves."

Two days later Javier escorted his Bother and Sister in law down to his cabin as the two agreed to sail back to New Orleans on his vessel. Although he wasn't in the business of transporting passengers, Javier saw to their every comfort, and actually found it quite enjoyable to have dinner with someone other than his crewmembers.

Leaving the two alone in his cabin for the night he slaps a mosquito and continues upward towards the deck to check with his second in command before retiring for the night.

Chapter Eleven

Javier swayed as he stumbled to the door of his second mate's cabin. He'd thrown up three times and had a terrible headache. He cursed as he now hurried to empty the contents of the chamber pot. Suddenly he felt as if his bowels were in a race against time to relieve him of whatever was left in his stomach. He was sure there couldn't be too much more left, he'd been throwing up for the last hour. Feeling as though he was feverish he swiped his hand over his eyes and continued on to the railing to empty the pot.

Hearing the terrible retching Beatrice sat up and looked around, wondering if Roberto was ill. Feeling him fast asleep beside her, she shakes him and says, "Berto wake up."

Turning to face her Roberto says, "Sweetheart go back to sleep, morning will be here soon."

"No Berto, someone is deathly ill, I have heard them several times now and it seems to be getting worse."

Listening intently now he straightens and swings his legs to the floor. He pulled on his robe and exited the cabin.

Roberto pulls up short as he realizes that his brother is the one hanging on to the railing of the ship sicker than he'd ever seen him before. Concerned he walks over and says, "Que Pasa, Hermano, do you think it was something you ate at the diner"?

Shaking his head wearily and with his teeth shattering Javier says, "Please get me to the bunk and go quickly to get el doctore."

Leaning on his brother's strong fame Javier stumbles to the bed and burrows under the blanket praying again for the second time that night that he hadn't been poisoned.

Beatrice came running in just as her husband was exiting and pulled up short at the site of Javier. He was sweating profusely and his face was flushed from what she guessed was fever. His teeth were knocking together and he was now having dry heaves. Sending up a quick prayer to the almighty she rolled up her sleeves and went to sit next to him while the doctor was being dragged out of bed. Frightened beyond her wits Beatrice sat and held his hand and sent up another prayer asking that it not be yellow fever.

Doctor Ramirez entered the room and pulled up short at the sight of his young captain. Regaining his bearings he rushed to the bedside to examine Javier. "Que Pasa, Capitane, did you eat something bad"?

Nearly delirious Javier manages to say, "NO, Nothing I ate. God I hurt all over."

"What do you mean you hurt all over, are you in pain, other than in your stomach, asked the doctor.

"Si, me duele todo, I hurt everywhere, my bones feel as if they are breaking apart", answered a weak Javier.

"Dios", muttered the worried doctor. "Javier, me puedes oir, can you hear me"? asked the doctor.

Before he could answer Javier was gripped by convulsions and was soon unconscious. Spurred into action by this turn of events the Doctor began barking orders for the ship to dock immediately and for a tub of cold water to be brought into the cabin. "We must bathe him to get the fever down, help me to get him undressed Senor Roberto", he said.

Orders were given to set a course for Orleans and the men began filling a washtub with cold water from the sea.

Docking in New Orleans, Roberto ordered that his brother be brought to his parent's home and sent a message announcing their arrival. He would go into the details later but for now thought it best to simply have them get a chamber ready and summon a doctor.

Nervously Senor and Senora de Soto paced the length of the hallway waiting for the doctor to emerge. Senora de Soto swooned to the floor in a dead faint when her eldest son had been carried in lying near death.

Senor de Soto sent out messages to the rest of the family to return to the mansion without delay. He had not imparted information about Javier's condition and only wished that they would take heed to the request he'd sent.

Julio was the first to arrive. He quickly was led to the upstairs chamber and nearly collapsed with relief at seeing that the summons had not concerned his mother.

Taking his mother in his arms he asks, "What is it Mama, is Abuela ill"?

Shaking her head no his mother swallows the lump in her throat and said, "No mijo, Abuela is fine, but your brother Javier is gravely ill."

Staring dumbfounded Julio looked questioningly at his father and said, "Excuse me Papa, but did she say Javier had returned?"

Taking a deep breath, Senor de Soto replies, "Yes my son Javier has returned but we do not know if he will survive. The doctors are in with him now, but it does not look good."

Just then Juan, Maria, and Graciela all came up the stairs into the hallway and looked to their father for an explanation.

"As I was just telling your brother, Javier has returned but is deathly ill."

At loud gasps and simultaneous what's, their father went on to further explain what was happening. "It seems that Roberto found him in Nueva Iberia and convinced him to come home. Javier took ill on the way here late last night. Roberto has no idea what could have caused this horrible sickness, they all had dinner together."

"This is incredible, how did Roberto find him papa", asked Maria.

"I do not know the particulars, only that they were all well until last night, when and if the situation improves, I am sure Roberto will tell us all we need to know", replied their father.

Beatrice, who was determined to right the wrong done to this elder de Soto son whom she'd just met, sat down and wrote out a note. After re-writing the note two times until she was satisfied with its contents, she went in search for Benito and instructed him of where to have the note delivered.

She made sure to tell him that it needed to be delivered as quickly as possible and not to return without a response.

Melinda sat in the room with the mid- wife and cast furtive glances towards her friend Suzanna or should it be sister? Suzanna had returned a few months ago almost ready to deliver and moved in with Melinda. Together the two had become almost inseparable, even often visiting the old Savoie plantation. The two young ladies had formed a special relationship filling the void in each other's lives. Melinda had never pressed Suzanna for any information of whom she had been involved with, and Suzanna had never voluntarily given any. Happy just to be welcomed home by someone Suzanna settled in and soon she and Melinda had bought a small store front and opened their own boutique.

Melinda rose and stretched her sore muscles and prayed to the Blessed Mother to intervene on Suzanna's behalf. It had been over two days since her friend's, no her sister's labor had begun. Deep within her heart she knew that something was wrong and had asked the mid-wife several times if all was well.

Hearing Suzanna whisper her name she walked to the bedside and took her hand. "Melinda, please promise me."

"What is it Suzy, I'll do whatever you want", she promised frantically.

"Please take care of my baby, don let nuthin happen to em."

Crying now Melinda tries to sound cheerful by saying, "Suzy you'll be just fine, the mid-wife said that it just takes time."

Weak from so much loss of her body's life sustaining blood, Suzanna ran her tongue over her dried, cracked lips and croaked, "No listen Melinda, I'm not gon make it and if'n my baby lives please raise him yo self."

Clenching her teeth together, she wailed like a banshee as another contraction hit her. The mid-wife moved quickly into position to help her bring forth the baby. She shook her head and said forcefully, "Dis be hard gal but you ken do it, the feet's is a comin furst, gon tear ya some but you's can do it."

Scared out of her wits Melinda said, "I'm sending for the doctor, we need help Ms. Lorraine."

"Suit yo self Miz Melinda, I says it won't do no good. Never heard of no man helpin to birth no babies, least wise no negra babies that is."

"Well they do it in other parts of the world, I can't see why it would be different here", retorted Melinda.

Running Melinda nearly knocked over Mrs. Thibodeau and Mrs. Owens in her search for old Doc Miller.

At the sound of incessant banging on the front door, Doc Miller rises to see who's causing all the commotion. Upon reaching the door and taking one look at Melinda's stricken face he turned around, grabbed his bag and said, "Lead the way little un."

Doctor Miller did all he could to save Suzanna, but she had simply lost too much blood. He had been infuriated at the lack of judgment the mid-wife had shown, and made a vow to talk to every mid-wife in the area about the birthing of breached babies. He looked over now as Melinda cradled the innocent babe to her heart and cried for the newly found sister she'd just lost. He wondered if she could handle all of this and made a mental note to keep an eye on her.

Melinda stood numbly as the black community of Bristol bid farewell to Suzanna. It was a beautiful day with not a cloud in the sky. She took it as a sign from God that he had accepted her sister into his bosom with rejoicing. The sky was so blue and clear that she could almost see the angels dancing and singing over Suzanna's home going.

Melinda fetched baby Camille from one of the neighbors and walked slowly towards the home she'd shared with Suzanna until two days ago. She was almost there when she realized that someone was calling her name. Turning she became a bit confused as the man came closer and delivered a handwritten note into her hands.

Taking the note she said politely, "Thank You sir, may I offer you something to refresh yourself"? "No Ma'am just a reply, I've been instructed to await your answer.

Melinda put the baby down for a nap, and sat down to read the note.

Javier vomited once again and wandered in and out of consciousness as his caretakers tried over and over again to get some liquid nourishment into his body. The Doctor had said that it was a necessity to give him some water each time he vomited so that he wouldn't lose all of his body's fluids.

The Doctor scratched his head, as Javier seemed to be getting weaker and weaker. He gave them his grim diagnosis and left them for the night, asking to be called if the patient began to pass blood.

Sinking down into a pool of tears, Senora de Soto cried until she had to be removed from the room by two of her sons. Senor de Soto looked as if he had not slept in a month. There were dark circles under his bloodshot eyes, and the lower half of his face was covered with unshaved stubs of hair. Roberto stood at his side consoling Maria Antonia who was crying loudly.

Graciela was crying into the front of her husband Cristano's shirt.

Into this scene walked Melinda carrying baby Camille with Beatrice at her side. Everyone including Roberto stopped to stare at the two young women. If one didn't know better they looked as if they could be related. Sure one was a darker hue than the other and had a deeper shade of auburn hair but there was no mistake about it, these two were related. Senor de Soto straightened at the sight of Beatrice escorting Melinda into his home and bristled with anger at her audacity.

Rushing forward, Roberto stood on the other side of Melinda and presented a picture of solidarity with his wife. "Padre I believe it is time to let things happen as God would have them."

Looking defeated his father thought things over for a moment and then moved away from the door.

Beatrice took the baby from Melinda's arms and placed the tiny bundle into Senor de Soto's, saying, "Say hello to your granddaughter Padre." Leaving them all open mouthed and wide eyed she entered the sickroom behind Melinda and Roberto.

Old Angie watched as Melinda, Roberto, and Beatrice filed into the room. As Roberto bent to check on Javier, the old servant took Melinda by the elbow and said, "Massa gon die lessen somebody do sumptin."

Hearing this whispered statement Roberto crossed the room in two strides, "What do you mean, the doctor's have been here night and day.

Looking fearful she took a step backwards and looked to Melinda for help.

"I don't think that is what she meant", said Melinda as she speaks directly to the old servant. "Are you a treater"?

Casting a furtive glance at Roberto Anna nods slightly indicating that yes she was a treater.

Placing her hand on her husband's sleeve Beatrice motioned for him to remain quiet and hear the old servant out.

Urging the old woman to speak Melinda said, "My grandma Ruthie was a treater, or so I've been told. Why do you feel the doctor's are not helping him"?

Moving to the bed she lifted the covers from Javier's arms and said, "When I's wuz cleanin him up I's found deez." Pointing to the mosquito bites she says once again, "He got the sickness from dem squitta bites."

"What do you mean he got sick from the mosquito bites", asked Roberto.

"Dem old squittas carry the Laria disease round deez parts of da world, massa."

Hope now running rampart through Roberto he ran a hand through his hair and asked, "How can we help him Miss Anna"?

"Well we's got ta get some China tree tea in em", she answered.

"China tree tea, where can I find this tea", asked Roberto.

"Got some tree bark back at da house, treated Old Ennis' boy fa da same thang couple months past", replied the old woman. "Well then what are we waiting for, I'll take you home in the carriage", said

Roberto. As he moved to lead Anna from the room she balked by saying, "Na jus hole yo horses dere Massa Soto, yo Maw and Paw not gon like dis one bit, no suh dey not."

"Miss Anna, we'll cross that bridge when we get to it, my bet is they'll be overjoyed that we can save him", Roberto assured the worried servant.

"All right Massa Soto you's da boss", she said finally bowing to his wishes. Melinda and Beatrice watched the two of them leave the room and said a prayer that this would work.

Chapter Twelve

"Moving closer to the light Javier blinked and stared up ahead. He could hear someone calling his name. Floating he moved onward trying to find the source of that beautiful angelic voice. For just a moment he thought that it sounded like...Suzanna, yes it was she, he was sure of it now. She was beckoning for him to come closer to the light. He could see her clearly now, smiling with her arms open wide. Just as he reached her side she disappeared. Turning this way and that he tried desperately to locate her. Calling to her he asked, Suzy where are you? He waited in vain for an answer and slowly began walking away from the light; maybe she was hiding near the door. He walked back towards the door where he entered this peaceful place; where was he anyway he began asking himself? Maybe he was in some kind of Hospital, at times he felt someone urging him to drink some bitter concoction, at others he felt someone wiping his forehead with a cool cloth. He tried to remember how long he'd been here or when he arrived but couldn't quite put it all together..."

Melinda sat in the dining room with Senora de Soto listening to Beatrice explain how she'd come about finding little Camille. She explained how Javier had told them about his relationship with Melinda and subsequently his arrangement with Suzanna.

"We met him in Neuva Iberia where we had dinner with him and then sailed home on his ship", Beatrice informed everyone present.

Just then Camille began to cry providing Melinda with the perfect excuse to escape the room. "The wet nurse will attend to my granddaughter Ms. Harmon", said Senora de Soto coolly. Continuing from the room without acknowledging the statement Melinda heads for the nursery. She simply needed to be away from Javier's family, she just couldn't handle all of their questions and snide remarks right now.

Melinda was very nearly on the verge of collapsing. She had not had a good night's sleep since before her sister's death, and seeing Javier in this weakened state was not helping matters at all. Almost to the top of the stairs she decided to let the wet nurse handle Camille and headed to her own room instead. She sat on the edge of the bed as a wave of dizziness hit her. She decided to lie down until it passed.

Blackness engulfed her as soon as she placed her head onto the pillows.

Her last conscious thought was of her sister Suzanna finding love and happiness with Javier, the man she'd loved for nearly 5 years.

"There it was again, the sound of a baby crying. Yes, he must be in a hospital. His body ached from head to toe and it felt as if someone had kicked him in the gut. Someone was wiping him down again and they were humming, he couldn't quite catch the tune but he felt certain that it was some religious song his grandma sang to him as a child. Yes, Abuela was there and she was singing to him, "Demos gracias al senor, demos gracias; demos gracias al senor. Por las mananas, las aves cantan, la alavansas del Cristo Salvador. Y tu hermano porque no canta las alavansas del Cristo Salvador. He wanted to sing along with her but couldn't find his voice.

He said the words over and over again in his head until he thought he'd go mad. What was wrong with his voice, why couldn't he speak, and why couldn't he remember what had happened to him.

Melissa A. Ross

If he could just open his eyes or say something he could get to the bottom of this puzzle. Listening quietly, he realized that the baby was no longer crying. No, no he screamed as the fog began to engulf him once again...

Chapter Thirteen

Jean Charles Livingston entered the little town of Bristol and searched for the Savoie place. His parents Alcide and Abbie Livingston had given him all the information they had concerning his birth parents. All of his life he'd lived as a white man, with the rights and privileges that came along with being a citizen of this great country, until now.

Jean Charles had even married the daughter of an influential family and worked in the family business. He and his wife Anatassia had three children, two boys and one lovely little blue- eyed girl. No one questioned anything when the boys had been born, as they were the spitting image of their father with Black eyes, black hair, a patrician nose, and swarthy skin. However questions had arisen after the birth of Noelle, she had been born with honey colored skin, blue eyes with golden specks and a stock of curly auburn hair.

It was then that he had gone to see his parents for some answers, little bits and pieces of conversations heard when they'd thought his was out playing had flashed through his mind. He'd gone over and demanded the truth, people who'd known his parents in their early days, had always seemed shocked that they had a son. A few of them had actually commented on how handsome and tall he was, so unlike his papa who was barely five feet six with stubby features and limbs.

Crying, his mother had finally given in and told him just how he'd come to live with them at the tender age of two. She told him of how they'd agreed to raise him until his parents found a way to come for him.

His father or at least the man he had called father all these years had then provided him with the name of his birth parents and told him where to find them.

Now here he was on the outskirts of a sleepy little town in the Deep South, in the illustrious state of Louisiana to be exact. He wondered if they even knew about Mr. Lincoln's Proclamation down in all these swamps. He rode his horse towards the massive plantation and again wondered if he'd somehow traveled back in time.

This place looked as if it hadn't been touched by the Civil War. He took in the look of the Plantation; workers were already out in the fields working along the endless rows of vegetation. Little Negro children were running around bare-foot dragging empty potato sacks. He watched them as they ran to where their parents were working down the dusty rows laughing and calling to one another.

As he passed under the oaks that lined the driveway he could almost feel and hear the cries of despair once uttered by the lost souls brought here in chains.

Shaking off those feelings, he continued onward towards the front door. As he approached the entrance a stable hand came and took his horse. He walked up to the large impressive door and lifted the knocker and counted out, one, two, three knocks before an old servant answered.

"I am here to see Mr. Jean Savoie", he said as the servant greeted him and took his hat.

Bowing the old servant pointed towards the foyer and said, "Yes suh, uh follow me suh."

Jean Charles followed closely on the old mans heels as he was led down the corridor to Mr. Savoie's private study.

He held his breath as he awaited permission to enter. Sweat began to bead upon his brow and he found himself tapping down fear as it threatened to rise. He reminded himself that he was a free man, a free citizen of the United States, whom by all accords was wealthy in his own right.

Neither man was prepared for what stood before him. Jean Pierre nearly had an apoplexy, and Jean Charles simply stood and stared open mouthed at this man who looked so much like him, only older.

Mutely Jean Pierre stood aside and motioned for him to come into the study. Taking a seat across from the huge mahogany desk Jean Charles waited for Mr. Savoie to speak.

Seating himself across from Jean Charles, Jean Pierre cleared his throat and said, "We always intended to go up an retrieve you, but we never got the chance."

"So you intended to come back for me, but just never got around to doing it, why may I ask", inquired Jean Charles.

"Things were so crazy back then, we were young and afraid and totally unprepared for the ways of the world", answered a dejected

Jean Pierre. "I know that doesn't excuse what happened but we thought you were safer there, and then your mother left."

"You said safer, were there threats against my life", asked Jean Charles.

Dropping his gaze to the floor, Jean Pierre stood and faced the window and began to explain everything to this man, his son, Jean Pierre Savoie.

He spoke of how his own father, Jean Pierre's grandfather had been instrumental in forcing them to send him away. He also told Jean Pierre of the Mother and Sister he'd never known.

He paused and wiped away a tear as he told Jean Charles of Mary's death.

"Oh my son, Jean Charles, Mary was a good and decent woman and I will love her forever. It was simply not to be", said a tearful Jean Pierre.

Finding tears in his own eyes, Jean Charles cleared his throat and said, "I'd like to see her grave sir, would you tell me how to get there."

"I can do better than that son, I'll take you there myself, but first I'd like you to meet someone."

Mrs. Camille Savoie sat and simply stared at Jean Charles, when she finally found her voice she managed to say, "Oh Good Lord son, he's the spitting image of my poor Gestave."

"Yes he does look amazingly like Papa and myself doesn't he", agreed Jean Pierre.

Dabbing at an errant tear she says, "This is all just so sad, my heart breaks at the thought of you being raised by others, but you have to understand that my husband, your grandfather was reared to believe in keeping the races separate. He wasn't a bad man, really he wasn't. You mustn't hate him, he did only what he thought was best for everyone."

"Actually I lived a very good life, one with all the freedoms of every other citizen of this great country", said Jean Charles.

Looking to her son for clarification Mrs. Savoie listened as Jean Pierre explained how the Livingston's had raised Jean Charles as a white child and therefore he'd never been subjected to the prejudices of society.

"Oh my word, you mean you had no idea who you really were until two months ago", asked Mrs. Camille.

"That's correct ma'am, recently my wife delivered a baby girl who I might add is the spitting image of you, only darker. After her birth I went to see my parents for some answers and was told of my past."

"You said she's the spitting image of me, my guess is she's the spitting image of Melinda Harmon", she answered casting a speculative glance at her son.

"Yes Maman he knows of his sister", chuckled Jean Pierre. "In fact we were about to leave to go in search of her, as well as, to visit Mary."

"Well then I suppose you'd better pack a bag if you're going to see Melinda, I suggest you visit with Mary first and then come back for dinner."

"What do you mean Maman, where is Melinda", asked Jean Pierre.

"Went to New Orleans last week after she buried Suzanna, Beatrice sent for her."

"Well,..., I see, come along Jean Charles I'll show you where Mary rests", he said while exiting the study. Calling back he said to his mother, "We'll return shortly Mother."

Mrs. Camille watched them leave and worried again just how they were going to explain this to her daughter-in-law, Laura Lee Savoie. It was well known that she hated the fact that her husband had children with other women. It deeply needled her that he'd loved someone else besides her, especially the fact that the woman he'd loved first was a Negro woman. She sent up a prayer for all to be well, this would probably send Laura Lee over the edge. She had never fully recovered after the death of the couple's infant son. Everybody knew that all she'd ever wanted was to give Jean Pierre a son to carry on the Savoie name. Now Mrs. Camille wasn't sure how she'd receive the news, that Mary had given Jean Pierre the one thing she couldn't.

"Oh Lord please make everything all right", she whispered as she rubbed her aching hands. "A son, Oh Gestave, a son, who would have thought that things would have turned out this way?" Muttering

to herself she said, "I'm getting entirely too old for this."

Chapter Fourteen

Melinda awoke and knew that it was time to return to Bristol. She couldn't stay here another day. The de Soto's would probably be glad that she was leaving, but she was sure that they'd fight her over letting baby Camille leave the estate. Javier was on the mend; it had been two days since his fever had broken. She was sure that he would wake up soon; his body was probably just exhausted from fighting the terrible sickness.

She had come only because something in Beatrice's letter had touched a chord of understanding within her soul. She'd thought along with everyone else that he was dying. She'd longed for closure of this chapter in her life. Now that it seemed as if he was going to pull through, her stay here had come to an end.

She had also come to terms that whatever she'd had with him; was over and done with. She'd sat by his bedside and listened to him cry out for Suzanna, until she thought she'd go mad. It was obvious to her and all present that he'd loved her half sister deeply.

Coming back to the present she opened her chest of drawers and closet and begin to fold the items neatly.

She spent the morning packing her meager belongings and went in search of Beatrice once this was done.

Knocking softly she awaited a response and upon hearing it she opened the door and entered her sister's private dressing room.

"Oh Melinda are you sure that you're ready to go back, surely you can stay just a little while longer", wailed Beatrice.

"No I must go home, regardless of what we thought, it is evident that Javier loved Suzanna deeply, there is no us Beatrice", interjected Melinda.

"Melinda it was just the fever that made him act so, I was there in Neuva Iberia, I saw first hand the love he had and still has for you."

"That was then and this is now, I was present when he began to cry out for her over and over again. I listened to him repeat those words I love you until I felt as if I'd go mad. No it's time to face reality and go home."

"Well if that is what you think is best, I just have one question though; how do you plan to convince the de Soto's that Camille will be leaving with you?"

Chapter Fifteen

"Most certainly not", raged Senora de Soto. Stepping beside Melinda Roberto says quietly, "I support Melinda in this Madre, it is her decision."

"How can you say this mijo, Camille is our flesh and blood, my granddaughter belongs here with her father, with us", she said hotly.

Unable to remain quiet Melinda said just as hotly, "Camille is also my flesh and blood or have you forgotten that Suzanna was my sister. I promised her that I would raise her child as my own. I will keep that promise with every breath that I have." No one seemed to remember the fact that Suzanna was actually her half sister, and both were daughters of Savoie servants.

Trying to calm everyone Senor de Soto said, "Now, now everyone I am sure we can come to some sort of agreement about Camille if we just calm down and talk rationally about this." "Please let us sit and talk about this as adults", pleaded Senor de Soto.

"I made a promise to my sister upon her death bed that I would see to the welfare of little Cami, and I intend to keep that promise", said Melinda.

"No one is questioning your promise to your sister Ms. Harmon, but we also have a right to our granddaughter", replied Senor de Soto.

"I will not deny you the right to visit her from time to time or the right to have her visit here with the family, but she will be raised in my home", stated Melinda.

"Never will I let my granddaughter be raised in such a place", stated Senora de Soto vehemently.

Rising from her seated position Melinda simply stated coldly, "Well I do believe that this discussion has come to an end, lets just agree to disagree. Camille and I will be leaving at first light."

Without waiting for a reply Melinda left the drawing room and headed upstairs to the nursery. She would sit next to Javier's bed with Camille for a short while and read before retiring for the night, tomorrow would be one of the longest she'd ever lived through. Cradling Camille in her arms she entered Javier's room and breathed a sigh of relief that she'd found him alone. She pulled the chair closer to the bed and began to talk to him, telling him of how big his daughter was getting.

She spoke of all of Camille's latest antics and laughed as the baby cooed. "Hear that Javier she's trying to tell you all about it herself."

Melinda looked up as the door to the bedroom opened and Graciella peered inside.

"Perdoneme, Melinda I will come back later", she said.

Wiping away an errant tear Melinda said, "Oh no it's getting late, we just stopped by before turning in."

Placing her hand on Melinda's sleeve Graciella says softly, "My mother can be very demanding at times but she means well."

Melinda seats herself next to Javier's bed again and said, "I promise to never stand in the way of Camille spending time with her family, but she must remain with me, on this I am not willing to compromise."

"There it was again the sound of a baby cooing, he could actually feel the child next to him on the bed. He could hear his sister speaking softly with someone, it sounded like Suzanna but he couldn't

be sure. He wondered again just who this infant was that they often brought to his room. The baby had to be Roberto and Beatrice's, and they were visiting him daily. It seemed logical to, that maybe they had found Suzanna. He remembered telling them about his relationship with her, but why would they bring her here, he was sure that he'd told them that he wasn't in love with her. He tried once again to open his eyes but couldn't quite manage the feat. He gave in and decided to let sleep overtake him, and determined to try again when he next awoke. Just as he was drifting off to sleep he felt someone place the baby's warm little mouth next to his face for a goodnight sleep. Smiling he gave in to the exhaustion and slept."

Excited at what she'd just witnessed Graciela jumped to her feet and ran to tell her parents. With Melinda following closely on her heels carrying Camille they found the family still assembled together in the family drawing room. Running to her mother she said, "Oh Madre, I think he is finally coming around, just as we were leaving Melinda held Camille close to him to kiss him goodnight, and he smiled."

Crying tears of joy Senora de Soto left the room with the rest of the family close on her heels and rushed to Javier's sick room.

The family took turns sitting next to Javier's bed waiting for him to acknowledge them in some way or another. It had been two weeks since Melinda had left with Camille to travel back to Bristol and everyone's nerves were on edge. Speaking in hushed tones they waited in the hallway as the doctor examined him yet again.

"What if he never fully comes back to us Juan", his mother asked.

"Shh, mi corazon, our son will be just fine", he reassured her.

Coming over to add his own reinforcements Julio said, "Si Mama Javier will be back to his old self in no time, don't worry so."

"Oh mijo, I only pray that it will be as you say", she responded. At that moment the door burst open and Roberto emerged with the biggest smile they'd ever seen.

"He is coming around Madre just as we thought earlier. El Doctore spoke to him and said if he could hear him and understand him to squeeze his hand, and Javier did it."

"Gracias a Dios", cried a relieved Senora de Soto. The family now waited for the doctor to emerge and tell them more.

Melissa A. Ross

Coming out and closing the door, the doctor removed his spectacles and said, "I believe that before long we will see him up and about. He is improving everyday; just continue to spoon-feed him with liquids and watch for any changes. Send someone round to fetch me no matter the time if he awakes."

Walking the doctor out, Senor de Soto asked quietly, "Do you think he will truly be all right, I mean will his mind be sound as it was before the illness"?

"That I cannot answer Senor, as with all types of illnesses involving deep sleep like this; it is impossible to say", the doctor said grimly.

Shaking his hand Senor de Soto gave him thanks and assured him that he would be called the moment Javier opened his eyes. "Thank you again Doctor, and we will send for you as soon as my son awakens.

"This time he was determined to open his eyes, he was so tired of broth he wanted to scream. He tried to exercise his vocal chords

again and found that they were a little tight. Swallowing several times he concentrated on making a sound...

Beatrice looked up from the small throw she was crocheting for baby Camille and stared at the bed. Was her mind playing tricks on her or did she hear Javier say hello. Moving closer to the bed she took his hand into hers and said, "Javier, it's me Beatrice are you trying to say something, can you hear me"?

She nearly fainted when he responded by squeezing her hand. "Oh God, I knew it, try again Javier, can you open your eyes", she said as she made her way over to the bell pull.

"Over and over again he sent messages to his eyes; open, he commanded them, all to no avail. He fell asleep trying and decided that he would wait until he felt a little stronger and then try again. There must be something else wrong with him, but all he could remember was an upset stomach. Maybe he'd fallen and hit his head on deck or something, whatever it was he refused to let it control him. He was sure that the next time he commanded his eyes to open they

Melissa A. Ross

would do just that. Surely he couldn't be blind, no he screamed over

and over in his mind until once again he fell victim to deep sleep."

Chapter Sixteen

Melinda stood open mouthed and stared at her father as he told her of the brother she had never known. How could her mother have kept a secret such as this? Surely she'd known of the loneliness Melinda had experienced as a child. How unloved and unwanted she'd been made to feel by everyone. No, this couldn't be true; her mother would never do something like this. It was simple, her father was lying.

"No, this can't be true, Maman would never do a thing like this, she wouldn't keep something like this from me", she shouted distraughtly. Trying to flee from the room she ran smack into the chest of Jean Charles.

Putting her a safe distance away he was shocked beyond words when he got a clear view of the young woman standing before him. Finding his speech again he says," Hello you must be Melinda." Extending his hand to her he says, "I am Jean Charles Livin…I mean Jean Charles Savoie, your brother."

Shaking her head no Melinda denies his assumption by responding, "No, sir you can not be my brother, my mother only had one child, me."

Coming around his desk to stand beside her Jean Pierre said, "Please sit down Melinda, I know that this is all too incredible to believe but it is true. If you'd let me explain things fully I'm sure that you'll understand why you were kept in the dark about this."

Obediently she sat and listened as he told her about the circumstances surrounding her brother's birth and why he was sent away. Turning to look at Jean Charles again she said, "So you had no idea who you really were until a few weeks ago"?

"Yes, that is correct, and as I said earlier there was no reason to doubt that I was anyone but the son of Alcide and Abigail Livingston. However when my daughter was born looking amazingly just like you everything came to the light."

Standing, Melinda said in a small barely audible voice, "All these years I felt alone in this world, how I wanted a sister or a brother to share my dreams and sorrows with. Someone whom I could feel connected to."

Rising to meet her Jean Charles says, "Melinda I know that this is a terrible shock to you just as it was to me, but if it will help I to often yearned for a sibling, someone to share things with." "If it is ok with you, I'd like to forge a relationship with you, get to know you, be a part of your life", he said tentatively.

Suprising them all Melinda asked, "Have you been to see Mama"?

Shaken by her question he responds by telling her that he had gone to her grave nearly everyday for the last few weeks. "Yes I have, in fact I've gone to see her everyday and brought fresh flowers just today."

Looking at him with tears in her eyes Melinda said, "So you're the one I must thank for pulling all the weeds around the cross and for whitewashing the little fence surrounding the grave."

Taking his sister into his arms Jean Charles cried silent tears of his own and said simply, "There is no need for words of thanks she was my mother also, besides, we had a lot of catching up to do, she and I."

Chapter Seventeen

"Yes, he could feel it. His eyes were opening. He could see the lamp burning in the corner where his brother Juan sat dozing. He swallowed several times and rehearsed moving his vocal chords silently over his brother's name. When he was sure that he could say it he opened his mouth and spoke groggily...

"Juanito." He spoke the words just as his sister Maria was entering the room. Screaming loud enough to wake the dead she dropped the tray she'd been carrying and rushed over to the bed.

Hearing the scream all of his family rushed upstairs to find them standing over an awakened Javier. Pushing the others out of the way his mother took his hand in hers and cried tears of joy saying, "Oh Javier you've come back to us."

With his vocal chords on fire from his efforts to speak he managed to eek out a request for water, "Aqua por favor".

Rushing to do his bidding Graciella poured a small portion of water into a glass and handed it to her father who was assisting Javier to sit up and drink slowly. Galvanized into action Roberto rang the bell pull and instructed Benito to send for the doctor.

The doctor had come at once and had ushered everyone out of the room while he conducted tests. Holding up two fingers he asked, "Quantos dedos tu des"?

"Two, two fingers", said a near exhausted Javier. "Good we are almost done Senor de Soto", answered the doctor. Running his hands down Javier's limbs he asked, "Sientes esto"?

Shaking his head yes Javier assures the doctor that he feels him running his hands over his weakened limbs.

The waiting was nearly unimaginable for the family and Senora had actually started to climb the stairs several times before being stopped by her husband. Finally the doctor emerged from the room and descended the stairs. Beaming he stated that Javier would be just fine. "Well from what I can gather Senor de Soto will make a full recovery, there doesn't seem to be any evidence that his brain has been hurt by this episode, with a little rest and some good food he should be right as rain in no time at all."

Grateful for the prognosis Senor de Soto shook the doctor's hand and escorted him to the door. "Thank you for all you've done doctor my solicitor will be by tomorrow to settle the bill."

"It has been a pleasure to serve your family Senor de Soto, just make sure that he gets plenty of rest and send for me if the need arises."

"Si, Buenos Noches", replied Senor de Soto.

Returning to the drawing room he smiled as an empty room greeted him. He whispered a prayer of thanks to God and climbed the stairs to his son's room.

It had been a full week now that he'd come back to the land of the living and while his family had filled him in on many things he was sure that there was something they were hiding. There was something that passed between them every time he asked about the baby he'd heard crying. His mother had quickly changed the subject when he'd mentioned it, which further confirmed his suspicions that something was not as it appeared. He decided to probe a little further when next he had a visitor.

Javier awoke when he heard someone moving around the room trying not to disturb his sleep. "Hola Abuela, como estas"?

Looking his way his grandmother replied, "Muy bien corazon, I tried not to awaken you."

"I am always glad of your company Abuela, besides I get tired of lying here all day."

"Yes but el doctore said that you must get plenty of rest so that you can regain your strength."

"Yes but I must exercise my muscles more or they will never strengthen enough to hold my weight", he argued.

"Just be patient amor, in time all will be as it used to be", she assured him.

"Abuela, I remember hearing a baby crying nearby when I was unconscious, whose child was it, Roberto and Beatrice's", he asked tentatively.

Not knowing what to say to this question she moves to the side of the bed and said, "These are questions tu Mama and Papa should answer Javier."

"Abuela, no one will tell me anything and I'm tired of being treated as an invalid." "Mijo, they are simply being careful not to upset you and cause you more harm."

Frustrated that even his grandmother would not divulge any information about the baby Javier sighed and said, "I don't understand why this is such a big secret and why it would cause me any harm, but I will wait and speak with them."

Moving an errant lock of hair she began singing an old childhood favorite of his and watched as he drifted off to sleep once again.

Javier's grandmother sat across from her son and daughter-in-law and sipped tea as she waited for them to digest what she'd just said. "I believe that it is time he knew about the child and the connection between child's mother and this woman he loves, Melinda." Finally her son spoke up and agreed with her that it was time to have a long talk with Javier about baby Camille. "Si mama, you are right, we will talk with him when he next awakens.

Melinda marveled at the beauty of her brother's home in Pennsylvania. She couldn't believe that all of this belonged to him.

His home alone was nearly the size of the Savoie Plantation and was surrounded by acres and acres of land.

Another shock had been his wife. While she'd known that he'd lived as a white man she was unprepared for the small, beautiful blond that now stood before her.

Extending her dainty hand Anastasia said, "Hello and welcome to our home." Hearing the baby cry she said, "Oh please forgive my thoughtlessness, do sit down and tend to your child."

"Oh she isn't really my child, but my sister's who died birthing this little angel", Melinda replied as she unwrapped Camille.

Gasping Anastasia rushed to her side to peer down at the crying bundle, "Good Lord she is the spitting image of Noelle."

Jean Charles who was just entering the room after overseeing the grooming of the team walked to this scene and said, "Well I see that the two of you have met."

Straightening Anastasia moved to her husband's open arms and said lovingly, "Oh I am so glad to have you home, I was so worried about you being down there, I..."

Stopping her with a kiss Jean Charles said against her lips, "Never fear my dear, I can take care of myself."

Melinda witnessed this little interplay between her brother and her sister-in-law with pure glee. She could feel the love and respect they had for one another and was overjoyed to know that true love did exist. Maybe just maybe there was a chance for her also to find that certain someone who'd make life worth the living again.

Melinda laughed again as her brother's two boys ran to their father and greeted him with pure joy. She and Ana sat holding the two girls and watched as the boys romped around on the floor of the foyer.

Dinner had been wonderful and for the first time in a long time she felt at peace in the company of others. It seemed as if her sister-in-law had gone out of her way to make her feel at home. Even her brother's parents the Livingston's had seemed happy to meet her. She sat and marveled at how different things were here in Pennsylvania as opposed to Louisiana.

She was brought back to the present by squealing as one of the boys toppled his father over with a huge feather stuffed pillow and they both jumped on his back to claim victory in their mock wrestling match.

Laughing, Ana suggested that they call this main event to a halt so that the babies could be put down to sleep.

"Ok men I think it's time to call it a draw, the babies need to get to bed."

In unison the boys protested loudly, "Oh no Mother surely we have time for another round to decide the winner."

"Oh no boys, I think your mother is correct, we have plenty of time for another match tomorrow", said their father trying to hold back his own laughter.

Clearly disappointed the boys muttered their goodnights and went down the hall to their bedroom, but not before the oldest came to stand before Melinda and said, "Will you tuck us in Aunt Mel"?

Melinda, whose heart nearly burst at the request, handed little Camille to the nanny and said, "I'd love to tuck you two gentlemen in, but only if you'll help. I haven't had a lot of experience with this.

Taking her hand in theirs the boys led her down the hall to their room promising to help her as much as she needed.

Chapter Eighteen

Javier tested his legs once again and was glad to find that he could stand just a little longer than the last time. He had to get stronger; he had to go to find Melinda and the baby, his baby.

He sat down and replayed the conversation he'd had with his parents and Roberto a couple of days ago. He'd never forget those words his brother had spoken...

"Javier we will answer your questions but you must remain calm. The baby you heard was, uh...Camille, she is your daughter." Javier had jumped to a standing position before anyone could stop him and demanded to know the full truth. It was then that his Mother broke down and related all they knew. "My son you must understand that we kept this a secret out of fear that you would have a relapse of some sort." His father had added, "We never meant to keep this from you forever it is just that the doctor did not want us to upset you with any unsettling news." "UNSETTLING NEWS", Javier shouted. "I have a daughter and no one bothered to tell me, I would think that this is more than just unsettling." Turning to his parents he asked

155

accusingly, "So may I ask why I haven't seen or heard her for nearly two weeks now"? Angrily his father stood and said, "I do not like your tone my son and further more we had nothing to do with her leaving."

Roberto had come forward then and said, "Melinda thought it best if..."

"Melinda", interrupted Javier. "What does Melinda have to do with any of this"? Asking his brother to sit and calm down Roberto then went on to tell Javier of Suzanna's death and of her connection to Melinda. Javier felt as if the wind had been knocked out of him and actually sucked in a gulp of air. Rushing to his side his mother asked with concern, "Mijo, are you ok." "Si, Mama, I am fine, would you all please leave, I need some time to think things through."

Alone he had cried tears of sadness and tears of joy all at the same time. He cried tears of sorrow for Suzanna and the tender age at which she'd died. He also blamed himself for her death and made a vow to her to do everything within his power to ensure the well being of their infant daughter. A daughter, wow he was actually a father and she was with Melinda. He vowed to find a way to have them both in his life again; he owed Suzanna nothing less. But would Melinda forgive him the transgression of having an affair with her sister. Somehow he had to make her understand,..., But what could he make her understand? That he'd lusted after her half sister and gotten her pregnant? He fell asleep pondering this last question.

Waking again later on that evening, he resolved to travel to Bristol as soon as he was able. Vowing to regain all he'd lost. Nothing would stop him this time, he wouldn't lose Melinda a second time no matter what her objections, she would not slip through his grasp. He sat there for some time, devising and revising his strategy. He determined to use whatever leverage he had to get Melinda to see things his way.

Javier smiled and wiped the sweat from his brow as he finally made it to the last step on the staircase. It had taken him five whole days to gain enough strength to make it this far and with a little more time he'd soon be able to walk out that front door and on his way to Bristol.

He leaned against the railing for a short time and then made his way to the family dining room. He knew that the family was gathered there now, as it was time for the evening meal. Slowly he walked towards them taking time to stop and rest along the way. He waved away all attempts of help from the servants and issued a warning for them not to announce his presence in the hall.

Entering the room he said, "Good Evening everyone, mind if I join you"? Forks and knives clanged against plates and glasses of wine nearly up to mouths dropped to the table staining everywhere it splattered.

Roberto, being the first to recover quickly, stood to assist Javier into a seat. However, Javier was determined to do this all on his own. Waving him off he said, "No hermano, I must do this alone." Walking on legs made out of wet rubber bands, Javier made it without incident to a seat next to his grandmother. Once he was seated he asked one of the servers for a place setting and waited to be served.

Dinner resumed after the initial shock had passed and all the spills were cleaned up. New glasses of wine were poured and rounds of toast passed around the room until what had started out, as simple family dinner now resembled a family celebration.

Melinda stood at the edge of the pond and watched her brother fish with his two young sons. She'd left Camille up at the house with Ana, Noelle, and Camille's nurse in order to spend some time with her brother and nephews. This was all so new to her, I mean, she really had a brother and nephews and a niece. All her life she'd wished for this and now it had come true.

At times she was tempted to pinch herself just to make sure that it was all real and that she was not asleep and having a wonderful dream.

Hearing her brother calling her name she realized that they were shouting for her to bring over the pail. One of the boys had actually snared a fish and it looked to be huge and,...wet. Taking care not to get the hem of her dress wet, Melinda edged closer to where her brother stood and handed him the bucket. He chuckled at the picture she presented and teased about getting her just as wet as the three of them were. Backing away, she tried to run in the opposite direction but was caught around the waist by Jean Charles and carried to the edge of the pond. Laughing he tries to throw her into the middle of the pond but stumbles into the pond as she gripped the front of his shirt and pulled him down with her.

Sputtering and laughing like fools, they surfaced to the chorus of the boys' laughter. Winking at each other they started in unison up the bank in the youngsters' direction. Chasing down their prey, they quickly overtook the boys and dipped them into the cold water of the pond.

Laughing, Jean Charles said, "Ok now that we're all wet and are nowhere near catching enough fish for dinner, I suggest we head back to the house and get changed."

"Here, here brother I do believe that you have the right idea", Melinda added merrily.

The four of them ran like madmen towards the house, laughing and shivering all the way.

Sitting there watching with fury rifling through him, Javier recalled his search for Melinda soon after her departure from his parent's home. Javier saw red as Jean Pierre Savoie informed him, that Melinda was away visiting relatives up north. He was further infuriated when Mr. Savoie refused to tell him where up north she'd gone.

"Listen Mr. Savoie it is imperative that you tell me where she has gone, I must find her", he stressed.

"I'm sorry Mr. De Soto, but I am not at liberty to disclose her whereabouts", replied Jean Pierre.

Beatrice hearing the raised voices from within, entered her father's study and pulled up short as Javier said, "Oh yes you will tell me where she's taken my daughter or I will make you, regret it."

Stepping between the two men, Beatrice laid her hand on Javier's sleeve and turned pleading eyes upon her father.

"Please calm down gentlemen. Papa I'm sure that you feel what you are doing is right but Javier does have a right to know where Melinda has taken little Camille."

"Thank You Beatrice, It's good to know someone here thinks rationally", Javier added sarcastically.

"I can assure you young man that my thinking is very clear in this matter, and I have no intentions of betraying Melinda's whereabouts to the likes of you", shouted Jean Pierre.

Roberto entered the study just as Javier began to advance upon his father-in-law. "Javier, please think this thru hermano", he shouted.

Coming out of the red haze of rage that gripped him Javier backed away saying, "Si, hermano you are right."

Roberto chose his next words carefully as he said, "Mr. Savoie I am sure that your reasons for keeping this information private are good ones but I think that there is something you should know."

Jean Pierre sat and listened as Roberto and Beatrice told him of the real reason Javier was so intent on finding Melinda. He listened as Beatrice told him of the love the two had shared and the grief both had felt over the breakup. Something in their story of joy and sorrow touched a chord within him and he suddenly felt compelled to do all he could to reunite the two.

Walking slowly towards Javier he extended his hand and said, "I am sorry for my behavior earlier, but I thought that you wanted to take Camille away, to hurt Melinda in some way and that I couldn't allow."

Taking his outstretched hand and shaking it firmly Javier replied, "It only speaks of your love for her sir, and your need to protect her, I commend you for your ethics."

Speaking up Beatrice said, "Now father I suppose you sit back down and tell us all about this brother of Melinda's."

Smiling brightly, her father motioned for everyone to take their seats again and dove into the story of the birth and life of Jean Charles.

Wiping tears from her eyes Beatrice says, "Oh papa how you must have longed to know what happened to him, I'm so sorry you had to go through this, and not be able to trust anyone enough to confide in them, oh papa I'm so sorry." "Shhhh, now Bea I don't regret the choices I've made in life, they were the right ones. Jean Charles is a very wealthy man, and has never been subjected to the hardships the Negroes face down here", Jean Pierre said as he took his daughter into his arms.

"But to live with such a secret Papa must have been like a living nightmare", wailed Beatrice.

"While I admit that it was unbearable at times, make no mistake I would do it again, to ensure the safety of my children", said Jean Pierre passionately.

"How dare you call them your children, they are the children of your sinful lust for a filthy negra woman", said a distraught Mrs. Savoie.

All heads turned in the direction of the voice and Beatrice broke away from her Father and walked slowly towards her Mother.

Hoping to diffuse the situation Beatrice said, "Maman how wonderful to see you again, I hope we will have lots of time to visit."

Turning hate filled eyes upon her daughter, Mrs. Savoie says, "Don't try to sweet talk me Beatrice, I know that you are in contact with that little half-breed bastard of Mary Harmon's, even had her at your home."

Barely able to contain the anger threatening to spill forth, Javier says, "I will not allow you to speak of Melinda that way Mrs. Savoie, she is not at fault concerning her parent's mistakes."

"How dare you speak to me in such a manner, this is my home sir, and you will not address me in that tone of voice", retorted Mrs. Savoie.

Stepping forward Mr. Savoie says, "Laura Lee you are out of line, Mr. De Soto is a guest here and will be treated as such."

"Well this is my home as well Jean Pierre and I will be respected by everyone here, including your guests", shot back Mrs. Savoie. Javier who was by this point ready to strangle Mrs. Savoie informed all present of his intentions of staying at the De Soto family home. "I will be staying at the family home, as a matter of fact my parents are also there awaiting Melinda's return." Turning to face Mr. Savoie he added, "I will keep you informed of my plans as soon as they are completed." Tipping his hat he said while leaving, "Sir, Madam, have a good evening. Berto and Beatrice I will see you at a later date."

Chapter Nineteen

Javier now sat at the edge of the oak lined drive and watched as Melinda played in the water with her lover and two small boys. He had traveled to her brother's residence only to find that she was now involved with someone else. He watched as the couple played lovingly in the small fishing pond and then dropped the two small boys into the water. Paralyzed by his anger he sat and watched as they ran hand in hand to the main house. Well it certainly hadn't taken her long to find someone with whom to get involved. He wondered how this man had convinced her to become his mistress. Certainly no white man would openly court a Negro woman, no matter how beautiful she was. Deciding that she was indeed this man's mistress he knew that he had no choice but to remove his daughter from her care. There was no way he was going to allow someone like this to rear his daughter. He wondered again at this conclusion he'd drawn. How could her brother openly allow this to go on under his roof? Once he knocked on that door all would be revealed. But would he be able to handle the facts once they were out in the open? Running his hand through his overly long mane he took several calming breaths. Finally he was able to control his rage and moved towards the house to announce his arrival.

No one was more shocked than Melinda when she descended the stairs to find Javier talking with her sister-in-law.

"My husband will be down shortly Mr. De Soto, please let us sit in the drawing room."

Looking up the stairs he nearly lost his footing and had to steady himself on the banister. Managing to find his voice he says, "Hello Melinda."

Feeling light-headed Melinda sat down abruptly on the stairs and tried to calm her racing heart. Surely her mind was playing tricks on her, this couldn't really be happening? Opening her eyes she nearly fainted as Javier said, "Well, I'm glad to see that you are as equally pleased to see me."

Coming down the stairs at that moment, Jean Charles stopped as he spied his sister sitting on the steps staring down at a young man. "Well what have we here my dear", he asked as he placed a kiss on Melinda's cheek.

"Uh, Uh this is Javier de Soto, Cami's father. Turning to Javier she says, and this is my brother Jean Charles Savoie." It was Javier's turn to feel light-headed. "Did you say brother, this is your brother", he asks laughing like an idiot for the first time since he'd arrived.

Turning puzzled glances towards Javier Melinda asks, "Well yes, who did you think he was"? Then becoming overcome by giggles she laughs and says, "My beau?"

"Something like that yes", replied an embarrassed Javier.

Suddenly aware of exactly what he'd thought Melinda descended the stairs and says with fire in her eyes, "Oh, I believe I know exactly what you thought Mr. De Soto."

"Well how do you think I felt when I saw the two of you down at the pond laughing like children and holding hands as you ran to the house with two small boys in tow."

"YOU WERE AT THE POND", asked an incredulous Melinda. Trying to explain Javier said, "I rode in on that side of the property and saw you with your brother, and..."

"JUMPED TO THE WRONG CONCLUSION", interrupted Melinda.

Looking to her brother and his wife for help Javier said, "What would you have thought if you rode up to find your future wife smiling up into the face of another man?"

Screeching like a harpy Melinda says, "WIFE, DID YOU SAY FUTURE WIFE? I WOULDN'T MARRY YOU IF YOU WERE THE LAST MAN ON EARTH."

"Now, now Melly lets hear the gentleman out", interjected her amused brother.

Glad for the support Javier said, "I know that I have a lot of explaining to do, but if you'd give me a chance, I'm sure that we could come to some kind of agreement."

"The only thing we need to agree upon is when and where you will visit with Camille. There is no longer an us Javier", assured Melinda.

Speaking up suddenly, her sister-in-law says, "Why don't we move to the study where maybe the four of us can come up with some sort of solution." Javier was so grateful for Ana's suggestion that he could have kissed her.

Once seated across from her brother's massive claw footed desk, Melinda allowed her gaze to sweep over Javier unobserved for the moment. Her heart did a somersault as' her eyes landed on his lips. After all this time all she could think about was the man's lips and how his kisses turned her insides to preserves. How could her heart betray her like this her mind screamed accusatorily. How could she still want this man, the one who'd betrayed her by carrying on with her sister? No matter how she tried she couldn't still her heart or stop her body from craving this man's touch. She made up her mind to simply not look at him, if she didn't look at him, his handsomeness wouldn't besiege her and make her feel things she shouldn't.

Turning to catch her staring at his mouth, Javier nearly jumped out of his skin. Desire dripped like honey off of a honeycomb from her eyes as she ran her tongue along her lips, and he swore he could actually feel the temperature in the room rising.

Loosening his top button, he pulled out his handkerchief and wiped his forehead where a fine mist of sweat had suddenly appeared out of nowhere.

Chapter Twenty

With a look of amusement, Jean Charles suggested that Javier start at the beginning. "Why don't you start at the beginning Mr. De Soto, that is; so that you can bring us all up to speed shall we say."

The four of them talked until the wee hours of the morning. Anastasia ordered the servants to set up a table in his study so that they could eat informally and continue talking.

It had taken Javier quite a while to tell of his adventures over the last five years; Jean Charles had flooded him with questions about Spain and the port of Cadiz.

Javier had dived into answering all of his inquiries with relish, after all his family had basically made their fortune from the busy port.

Finally Anastasia had to kick her husband discreetly under the table before he suggested that they retire and leave Melinda and Javier to their own devices.

"Well, we must turn in for the evening I have an…early meeting in the morning, yes that's it, an early meeting. You two feel free to stay and talk as long as you like." Extending his hand again he said to Javier, "Well it was a pleasure getting to know you, we'll do this again soon. Bentley will show you to your quarters when you are ready to retire."

Placing her hand at her husband's elbow, Anastasia turned, wished the couple a good evening, and walked out of the room on her husband's arm.

Finally alone, neither of the two knew what to say nor when to say it. Looking into the fire Melinda finally managed to say nervously, "Camille is growing by leaps and bounds she can already roll over."

Looking at Melinda as if she were a sweet morsel Javier said, "I'd rather talk about us Melinda, tomorrow we can speak of my daughter."

"What do you mean us, there hasn't been an us for quite some time now Javier."

"Is it really so impossible to believe that I've never stopped loving you, Melinda."

"LOVE ME?" Really Javier I was at your bedside, it's not me whom you love and we both know it."

Confused Javier said, "What do you mean by that statement, of course you are the one I love, who else could there be"?

"Suzanna, I was there Javier and listened as you called for her over an over again", replied Melinda.

Coming to cup her face he said, "No mi amor, I was dreaming about Suzanna and saw her near the light, then she disappeared and I couldn't find her. Maybe it was a vision to tell me of her death and she was warning me not to follow. I only called to her because I could hear her but no longer see her."

"But there were times when I heard you call out to her and then say I love you. No Javier I am not mistaken you are only trying to get to me so that you have access to Camille."

"Listen to me sweetheart, Suzanna was a part of my life for a short while and truly it was not a love relationship but one of lust and longing to feel again, after years of numbness."

Turning away so that he could not see the moisture in her eyes Melinda shrugged and asked, "So she meant nothing to you, just a tumble in the hay, Javier, is that what you are saying"?"No, amor, don't cry", he said while walking up behind her and placing his hands on her shoulders. "I didn't mean that at all, sure I cared a great deal about Suzanna, but I didn't love her, not the way that I love you. I could never, ever love anyone else the way that I love you, Melinda."

Breaking away from him and swiping at the tears falling to her cheeks, Melinda said, "How am I to believe you, what assurances do I have that you are not just trying to trick me with your claims of undying love"?

"Tell me, tell me Melinda how can I prove that all I say is the truth", asked a near desperate Javier.

"I don't know if there is anything that you could do Javier", cried Melinda as she left the room and headed up the stairs.

Following her out of the room Javier decided against calling out to her as he took notice of all the turned down lamps and the stillness of the house. Swallowing the cry upon his lips he walked back into the study and poured a drafter of brandy as he pulled the bell chord.

Chapter Twenty-one

Knocking softly, Javier waited for a reply from within. Finally he heard a response from Jean Charles and entered the study.

"Good Morning Jean Charles, I hope I'm not interrupting", said Javier cordially.

"No, not at all, In fact I made plans to seek you out this morning after I finished with this correspondence to my solicitor. So what brings you to see me instead of being in the company of my lovely sister" asked Jean Charles.

"That's why I'm here, your sister doesn't seem to believe that I love her", said Javier.

Amused Jean Charles chuckled and asked, "How can I help you Javier.

"Smiling back Javier says, "Well this is what I had in mind…"

Melinda descended the stairs with baby Camille in her arms and headed off to find her sister-in-law. Searching the house, she finally found her in the kitchen going through dinner menus with the cook.

"Good Morning Ana, you are up and about quite early I see", Melinda observed.

Smiling Anastasia replied, "Old habits are hard to break." Waiting for Melinda to say something about her conversation with Javier Ana looks at her expectantly before she could finally hold out no longer. "Ok, tell me everything, how did things go last night after we left the two of you alone", she asked.

Melinda who'd dreaded such questions from her sister-in-law agonized over what to say. Finally she came up with what she thought was as good an explanation of their conversation as any. "We talked that is all."

Incredulous Anastasia stared at her as if she had suddenly sprouted two heads and said, "You talked, and that's it, nothing else?"

"Yes we talked, you seem surprised at that, what else were we supposed to do", asked Melinda.

"Never mind me I am just an incurable romantic, I thought that perhaps he'd expressed his feelings for you in some way…"

Taking a deep breath Melinda swallowed and said, "Well he did try to convince me that he has feelings for me but I clearly saw through his plan."

Truly at a lost for words Anastasia said a little too loudly, "Plan, you saw through his plan? Melinda, can you not see that the man simply adores you?"

Shaking her head in disagreement Melinda replies, "No that's where you are wrong, you see it's my dearly departed sister Suzanna whom he loved and still does. Now that he knows about little Camille he's simply trying to trick me to get to her."

A clearly agitated Anastasia replied more sharply than she would have liked at Melinda's synopsis of the situation. "Melinda do you actually believe that utter nonsense, anyone with eyes can see that it is you he loves, not your poor unfortunate sister."

"No, Ana you weren't near his bedside to hear him call to her over and over again. I thought I'd simply go mad if I didn't escape his sickroom sometimes", said a stubborn Melinda. Walking over to her, Anastasia placed her arm around her sister-in-law's shoulders and tried to get through to her once more. "Listen to me Melinda, the moment I saw the two of you together in the same room last evening I knew that you were meant to be together." As Melinda tried to interrupt she held up her hand and continued on saying, "Oh Melinda people often say all sorts of things when they are fevered, I don't believe for one moment that that young man of yours has ever loved any other woman but you my dear."

"I agree, that there may have been a time when he did love me. Several years ago, but then he met Suzanna and together they have a daughter. How can I compete with that", asked Melinda.

Beginning to feel some ebbs of hope arise Anastasia chanced to ask, "Oh Melly, do you want to compete with that?" Rushing on she adds, "Because if you do then that means deep down inside you know that it's you he loves."

Not waiting for an answer from Melinda, Anastasia exited the room and left her sister-in-law to ponder those thoughts.

Round and round went the words that Ana has just spoken. Melinda paced back and forth in front of the huge bay window until she wanted to pull her hair out. She was torn between feelings of elation at the possibility of Javier loving her. Yet there lingered

179

feelings of anger over the supposed betrayal of Javier because of his relationship with her sister. Finally she threw up her hands and decided to find something to do to get her mind off of the situation.

Leaving the drawing room, Melinda headed to the nursery. Spending time with little Cami, was just what she needed to keep her mind off of things.

They were up to something mused Melinda, twice now she'd caught Jean Charles, Javier, and Anastasia whispering with their heads close together, and once again they all jumped apart and grew silent as she entered the room.

Angry now that they were all scheming against her, she let it be known that she would not be dining with them this evening as planned, but instead had accepted an invitation to dinner and the theater from Dr. Jones. "Please don't set a place for me this evening, I will be out. Dr. Jones has invited me to the dinner and the theatre."

Crossing the room in two strides, Javier moved to block her exit and shouted to everyone within hearing distance that she would do no such thing.

"Out of the question Melinda, no certainly not, send this Dr. Jones a note telling him you cannot meet him as planned", he commanded.

So furious that she could hardly get the words out, Melinda shouted back, "Just who do you think you are telling me what to do?"Realizing that he'd gone a little too far Javier tried to back track by saying, "I'm sorry Melinda, but please for all our sakes, cancel this outing."

Tempted to do just that, Melinda turned away where she could not see the pleading in his eyes. "No I'm sorry Javier but it is time for me to go on with my life, and you should do the same."

Melinda nearly ran from the room because no matter what her mind said her heart was breaking into a million pieces. It didn't matter what Anastasia had said earlier, Javier had loved Suzanna dearly, and that was not something she could forget or forgive. After all, if he'd truly loved her why had he stayed away so long and left her to suffer alone for five long years. Besides only a blind man couldn't see the strong resemblance she and Suzanna had born one another.

It never occurred to her that he could have actually been using her sister as a substitute for her. No, instead she was sure that he had great love for her sister. Now he was simply trying to ensure that their daughter would be raised under the de Soto family's roof. Never mind that she would be extra baggage, she figured that Javier would just go about business as usual and would eventually plan to dispose of her in some way.

Well, she'd put a wrench in his plans and come up with a good one of her own.

Unfortunately the only thing she could come up with was the idea that she needed a husband. Not just anyone, but a very influential husband. Walking to her room, she foraged through the wardrobe looking for her ice blue silk chiffon gown with the lowly cut neckline. Yes, this would do nicely to serve her purpose, which was to knock Dr. Jones off of his feet.

She chose to ignore the fact that her heart was breaking in two at the prospect of marrying anyone other than the man who'd stolen her heart years ago. Melinda conceded to the fact that he was very close to wearing her down. Javier had been there for three weeks now declaring his love for her nearly every waking moment. Melinda could feel herself falling for him all over again and was determined to do something about it.

Pacing back and forth in front of the fireplace, Javier stopped long enough to say, "I will not let her do this to us again. I mean it Jean Charles I will do whatever it takes to make her see that we belong together."

Walking to meet him Jean Charles said, "I agree that she can be overly stubborn at times but it is her choice. I will not allow you to bend her to your will Javier."

With deadly calm, Javier issued a warning of his own, "And I will let nothing or no one come between us ever again."

Anastasia wishing to keep the peace said simply, "Now, now boys we're all in agreement here, Melinda's place is with Javier, she just doesn't realize it yet."

Kissing his wife's delicate hand Jean Charles agreed that she was correct and that they were all on the same side and shouldn't quarrel. "As usual you are right again my love." Turning to the side bar he offered Javier a drink as they all sat and once again tried to come up with a plan of their own.

Melinda turned this way and that as she examined her appearance in the mirror. She pulled on her gloves and picked up her matching handbag. She looked a vision in this ice blue confection and Dr. Michael Jones wouldn't be able to keep his eyes off of her.

Hearing a soft knock she called out softly, "Come in" suspecting that it was Ana once again coming to talk her out of going to the theater with Michael.

She nearly fainted when she spied Javier walking through the bedroom door. Gasping she screamed, "How dare you enter my private bed chamber."

"Didn't you just tell me to come in", asked a confused Javier.

"Yes, I said come in, but I thought you were Ana. It is unseemly for you to be alone with me in my sleeping quarters", huffed Melinda.

Thoroughly enjoying her discomfort, Javier chuckled and teased her further by saying, "I thought that maybe you knew it was me and wanted to be alone with me."

Determined not to give him the satisfaction of knowing how flustered she was, Melinda said calmly, "Don't flatter yourself Senor de Soto, and now if you'll excuse me I have a night at the theatre planned."

"Oh yes, how could I forget? You announced to everyone within hearing that you were meeting some...doctor this evening", Javier said with a snarl.

Startled at the venom dripping from him, she backed away slightly and said, "I really must be going and I must check on Camille first before I go out."

"Don't worry about my daughter. She has all she needs, please enjoy yourself", answered Javier.

A shiver ran through Melinda at that moment, there was something she'd seen briefly as it flashed through his eyes. She wasn't sure exactly what Javier was up to, but she knew that he had something up his sleeve. She refused to respond to his taunting comments and instead left the room and headed for the nursery anyway.

Javier followed her down the hall and entered the nursery close on her heels. He waited quietly as Melinda gave the wet nurse her orders for the evening. He watched as she leaned down to kiss Camille goodnight and wished for the thousandth time that Melinda wasn't so stubborn. He hated the idea of punishing her, but she left him no choice.

Melinda sat through another endless act of the play and lost herself to her own musings. What in the world had compelled her to come to the theatre tonight with Dr. Jones? She told herself that she was truly interested in him, after all he was tall, dark, handsome, and wealthy. Not to mention respectable, yes he was definitely well respected and well liked by those in the community. He was everything a girl could ask for, so why wasn't she enjoying herself? She tried to convince herself that Javier had put a damper on things with his scheming, but if she were to be truly honest with herself she knew the truth. Deep down she knew that she could never commit herself to anyone but…

Chapter Twenty-two

Melinda waited for the carriage to stop before saying goodnight to Michael. "Well I guess this is goodnight, thanks again for a lovely evening." Not fooled for a moment Michael asked, "Well if it was so lovely why were you absent for the most part of it?"

Not knowing what to say Melinda chose instead to apologize for her absentmindedness. "I'm so sorry for my behavior tonight please accept my apology. I have so many things on my mind that I'm afraid I was quite preoccupied."

Taking her hand into his, he lifts it to his lips and places a small unthreatening kiss on the back before saying, "Only on one condition that you have dinner with me sometime in the near future when you can be more attentive."

"I promise", was all she said while smiling up into his face.

Leading her to the door Dr. Jones raps softly three times and bids her farewell once they were admitted into the foyer.

Melinda gently padded her way up to her room and nearly jumped out of her skin when she entered her bedroom to find Javier asleep in the armchair near the bed. He looked so peaceful as he slept, almost like a cherub. A lock of hair had fallen over his forehead and she was sorely tempted to push it away from his face. Moving closer, her heart did a little dance as she looked upon his sleeping form. She imagined a life with him, this man who'd stolen her heart over 5 years ago; and if she had to be honest with herself still owned a great deal of that heart. If only things had been different maybe they could have been happy together. Now here he was once again claiming to still love her. All of her dreams could come true if only she was willing to trust him again and submit her will to his. But was he truly being honest with her, did he really love her or was this all just a scheme to get Camille in his clutches?

Yawning she decided to sleep on it and make an intelligent decision in the morning. But, what to do about Javier tonight? Should she leave him here in the chair in her sleeping chamber or awaken him? She decided to leave him asleep, which would prevent them from arguing in the middle of the night. She was certain that she just couldn't handle anymore of his badgering. Placing a throw over him, she takes one last glance at him and goes into her dressing room to change into her nightclothes.

Returning she walked forward on unsteady legs and placed a feather light kiss on his cheek. He stirred, and for a moment she was frozen in place, as she feared she'd awakened him after all. After he didn't open his eyes, she determined that he was simply re-positioning himself trying to get more comfortable. Then and only then did she let go of the breath she'd been holding.

Tip toeing back to the bed she turned down the lantern and pulled the covers up over her shoulders. It didn't take long for her to fall asleep as she was exhausted after such a long evening and soon she was sleeping soundly.

Javier stirred and couldn't quite recall his surroundings. He sat up and spied a sleeping form on the bed. Searching his memory, he suddenly remembered whose bedchamber he'd fallen asleep in and smiled to find that he was still there.

Another thought immediately came to mind also. He was late getting started with his plan to teach Melinda a valuable lesson. He took one last look at the bed and was nearly tempted to stay but decided against it. Finally after fighting an inner battle not to walk over to that bed and awaken Melinda with kisses and whispers of love he arose quietly and left the chamber in search of Jean Charles and Anastasia whom he knew would be waiting for him in the nursery. He could just imagine the questions they'd have for him as he tipped from the room and headed down the hall.

"Where have you been", came the anxious question from Anastasia. "Jean Charles has been searching for you for well over an hour."

"I'm sorry, I fell asleep in Melinda's chamber while waiting for her to return last night and found myself still there this morning, she didn't awaken me as I thought, but instead left me sleeping on the chair."

Clapping her hands in delight she asked, "So that means you don't have to do this, if she didn't awaken you then you have to agree she's had a change of heart."

Shaking his head no, Javier said, "It was more a decision of not having another argument more likely that prompted her not to awaken me."

Just then Jean Charles entered the nursery and said, "Where have you been man? It is nearly dawn and the servants will all be about soon, we can not be connected in any way to this mad scheme of yours Javier."

"Yes you are right, she would never forgive you for aiding me if we were caught." Shaking Jean Charles' hand and placing a small kiss on Ana's cheek Javier adds, "Thanks for all your help and trust me all will work out between us."

"Yes well I am sure we'll be seeing one another soon enough. I pray that you know what you are doing, for all our sakes", replied Jean Charles.

Kissing the cheek of the still sleeping Camille, Anastasia hands her over to her father and motions for the wet nurse to come forward. Giving her some last minute instructions, Ana then exits the room and walks quietly back to her own sleeping chambers. She walked to the bed and sat down to whisper a little prayer for a safe journey for

Javier and Camille. She also sent up a prayer that Melinda wouldn't flay the skin off all their backs when she awoke later this morning.

Jean Charles watched as Javier, Camille and the wet nurse pulled away in the carriage. He prayed once again that all would be well when his sister awoke to find Javier and Camille gone. "Please sir if you're listening, help us just a little and let those two work out their differences."

Turning, he walked back into the house and up to the sleeping chambers he shared with his wife. They would need all the rest they could get before Melinda discovered what had happened under the cover of darkness this night.

Chapter Twenty-three

Melinda couldn't shake the feeling that something was not right as she awoke from her troubled sleep. All at once, memories of Javier sleeping peacefully in a chair near her bed washed over her. Looking around she was almost relieved not to see him there.

Stretching languidly she placed her tiny feet on the floor and rose to wash away the sleep from her eyes. While moving to the wardrobe to select what she'd wear, she stopped and listened carefully. Again she felt as if something was not quite right but couldn't put her finger on what was wrong. Looking at the clock on the mantle of the fireplace, she was shocked to find that it is nearly ten o' clock in the morning. "Oh dear, how could I have slept so late? Cami must be wondering where I am this morning", she said aloud to herself.

Then at once she knew what was wrong, no babies were crying. In fact the house was unusually quiet. Leaving the room in a dead run, she ran first to the nursery and finding no one there went in search for her brother. She was told by the butler that her brother and his wife left earlier that morning for an appointment in town and had taken their three children along. When she asked about Camille and the wet nurse the butler hesitated briefly and then said, "Well madam now that you mention it I don't recall seeing them at all this morning."

Fear nagging at her insides Melinda asked; "Tell me Bentley have you seen Mr. De Soto this morning?"

"As a matter of fact, I haven't seen him since last night. His bed was unruffled this morning. Leading one to think that he hasn't returned from his adventures of last evening Ma'am", answered a slightly embarrassed Bentley.

Bentley may not know where Javier had slept but she did and something was not right here. She decided to go in search of anyone that may have seen Javier. By the noon hour she was thoroughly convinced that Javier had taken Camille and was headed back to New Orleans.

So distraught was Melinda that she didn't hear Jean Charles and Ana return and head for the dinning room.

Passing the drawing room, Jean Charles spied Melinda's tear streaked face and halted in his footsteps. Ana who had been following closely bumped into his back and asked, "What is it darling?"

Motioning towards Melinda he whispered, "I do believe that it is time to face the music my dear."

"Oh dear face the music is right. I'm not sure if I can do this Jean. Look at her face, it is riddled with pain", responded Anastasia.

"Well ready or not the hour is at hand my love", turning to the children's nanny he said, "Take them up and let them eat in the nursery before nap time Mrs. Pipkins, we'll be around shortly." Pulling Anastasia into the room with him, Jean Charles said a little too loudly, "MELINDA, how has your day been?"

Jumping Melinda ran into her brother's arms and cried her heart out. Producing a handkerchief from his coat pocket Jean Charles said, "Now, now what seems to be the problem, Javier being difficult again?"

"Javier, who said anything about Javier", asked Melinda suspiciously. Uncomfortable at her assumption he responded, "Well I…just assumed that the two of you had another argument and…"

"And what Jean Charles", asked a now angry Melinda. She was sure now that her brother had a hand in Javier's disappearance. She wasn't sure just what had given him away but she knew beyond a shadow of a doubt that Javier had confided in her brother.

Trying to soothe things Anastasia cleared her throat and said, "Melinda, why don't you tell us what is bothering you?"

Turning to look at Ana, Melinda searches her face for any tell tale signs. When she was convinced that Ana couldn't possibly have participated in this mad scheme she said, "I think that Javier has taken Camille back to New Orleans to his family's ancestral home."

"WHAT", exclaimed Jean Charles with what he hoped to be a shocked expression.

Not convinced Melinda went on to say, "And I think that you my brother, know that I am correct in this assumption."

Flustered that all would come to light Ana said, "Oh Melinda how could you suggest such a thing? Jean Charles was with me all morning. We left at first light with the children to go into town."

Confused, Melinda apologized and added, "I'm sorry Jean Charles its just that when you automatically assumed that Javier had done something, I jumped to conclusions and thought that you were in on this foolhearted plan of his."

Relieved that they'd somehow convinced her of his innocence Jean Charles sighed and motioned for her to sit and to tell them about her suspicions. After hearing all she had to say, Jean Charles agreed to go with her to New Orleans to retrieve baby Camille. Rising Anastasia extended her hand to Melinda and said, "Come sister, let me help you. Morning will come soon enough, and I want you to get an early start.

Jean Charles sat and wondered after the two retreated upstairs just how he was going to convince Melinda to go to Javier's true destination. He knew that they'd be wasting time going to New Orleans but couldn't say a word. Turning his face upward he whispered another prayer to the Almighty on behalf of his sister and his future brother in law.

Chapter Twenty-four

Javier was furious, there was simply no other way to put it. He had been so sure that Melinda would follow him immediately to Bristol after she discovered he'd taken Camille. Today was the tenth day he'd been here and Melinda still hadn't shown up.

Coming to her small home, he thought had been an excellent idea of showing her that he wanted to be here, with her; raising Camille together. How dare she lie to them all about her supposed love for Camille?

Looking down at his sleeping daughter he said out loud, "So, I guess everything she said was a lie, mija? The only thing she cares about is herself and her future with this Dr. Jones fellow."

Deciding to pack their things and head for his family's home in New Orleans, Javier left to find the wet nurse to inform her of their departure.

Melinda stood before the de Soto family fuming. She knew that they would do anything to aid Javier. She was certain that they were lying when they claimed to not have seen him. He'd left over two weeks ago with little Camille. Indignant at their deceit she said, "I do not believe for one moment that you do not know where he has gone."

Rising, Roberto walked calmly to where she stood and said simply, "Melinda may I ask you something?"

Opening her mouth and closing it several times Melinda finally found the words to answer his question. "Yes, what is it Roberto?"

"Well, it has struck me as odd that Javier would take Camille and come here that is all. I wondered if you'd checked in Bristol for him", asked Roberto.

Feeling as if a a ton of bricks had been lifted from her shoulders, Melinda ran to Roberto and kissed him soundly on the cheek before saying, "Oh Roberto, you are an absolute genius."

Running from the room like a lunatic, she grabbed her startled brother's arm and shouted, "I think I know where he's gone."

Releasing a pent up breath Jean Charles said, "Thank Heavens for that, where are we headed now sister", as if he had no idea. It had taken him until just this morning to finally get Roberto alone and confide in him what Javier's plan had been.

He had to stifle a small laugh now at the thought of how easily Roberto's comment had sent them finally in the right direction. He whispered a silent prayer of thanks that all was once again back on track and listened as his sister told him where they were headed to next.

Javier rode in gloomy silence as the carriage slushed along the wet roads through the outskirts of New Orleans. He'd left Bristol two days ago and had hoped that the condition of the weather would somehow change to his favor. He hadn't bothered with sending a note to alert his family of this impending arrival but had simply left Melinda's small home for what was surely the last time. He cursed softly as he thought about her uncaring ways concerning his infant daughter; all her talk about raising Camille and her duty to Suzanna had been just that, talk.

Interrupting his musings, the nurse said suddenly, "Sir, look someone is stuck in the mud on the other side of the road." Looking to where she indicated Javier yelled for the driver to stop and jumped down to help the poor unfortunate souls.

Calling out he said, "Hello, would you like some help getting your wheel out of the mud?"

Turning Jean Charles and Melinda looked into the face of a shocked Javier. Before anyone could stop her, Melinda became a flurry of action swinging her balled fists and kicking out at the same time. Shouting she said, "How dare you do this, how dare you steal Camille away from my brother's home and away from me!"

Trying to contain her before she did some real damage, Javier dodged a right hook, grabbed her up in a bear hug, and responded by saying, "I only did it so you'd come to your senses." "Melinda, I have been waiting for you for ten days, where in God's name have you been"?

Javier, totally unaware of Melinda's intent, was ill prepared for what she did next. Bringing up her knee she caught him in a very vulnerable spot and fell to the ground with him as he lay there panting in pain.

Jean Charles, who'd try to cry out a warning to Javier stopped in mid stride and stared wide-eyed from one to another.

Melinda, realizing that she'd truly injured Javier scrambled over to his side as he rolled from side to side and apologized profusely. "Oh Javier I'm so sorry, I didn't mean to hurt you."

Javier who was in agony and more angry than he'd ever been, managed to say through gritted teeth, "Get far away from me Melinda, I am going to kill you when I'm able."

Hearing the threat Jean Charles said, "Melinda I think you should do as he says for now", while placing his hand on her forearm.

"But how Jean Charles, the wagon is stuck", wailed Melinda. Shaking his hand away she moved back towards Javier and said, "No Javier I will not run away again, I'm sorry if I hurt you, I was just angry, and…"

"Melinda I said go!", managed Javier as he was finally able to get to his knees. "Take my carriage and return to New Orleans", he added.

Seeking to argue Melinda said, "But Javier…"

"NOW!!", he shouted. This time his one word statement worked wonders and Melinda scrambled to his carriage where she found Camille and the wet nurse waiting anxiously. She gave a small cry of delight when she spied Cami, fast asleep and wrapped warmly in her favorite blanket.

She glanced back briefly as the carriage pulled away and saw her brother trying to help Javier up from the rain soaked road.

Helping Javier to stand Jean Charles said, "Please try to find some way to forgive her for this, she simply was over come…"

"Don't make excuses for her", interrupted Javier while he tried to control his raging temper. Bringing his breathing under control once again he smiled and said to a worried Jean Charles, "Don't worry I will not harm her, amigo."

Taking his outstretched hand and pumping it up and down, Jean Charles chuckled and said, "You got to admit my friend that she does have fire."

"Fire indeed, muy caliente", said Javier with a look in his eyes that Jean Charles wasn't sure he cared for, she was after all his younger sister.

Now it was Javier's turn to laugh at the pasty look on Jean Charles' face, "Don't worry amigo, I will marry her first."

Chapter Twenty-five

Benito stared open mouthed at Melinda as she stepped down from Javier's carriage covered in mud from head to toe. There was a ring of mud surrounding one eye, which made her look like young master Juan's little terrier. Her hair was stiffly standing in place on the left side of her head and her once yellow and white dotted gown was now light brown with yellow dots. He quickly masked the desire to roar with laughter and busied himself with ushering her inside and finding drying towels to wrap around her.

Melinda caught his attempt to hide the laughter bubbling inside and said, "I've decided to start a new fashion trend, Benito, so don't look so shocked", "Please show me to an empty chamber."

Coughing to hide the bubble of laughter that threatened to escape any moment Benito said while leading her upstairs, "Uh…Right away Madam please follow me."

They walked past all the wide-eyed servants they encountered and down the hall to the chamber Melinda had most recently occupied.

Leaving her inside he instructed the maid to help Melinda change and get into a warm bath. He also showed the nurse to the nursery and got her settled in with the baby. Finally he went to the butler's pantry to let go of the laughter threatening to smother him. After laughing himself silly, he went in search of his employers to inform them that Melinda had returned with little Camille, and that he expected Senor Javier to return at any moment.

Knocking softly, Benito waited for acknowledgement to enter the family drawing room.

Calling out softly Senor de Soto said, "Entrar". Stepping into the room Benito informed them of Melinda's return, "Yes I hate to disturb you but felt I should inform you that Ms. Harmon and the baby have returned."

Jumping up Senora de Soto exclaimed, "Oh that is quite interesting indeed, but what about Javier, is he not returned also?"

"I expect him shortly Senora, as well as Senor Savoie, Ms. Harmon's brother", said Benito.

"This is just wonderful, please tell cook and her staff to set three more places at the dinner table", she said as she dismissed Benito.

Coming to her side her husband asked, "So you have decided to accept this woman into our son's life?"

"What choice do we have Juan? I am not willing to loose him again, and if he is decided upon making her his companion, then so be it", she said.

"But what if he wants to make her his wife my dear, is that still acceptable unto you", her husband asked.

"Wife, don't be ridiculous Juan, he can't, we all know that it is against the law to do such a thing. In time he will come to see that he must marry a legitimate bride for the good of the family", said Senora de Soto confidently.

Not wishing to dispel her of what she knew to be the truth, he kept the information of couples going to other countries to marry to himself. He would allow her this false security until he was absolutely sure about Javier's plans. Smiling he said, "Now lets go up and tell the others the good news, but first let's go see our granddaughter."

Javier swore repeatedly on the way to his parent's home. He and Jean Charles had decided to leave the carriage where it was. It was simply impossible for the two of them to dislodge the wheel. He regretted sending everyone else back with the women but had seen no point in making everyone miserable.

Finally the two of them had decided to unhitch the horses and ride them back after several unsuccessful attempts. While it had seemed like a good idea to leave the carriage, now he wasn't so sure. He was soaked through and through. He was covered in mud that clung to him like a second skin. Although he had promised not to strangle Melinda for tumbling him into the mud his resolved weakened with each step the horse took towards New Orleans.

Jean Charles who'd remained silent for the most part of their soggy journey broke his silence by saying, "You may not harm her but I certainly will, I have never been more uncomfortable in all my life."

Finding it amusing that both their thoughts were in the same place Javier laughed aloud and said, "Now, now, amigo we mustn't let our sour moods take over our brains and make us do something we'd regret."

"We, so you're hard pressed to not do her bodily harm also", asked Jean Charles.

"Only for a moment amigo, only for a moment", answered Javier.

"Well, I, for one could shake her until her teeth rattle", muttered Jean Charles.

Chuckling Javier said as they came around the bend, "Come my friend we are nearly there." Spurring their horses forward the two men rode swiftly towards the de Soto mansion.

Melinda was once again warm and dry and sat before fire while the maid brushed the tangles from her hair. Hearing a knock she sat up and instructed the maid to turn away all visitors citing her state of undress.

Opening the door the maid gasped as she looked into the eyes of a very wet, very dirty, and a very, very angry Senor Javier de Soto. "Oh, pardona me, Senor but the Senorita is not dressed to receive visitors at this time."

Sweeping past her he strode into the room and said to Melinda, "Make sure that you are at that dinner table in one hour Melinda or I will come to get you myself; dressed, or not." Not waiting for a response from her he pivoted on his heel and walked past the staring maid and down to his personal sleeping quarters for a much- needed bath.

Seething that he would issue such a warning to her, Melinda screamed her frustration and threw aside the lovely dress she'd selected earlier in exchange for the black muslin she'd worn for Suzanna's funeral. Smiling into the mirror at the image she presented she said to the horrified maid, "Well how do I look?"

Clucking her tongue the maid said, "Perdoneme for saying so Senorita Harmon but it looks as if you are going to a funeral."

"Perfect", exclaimed Melinda and exited the room.

The de Soto family assembled together in the dining room and awaited Melinda's arrival. Javier bristled that she would ignore his earlier warning. Standing he began to exit the room just as she entered. Nearly colliding Javier reached out to steady her and then saw all shades of red as he took in her appearance.

Bending closely to her ear he threatened to tear the mourning gown from her if she didn't change it. "How dare you come to dinner looking like this, go change it or I will tear it from you."

Thinking to call his bluff Melinda opened her mouth to speak but took one look into his eyes and knew that he meant what he said. Squawking she turned and ran back up the stairs to change her gown.

Javier turned to face the family and explained that he and Melinda would return shortly. "Un momento por favor, we'll return soon", he said as he ran up the stairs to her sleeping quarters.

Opening the door Melinda shouted for the maid and began trying to unfasten her gown. Still struggling with the buttons at the back of her gown she did not see Javier enter the bedroom and send the maid scurrying from the room with a simple look.

With the gown finally unbuttoned and almost over her head Melinda accepts the help of the maid but is puzzled over why she doesn't speak. "Oh come now, Anita, say something, say I told you so, anything", urged Melinda.

Instead of speaking Javier bent his head to her lovely exposed back and lightly ran kisses over her flesh.

211

Scandalized Melinda tried to jerk the dress back down to cover herself, but met with resistance as Javier held her in place and pulled the dress over her head.

Melinda dashed towards the screen but Javier was on her in a flash. Before she could reach it, he was kissing her soundly and she was responding. Try as she might she couldn't seem to get her body to do as her brain screamed. Instead of pushing him away she inched closer by placing her arms around his neck.

"Well I think we'd better get on with dinner somehow I feel they will be occupied for the rest of the evening", said a tight-lipped Senor de Soto.

Offended beyond words Jean Charles stood and excused himself. "Excuse me but I find that I'm not very hungry this evening."

"No please stay Jean Charles my father meant no disrespect", interjected Roberto.

Turning to face Jean Charles he remarked, "Please accept my apology, I certainly meant no harm."

Still refusing to take his seat Jean Charles replied, "Apology accepted, now if you'll excuse me I must see to something right away."

Rising to block his path Juan waited until Julio also stood in the doorway and then said, "Please sit Jean Charles, they deserve this time together, and we intend for them to have it."

"No, I must protect my sister's virtue, I must…"

"Your sister is also my sister Jean Charles and I agree that they deserve this time alone, please sit down", stated Beatrice.

Looking at all of them as if they'd lost their minds Jean Charles said with contempt, "Do you all realize what will happen if we leave them alone in her bed chamber? No I cannot allow this to go on."

He advanced towards the door once more only to pull up short as the younger sons of his hosts moved to block his exit.

"Listen I do not wish to harm anyone but if you do not remove yourselves from my path I can not be held accountable for what happens", he warned.

Melinda and Javier were oblivious to what was transpiring downstairs. They were so caught up in the storm of feelings washing over them. Before long Javier heard her moaning deeply as he trailed kisses down her neck and over the tops of her perfect breasts.

Javier whispered words of love as he continued kissing her until she was nearly mindless with desire. He trailed feather light kisses up and down her long slender arms and over her lovely shoulders. On and on the assault went until she was a quivering mass of flesh made up of nerve endings only.

He picked her up and started heading for the bed all the while still kissing her passionately. Just as he began to lie her down upon the huge four- posted bed, a loud crash sounded downstairs.

Javier lifted his head and listened for more sounds to follow, the shouts that came from downstairs told him that he needed to go an investigate.

Melinda who had come to her senses lay there and listened as her brother's voice rose in an angry shout.

"Oh no, its Jean Charles", she said with fear running rampid throughout her body.

"Shhh, get dressed and I will take care of this", promised Javier before rising to leave the bedchamber. Turning back before going through the door he kissed her briefly and promised to return soon.

Pulling on a dress with buttons in the front Melinda barely had time to finish dressing as she heard the sound of raised voices near her door.

Meeting the party nearly at Melinda's door, Javier stopped and looked with puzzlement at Jean Charles struggling with his two younger brothers.

Laughing he crossed his arms over his chest and asked, "What is going on here, I thought I left you downstairs having dinner with my parents?"

He was taken aback by the look of raw anger he saw in the depths of Jean Charles eyes, and actually moved back a step.

"I trusted you with my sister's virtue and you betrayed that trust Javier", shouted Jean Charles.

"Listen amigo I did not compromise her in any way, we were only sorting things out..."

Javier landed with a thud as a left hook thrown by Jean Charles connected with his jaw.

Grabbing Jean Charles, Juan and Julio held him down as Javier shook the cobwebs out of his head. Javier struggled to stand on rubbery legs and messaged his jaw.

Melinda walked out at this point and screamed at the top of her lungs, which promtly brought the rest of the de Soto family up the stairs.

Going down on one knee she ran her hand over Javier's face. Checking for any broken bones, she breathed a sigh of relief when all she found was a bruise starting to appear near his jaw line. "Javier are you all right", she asked anxiously.

Waving her away he said, "Yes I'm fine, your brother and I simply had a slight disagreement sweetheart."

Javier was just starting to rise when his parent's arrived on the scene. Rushing to help his brother stand, Roberto said, "Juan, Julio let Jean Charles up. Now could we all go downstairs and talk about this calmly?"

With downcast eyes Jean Charles apologized for his actions and begged his hosts' forgiveness. "Please forgive my actions, I was simply overcome with the need to protect my sister."

Moving to slap him gently on the back Javier said, "Amigo it is water under the bridge as we say. I applaud your need to look after your sister, come let us eat."

Javier's parents were the first to turn and leave with Juan and Julio following, next went Jean Charles and Javier, with Roberto extending his arm to Melinda.

Bending closely to her ear Roberto whispered for her to fix the buttons of her gown near her throat. "Please Melinda fix the buttons at your collar or we will have another row."

Mouthing a silent thank you, Melinda attended to her dress and entered the dining room smiling brightly. She took a seat next to Beatrice, across from Javier and tried to avoid looking at anyone directly.

Senora de Soto signaled for the start of dinner and everyone soon forgot about the previous activities as they lost themselves in the scrumptious dishes prepared by the cook.

The wine flowed merrily and soon all were back in the best of spirits. Melinda accepted her third glass of wine and felt it's soothing powers wash over her. Beginning to relax she chanced a glance in Javier's direction and smiled boldly as she caught him watching her with desire laden eyes.

She wasn't sure if it was the wine making her feel so heady or if it was the knowledge that her dreams were finally coming true. However she reveled in the feel of it. She marveled at how accepting the de Soto's were of her, and for the first time in a long time felt as if she belonged.

Chapter Twenty-six

Javier waited until they had all removed from the dining room and to the drawing room before he surprised them by asking Melinda to wed with him.

Rising he went to stand in front of her before dropping to one knee. Taking her hand into his he looked into her eyes and asked with the entire family watching, "Melinda will you do me the honor of becoming my wife"?

Pandemonium broke at that moment as everyone shouted to be heard over the other. Roberto and Jean Charles were shouting their congrats as were Beatrice, Graciela, and Maria Antonia. Javier's parents however were another matter all together. Melinda, still in shock by Javier's question stood mutely as his mother shrill comment cut through the air and fell heavily between all present.

"Never! Can we allow this to happen", she screeched.

Turning to face his parents Javier pulled Melinda closer to his side and stood his ground. Speaking he said, "Once I allowed you to separate us but never again, Madre. No, this time if we must leave we will do so, the choice is yours."

"But Javier you must listen to reason, not only did we have other hopes for you, but it is illegal to marry someone of her race", pleaded his mother.

Javier was not to be deterred and so simply restated his answer saying in no uncertain terms he would never be separated from Melinda again. "If we must, we will go elsewhere to be married, Madre, but we will be married. You can choose to accept Melinda, or to turn your back on the both of us and any children this union would produce."

Stepping forward his father said, "Javier are you absolutely sure that this is what you want? To turn your back on all of this, for someone who brings nothing in return into this marriage?"

Lunging forward Jean Charles is restrained by Roberto who took center stage in Javier's defense. Shaking his head for Jean Charles to remain seated he said, "Madre, Padre, they have suffered enough. Truly you can see that to further keep them apart would do no one any good."

Adding her support Javier's grandmother entered the room and said calmly, "My son, Maria, it is time to let him live life as he wishes." Walking further into the room she sat in a chair near her son and continued speaking, "I support his choice in a wife".

Extending her hand to Melinda she finished by saying, "Bienvenida a la familia."

Nudging Melinda forward Javier bent down to kiss his grandmother's cheek and thanked her for her support, adding that he loved her. "Gracias Abuela, Te' amo."

Moved to tears Melinda was speechless as one by one the de Soto clan filed past her to offer felicitations.

Graciela stopped a few feet away from her, and while embracing her said, "As my grandmother said, Welcome to the Family, Melinda."

Grateful for the elder Senora de Soto's support Javier said to all present, "Melinda and I will leave for Canada soon, where we can be married legally. I'd like for all of you to be there, but will understand if you cannot for reasons of your own."

His mother, Senora de Soto, who had not uttered a single word since her mother-in-law's surprising declaration, bent to her mother-in-laws wishes. Stepping forward she said, "While I do not support your choice of bride at this time, I will honor your wishes and attend the ceremony." She cast a furtive glance at Melinda and added, "Who knows in time maybe I will find a way to accept this decision you've made."

Trying to lighten the mood Juan said, "But Javier I have not heard the young lady agree to marry you yet, please Ms. Harmon let us hear your response."

Chiming in his voice Julio added, "We'll understand if you choose not to align yourself with one such as he."

Laughing she sent them looks of deeply felt gratitude that said all she couldn't quite manage to utter. Swallowing the lump in her throat she said slowly, "Si, yes, I will marry you."

Lifting her feet from the floor Javier swung her around as he kissed her. Placing her feet back onto the floor he turned and received congratulations from Jean Charles.

His father, who'd remained quiet through this entire exchange was the last to come forth. Leveling his son with a steely glare he said, "I am not so easily won over. I will never accept this dishonor you are forcing upon this family. Nor do I accept your terms concerning your marriage ceremony."

Calmly his mother, the elder Senora de Soto, stood and said without blinking an eye, "You will do as I wish in this matter my son. My grandson will have his entire family at the ceremony."

Instead of arguing the point Juan turned to look at his mother and said simply, "As you wish Madre, as you wish." After making this stunning declaration he turned and walked from the room leaving all to stare and wonder over what had just transpired.

No one moved for several moments following Senor de Soto's hasty exit. Javier gave Melinda's hand a slight squeeze to reassure her and moved to once again thank his grandmother for siding with him.

Maria de Soto surprised everyone by not following her husband from the room. Instead staying in the room for the endless rounds of toasts being offered to the happy couple.

Soon the room was filled with gaiety as the wine flowed freely from one glass to another. When Melinda would have accepted her fourth glass of wine however Javier stayed her hand and whispered softly, "No more amor, or you'll pay dearly in the morning."

Giggling, she agreed that she'd had her fill and said with a slight slur, "You are right I've had enough."

With his heart bursting with love for his beautiful soon to be wife, Javier leaned over and placed a feather light kiss on her lips. He dipped his head twice more to kiss her rosy colored lips and murmured for her ears only of the love he had for her. "I am filled near to bursting with my love for you, corazon."

Caressing his cheek Melinda kissed him back and whispered against his lips, "So am I my love."

Looking on, his brothers began teasing him unmercifully and only stopped when their grandmother and mother rose to retire for the evening.

Rising the elder Senora de Soto smiled once again at the loving couple and said, "Come ladies I think that we can now leave the gentlemen to their own devices." Turning to each of her Grandsons she bid them all a good night and walked from the room with all the women trailing after her.

Javier bade Melinda a good night after kissing her yet again, to the chorus laughter of his brothers.

Watching her disappear up the stairs, he replaced the carefree smitten look he'd wore all night with a serious worried one. He informed all present that his Father's reluctance to accept Melinda did not bode well. "This position adopted by Papa is not good, please help me keep an eye on him."

Laying his hand upon his shoulder, Roberto tried to give him some measure of assurance that things would work out for the best. Not totally convinced Javier said, "While I pray that what you say will be so, I cannot help but feel as if something will happen to hurt us in some way."

Agreeing with Javier, Juan added reluctantly, "I agree with Javier, Padre will never accept this quietly."

"What are you saying Juanito, that he will do something to harm them in some way", asked and incredulous Julio.

"No, I,…,uh, I'm not saying that either, I just think that we should keep an eye on things until after the ceremony", replied Juan.

"I agree with Juan. We must watch Papi carefully until then. While I don't think he would harm her physically, I do believe that he may try and convince her to leave", said Javier.

"Yes you have a point there, hermano, Padre can be pretty convincing when he chooses", agreed Roberto.

Throughout this exchange Jean Charles had not spoken a single word, but now stood and addressed the de Soto brothers, "I will not allow my sister to be hurt again in anyway Javier."

Standing Javier made a vow to Jean Charles that Melinda would come to no harm. "I will protect her with my very life amigo, please don't worry. All will be well."

Chapter Twenty-seven

Jean Pierre was delighted to hear the news of Javier and Melinda's upcoming marriage. Rising he kissed Melinda lightly on the cheek and said, "I know Mary would be delighted if she were here with us today."

Swallowing past the lump in her throat Melinda simply shook her head in agreement. Hugging her tightly her father said, "If you will allow it, I'd like to be there, I know that I have rarely been there as you needed, but would like to do so now."

Bursting with gladness and her eyes blurred with tears she said happily, "Yes I'd love to have you there."

Stepping back Jean Pierre extended his hand to Javier and said briefly, "Love her forever young man, love her forever."

The de Soto's boarded one of the family's ships and headed for Nova Scotia. After sitting and speaking at length with Jean Pierre, it was decided that Javier and Melinda would go to Clare, Nova Scotia where they could safely be married.

Jean Pierre also wanted to make sure the family she'd never known would finally surround Melinda on this special day. Clare was a Savoie stronghold and had been since the expulsion of many of the Cajun families from other parts of Canada. Many Savoie family members still chose to live there and prospered greatly from the bountiful fishing to be had near the port. The trip to Canada proved to be adventure for the soon to be newlyweds.

Sitting down to dinner one evening Senor de Soto finally reconciled himself to the marriage and joined them for the evening meal.

Entering the dining compartment he said simply to Javier, "With your approval I'd like to join you for the meal and offer my support to you in any way."

Moving to embrace his father Javier said gratefully, "Gracias Papi, We will certainly need the support of everyone to make this work when we return to the states as a married couple."

"I will do all that I can to help present a united front to smooth the way with our business partners and peers."

Coming to stand beside her husband, Maria smiled brightly raised her glass in tribute and said, "To the de Soto familia."

Sounds of glasses clinking were heard throughout the room as one family member lightly tapped their glass to another's.

Melinda clinked her glass with Javier and then turned to her future father-in-law and expressed her heartfelt thanks by saying, "Thank you Senor de Soto for your support, this means the world to me."

"No, the thanks belongs to my mother, who made me see that love is what really matters. Not my hopes and dreams, but my son's hopes and dreams." "Besides there was once upon a time when I was not the chosen bride", added Maria to everyone's astonishment.

Rubbing her hands together in anticipation, Graciela said, "Oh you simply must tell all madre." Everyone sat and listened as Juan and Maria recalled how they had met and fell in love to the dismay of his own parents. Juan told of how his parents had also sought to put an end to their relationship, but how they had eventually assented to the wishes of their son.

Melissa A. Ross

"Abuela, how can I ever thank you for all you've done for us", asked Javier.

"Just give me some little ones to cherish in my old age", she replied cheerily.

"That will be the first thing on our agenda", Javier said to Melinda's embarrassment.

Stepping forward Jean Charles said, "I hope that your agenda is to be executed after you are married."

"Why of course amigo", answered Javier grinning broadly.

Blushing profusely, Melinda chanced a look at Javier's parents only to find them also laughing at Javier's antics and bold remarks.

Life was finally becoming all that she had dreamed about since childhood. She whispered a silent prayer towards Heaven for continued happiness and prosperity.

She pushed aside the nagging feeling that something would happen to dampen their spirits. She couldn't prevent the thought from coming to mind of the old adage that whenever things were going too good something bad was always just around the corner.

Javier noticed the slight shiver that ran through her body and pulled her closer to his side. Nuzzling her cheek with his lips he whispered, "I love you Melinda Harmon, and don't you forget it."

Gazing into his eyes, she felt all the uneasiness disappear and in its place a warm fuzzy feeling permeated her very bones. Snuggling closer to his side she sipped her wine and lost herself in the gaiety of the moment.

Jean Pierre's cousins, Germaine and Jean Claude Savoie, who had brought along their wives and children, greeted them on the banks as they embarked from the ship. Jean had thought it befitting for another generation of the Savoie clan to return home for such an occasion.

Melinda was shocked to see that this Savoie clan was of a darker hue, with dark hair and eyes. She searched her Father's face and realized that he had known exactly what he was doing in bringing them here.

She listened as the men spoke in a dialect of French closely related to the one she'd grown up speaking and even laughed at a joke they shared.

It was plain to see that her Father felt right at home amongst his distant relatives, and it was plain to see also that they knew of her existence.

Had her father told them of her existence before now or had this been something he'd shared with them only recently?

She took a deep breath and stepped forward as her father motioned for her to be introduced to his family.

Taking her hand Germaine said, "Ah she looks like Aunt Camille." Smiling he continued on with saying, Bienvenue Melinda." He kissed her on both cheeks in the old European fashion and handed her over to his brother Jean Claude before motioning for his wife and children to come forward.

Hugging her tightly Jean Claude said, "In the words of my brother, Bienvenue, Welcome Home.

With tears glistening in her beautiful eyes Melinda returned the hugs and brought Javier forward to meet her Father's cousins, now her cousins.

After all the introductions were made they were led to the home of Jean Claude and assigned rooms where they would stay for the duration of their time in Canada.

Chapter Twenty-eight

The day of the wedding dawned with all the ingredients of a perfect setting. The sun rose early and shone so bright that one had to squint upon first looking outdoors. Birds sang to the fullness of the Lord's glory and the flowers bloomed brighter than at any other time. The heavy scent of roses and gardenias filled the air with their perfume.

Melinda sighed and pinched herself to make sure that she was actually awake and not caught up in some beautiful fantasy.

She turned as the bedchamber door opened and in walked her future sister-in-laws, Anastasia, and both Senoras de Soto.

Coming to stand in front of her Javier's mother said softly, "Come Melinda let us prepare you for your marriage to my son, everything must be perfect."

As if on cue Anastasia stepped forward and held out a choker of pearls saying, "I'd be honored if you'd wear these today, think of them as your something borrowed item."

Next came Graciela with a beautiful blue silk underslip and said, "And don't forget this, you simply must wear something blue." Unable to stop them, the tears now burst forth and ran unchecked down her cheeks as Javier's grandmother stepped forward and took her hands. Walking Melinda over to the dressing table she motioned for her to sit as she placed a very old looking velvet box in front of her.

Opening it slowly she said, "These pearl earrings have been in our family for over two generations, and I would be honored if you wore them as do all the de Soto brides on their wedding day."

Nearly blinded by the tears in her eyes she swiped them away to see Javier's mother come forward next to present her with beautiful mother of pearl set of combs for her hair. Placing them in Melinda's hand she said, "We cannot forget the something new item, I had these made a few days ago, they will look lovely in your beautiful hair." Looking at all of them Melinda suddenly began to giggle as she noticed that there was not a dry eye in the room, and soon everyone was giggling and talking all at once.

"Come, come we must hurry we only have one hour till the ceremony", said Javier's mother.

Surrounding Melinda they worked their magic until finally they all stepped away and gasped at the vision standing before them.

Maria Antonia, Javier's youngest sister whispered in awe, "Melinda you look like...a princess."

"Yes an absolute princess", agreed Beatrice.

"Surely princess is not accurate..." said Melinda before she was cut off by Javier's mother.

"No Princess is right mija", motioning for Melinda to stand before the mirror she continued on by saying, "Take a look for yourself."

Bringing her hand up to her mouth Melinda said unbelievingly, "Is this really me?"

Truly pleased their handiwork the ladies laughed with glee and assured her that yes it was she.

"You are absolutely beautiful my dear. My grandson will not be able to take his eyes from you today", said the elder Senora de Soto.

Ushering the ladies from the room Javier's mother said, "Now ladies if you'll wait for us downstairs I'd like to speak with Melinda alone for a moment."

Turning to leave they each placed a small kiss upon her cheek before exiting.

Melinda, not knowing what to expect, sighed nervously and waited for Senora de Soto to speak.

Taking a seat upon the side of the bed she invited Melinda to sit next to her. "Please Melinda have a seat next to me."

Melinda sat and looked at her expectantly.

Senora de Soto took a deep breath and then said, "I don't know if your dear mother had a chance to speak to you before her death. Concerning what happens on the night of your marriage? If you will permit it, I would like to advise you on what will happen."

Blushing with embarrassment, Melinda said barely audibly, "No she didn't have time to explain what happens between a man and his wife. I would be humbled if you'd go over it with me."

"First, let me say that there is nothing to be afraid of. In fact it will be the most beautiful thing you've ever experienced", Senora de Soto went on to say.

Javier looked up as his sisters and grandmother entered the small Chapel. He stretched to see if he could locate Melinda, and not finding her went to inquire of her whereabouts. "Graci, where is Mama and Melinda", he asked suspiciously.

Smiling reassuringly she said, "Not to worry they will be along shortly."

"But why are they not here with you", he asked further.

Placing a hand on his sleeve his grandmother said, "Maria is performing the duties of a mother today Javier and will be down shortly. In fact she should be arriving any moment, now take your place at the altar."

Smiling with understanding he simply said, "Si, Abuela", and headed to stand next to his brother, Roberto.

Jean Pierre knocked softly on the door to Melinda's chamber and waited for an answer.

Calling softly from within Senora de Soto said, "Come in."

Pulling up short at the sight of Melinda he swallowed the lump in his throat and said, "A more beautiful bride I've never seen Melinda. I wish that Mary were here today to see you in all of your loveliness."

Walking into his arms Melinda cried softly and managed to say, "Oh but father she is here", pointing to her heart she said further, "I feel her here."

Looking on the scene with tenderness Senora de Soto cleared her throat discreetly and said, "We must go now, I'm sure that Javier is on pins and needles wondering where we are."

Wiping her tears away with his handkerchief her father said, "Come my dear let us go down now, before he comes up here to us."

Placing her hand at his elbow she allowed him to escort her down the stairs and out of the house to the nearby chapel.

Senora de Soto placed her veil over her face once they were outside the chapel. Kissing her softly she left her at the entrance with her father and walked down the aisle on the arm of her husband.

Smiling brightly at her son standing at the altar she mouthed the words "I Love You."

Slowly, Melinda's father led her down the aisle towards Javier and the priest, Father Costeau.

Javier felt as if his heart would burst with pride as he glimpsed Melinda for the first time. He felt tears sting his eyes as he thought she looked like a fairy princess gliding towards him on crushed rose petals.

Melinda, upon spying the tears in his eyes, felt her own eyes moisten and began to tremble slightly.

Reassuring her, Jean Pierre whispered softly, "Cheer up Cherie, the man of your dreams awaits."

Placing her hand into Javier's, Jean Pierre lifted her veil briefly and placed a kiss upon her cheek. Returning her veil to its original place he turned to Javier and said, "I give my daughter into your hands now, to love and cherish as I have come to love her."

Moved nearly beyond words, Javier took Melinda's hand and whispered, "I will cherish her all the days of my life, sir."

Turning to face the priest, they knelt before him and became husband and wife before God and man.

Finally Father Cousteau pronounced them Husband and Wife and instructed Javier to raise her veil and seal their vows with a kiss.

Lifting the veil Javier smiled lovingly into her eyes and momentarily lost himself in their depths. Bending his head slightly, he slanted his mouth over hers and kissed her closed lips. Coaxing her to open her mouth by running his tongue along her bottom lip.

Shyly Melinda kissed him back allowing him to lead her in this dance of their fused mouths.

· They pulled apart to tunes of shouting and clapping as the attendants at their wedding cheered them on. "Well Mrs. Augustos Javier de Soto, how does it feel to finally be my wife", asked Javier lovingly.

"Like it has been this way forever", she answered adoringly.

Walking hand in hand they exited the small Chapel with their family members trailing behind and stopped a short distance away on the lawn.

Placing his hands over her eyes Javier said, "I have a surprise for you my beautiful bride."

Motioning for the Stable Master to come forth, he slowly removed his hands and said, "Now you can look."

Gasping, Melinda gazed in wonder at the sight before her. Standing just a few feet away was a carriage drawn by six white horses and a driver dressed in white and gold livery. Turning to Javier she asked, "How, how did you know I always dreamed of something like this on my wedding day?"

"I know your hopes and dreams so well Melinda, because they are the same as mine, corazon", he answered.

Walking into his arms she initiated the kiss this time. Tentatively placing her lips against his, she ran her tongue against the edge of his and kissed him with all the feeling she could muster.

Groaning deeply in his chest Javier broke the kiss abruptly and said, "Bebe, we must stop this or we'll never make it through the reception."

Watching something play over her face, he said asked, "You don't have any reservations about later do you sweetheart?"

"No, your mother explained it all to me earlier", she responded quietly.

Interrupting the happy couple a shout arose among the guests, "Throw the bouquet."

Laughing, Melinda turned her back on the crowd and on the count of three threw the bouquet over her head.

Turning around she erupted into laughter along with everyone else as Juan, Javier's younger brother caught the flowers. Realizing just what this implied he quickly passed them over to his unsuspecting twin Julio.

"Oh no dear brother, this is your prize", chuckled Julio handing them back to Juan.

Their mother whose fondest wish was to see all of her children happily wed, clapped her hands in delight.

Senor de Soto, who to everyone's delight, had actually come to terms with things, joined in the playful banter.

"Praise God, maybe now I will get a chance to see all of my grandchildren while I still have my teeth."

"Hear, Hear", said his mother, "I too would like to get to know all of my future relations while I am still coherent."

Holding up his hand for silence Germaine stepped forward and said, "Congratulations to the happy couple, now if you will all follow me, we will dance until morning."

Shouts of "Lassier le bon temps rouler." were heard throughout the crowd. One by one they moved towards the grand estate, laughing gleefully as they celebrated Javier and Melinda's wedding.

Chapter Twenty-nine

Laura Lee Savoie sat in the darkest corner of her sleeping chamber and seethed at her husband's actions. How dare he go off to attend the marriage of his half- breed illegitimate daughter? It was against every fiber of her being to sit idly and allow something like this to happen.

Jean Pierre had even helped them to plan this digusting act. He'd even had the audacity to take them to his ancestral family home in Nova Scotia. Well, she for one would not allow him to bring this kind of shame upon the Savoie family. She wondered how the de Soto's felt about this scandalous affair? Sitting down at her desk, she lit a lamp, and sat down to write a note to Mr. And Mrs. De Soto. She was sure that those wealthy upstanding citizens were against this match as much as she. When she'd finished her note to the de Soto's she wrote another to Beatrice, stressing her disappointment over her daughter's approval of such a match. Afterall, Beatrice would be the little negra's sister-in-law. No she couldn't allow Beatrice to be associated in any way to one such as Melinda Harmon. She reconciled to do whatever it took to protect her family and their reputation in the community.

The servant returned a few days later to report that the entire de Soto family had taken a trip to celebrate the eldest son's wedding. "Sorry ma'am but no one there to deliver these to, cept the servants."

"What, why is that, Benjamin", asked Mrs. Savoie.

"Seems they all took a trip for the oldest boy's wedding ma'am", replied old Ben.

A temporary madness overtook her then. The servant's were unsure of what to do and went in search of old Mrs. Camille.

Mrs. Camille entered the room to find Laura Lee screaming at the top of her voice with blood running down her face. It looked as if someone had clawed at her face.

Clutching her heart she called for a servant to fetch Doctor Miller. Walking slowly towards Laura Lee, she stopped a few feet away and she said softly, "Laura Lee, can you hear me child?"

Slowly Laura Lee looked through the dense fog to locate the voice calling her name.

Finally when the red haze lifted she spied her mother-in-law standing before her with frightened eyes.

The stricken look upon her face struck a chord of humor in Laura Lee, and before a dozen servants and Mrs. Camille she began to laugh hysterically. She laughed until she was out of breath and fell to her knees. Fear paralyzed everyone in the room preventing them from moving to help her.

In walked Doctor Miller while Laura Lee was on her knees laughing like a mad woman. "Mon Dieu", he whispered and strode further into the room. Immediately taking charge he went to her side and spoke to her in a tone that made her head snap up and the laughter die on her lips, "Laura Lee, get hold of yourself girl!"

He galvanized the frightened servants into action by dispersing them to complete their tasks and ordered a couple of the young men to help him assist Mrs. Savoie upstairs. "Get back to work everyone, Jesse, Moses help me to get her upstairs to her chamber."

Stopping on the way out of the room, he turned to speak with Mrs. Camille. "Are you are okay Mrs. Camille."

"Yes", she said sadly, just help that poor child upstairs."

"Try to get some rest ma'am and I will see to you as soon as I'm done with your daughter-in-law."

Almost out of the room he turned to ask, "Any idea what brought this episode on?"

Realizing that the truth could mean danger for her family, Mrs. Camille said simply, "I'm afraid not, I was lying down when the servants came for me."

"Ok, I'll be down shortly, Mrs. Camille", said Doctor Miller. Mrs. Camille sat and lost herself in her musings. "Dear God", she prayed, "let this bitter cup pass."

She also made a mental note to say an extra Hail Mary for the lie she'd just told to Doctor Miller.

Chapter Thirty

Finally after what seemed like an eternity Javier was able to take Melinda's hand and lead her to their chamber.

As he stood his brother Juan joked about their departure, "Well I see the happy couple wishes to be alone."

Holding his hand up Javier said, "Please continue to celebrate as long as you wish and thank you all for everything you've done to make this the happiest day of our lives."

All the women of family rose at that moment and moved to escort Melinda upstairs to prepare her for Javier.

Seeing this Javier said simply, "No mama, I will assist my wife this evening but thank you all for your thoughtfulness.

Seeing the determination in her son's eyes, his mother gave in to his wishes by saying, "As you wish my son, besides all is in readiness." Blushing to the roots of her hair, Melinda kept her eyes downcast and allowed Javier to escort her to their private chamber.

Melissa A. Ross

She turned a deeper shade of red as she overheard some of the outlandish comments made by some of her male relatives concerning the marital bed.

Javier lifted her into his arms and carried her through the bedchamber door. He placed her feet gently on the floor and took in the appearance of the room. True to his mother's words all was in readiness.

There were crushed flowers spread upon the floor and huge mahogany carved bed. A bottle of wine with two glasses had been deposited on the night table near the bed. The room was aglow with candlelight as candles were littered across the room. His eyes took on another gleam however as he spied the filmy white nightdress that had been laid across the top covers on the bed.

Overcome by nerves, Melinda tripped over the carpet and would have fallen if not for her husband's steadying hands.

Taking her into his arms he kissed her gently and said, "Come let me help you remove your gown."

Melinda, who'd never undressed in front anyone before particularly not a man, was rooted to the spot. Seeing the anxiousness

250

on her face, Javier decided not to rush her and invited her to sit and have a glass of wine with him. "I am sorry corazon, I don't mean to rush you. Lets have a glass of wine and talk awhile."

Glad for the reprieve, Melinda walked to the place he indicated on the bed and sat as he suggested.

Javier poured them both a glass of wine and then turned to face her and offered a toast. "May we find happiness together always."

"Always", she whispered and then sipped the heady wine.

Soon Melinda was laughing aloud at Javier's antics and began to relax in his company. Javier was pleased to see that his strategy was working and after her fourth glass of wine suggested that they get more comfortable. "Would you mind if I got out of some of these clothes sweetheart?"

"No, not at all, in fact I was just going to suggest the same thing", said Melinda with a slight slur.

Standing he said "Come let me help you undo the buttons and if you wish you can then go behind the screen and change into this beautiful garment."

Rising, Melinda offered him her back. Javier began to undo what seemed like a hundred buttons and sooner than he thought had her nearly free.

Melinda, who found that she was a little unsteady on her feet, reached out a hand to the back of the fainting couch. Together she laughed along with Javier as he had to reach out to keep her from falling.

Teasingly Javier said, "I don't know if you'll make it to the screen, but I have another idea."

"Ok, lets hear this brilliant idea of yours", said a slightly tipsy Melinda.

"Why don't I blow out some to these candles and help you undress. Then you can get under the covers while I undress", suggested Javier.

Giggling at his suggestion Melinda said, "Sounds like a good idea to me, husband."

Grateful to be making some progress Javier diligently set to blowing out many of the candles and left only a few lighting the room.

Removing all the layers of clothing was a bigger task than he'd thought. Finally she sat before him with the sheer nightgown now in place. Slowing his breath to a normal pace he thanked even the stars above.

Looking at her thus, it was hard to keep his promise not to rush her as he found himself kissing the back of her neck.

Melinda wasn't prepared for the jolt of electricity that passed through her as his lips touched her skin. Her skin felt as if it was on fire wherever his mouth touched her.

Turning her in his arms he looked into her desire laden eyes and nearly lost control. Fusing his mouth to hers he kissed her passionately until she was quivering with need in his arms.

He crushed her to him as he deepened the kiss. Lifting her in his arms once again, he walked to the bed and placed her gently upon the mattress.

Breathing raggedly he broke the kiss and said, "Tonight Melinda I will make you my wife in every sense of the word."

Melinda, who was still caught up in the myriad of feelings he'd created with his kissing, barely noticed that he was undressing right before her eyes.

She had never felt this way before, while she had imagined that it would be magical, there was no way she could have been prepared for this. It felt like her very soul was on fire, and all she wanted was to feel his mouth upon her body over and over again. Moaning, she came up on her knees and met him half way as he knelt down on the bed. Kissing her with all that he was feeling, Javier reminded himself to go slowly so as not to frighten her.

With loving gentleness he laid her upon the bed and kissed her worries away.

He trailed kisses down her neck and onto her firm breasts. As she began to moan deeply and without restraint he trailed kisses down her stomach. He took one of her shapely legs in his hands and rained kisses up and down it until she was nearly incoherent. Just when she thought she could take no more he picked up the other leg and bestowed the same attention upon it as the other. Before it was all over she swore that he'd kissed every inch of her scorching skin. Her body felt as if it were all nerve endings and every inch of her was on fire. Nearly mindless with desire she didn't fight him as he cast aside her flimsy nightgown and came down upon her burning flesh. She briefly felt the pain as he entered her but soon was lost to the sensations flowing through her body.

Unsure of what to do, she was relieved beyond belief when she heard him whisper, "Move against me, mi amor."

She moved against his male hardness and gave herself up totally to this man whom had captured her so completely.

In a dance as old as time itself, Javier made Melinda his wife in body and soul.

Chapter Thirty-one

Melinda awoke to the sounds of the birds welcoming a new day and to the feel of Javier placing kisses along the curve of her slender thigh.

A shiver of delight coursed through her as he concentrated on initiating her in the ways of lovemaking between a man and wife.

Lowering her hand to run her fingers through his magnificent hair she moaned her pleasure.

Lifting his head from his task, Javier smiled lovingly and moved up her body to take her fully into his arms.

"Good morning Senora de Soto", he said against her lips. She answered with a kiss of her own. Melinda who'd learned much in the last few hours kissed Javier with all the passion she felt. Feeling like Eve herself, Melinda worshipped her husband's body just as he had worshipped her's only moments ago.

Soon they were lost in the throes of passion washing over them and cried out simultaneously of their love for each other as they reached the explosive end they sought. They fell asleep with their limbs intertwined, and their joy complete.

With much effort they were finally able to tear themselves from their chamber. Javier and Melinda made their way downstairs, where they were greeted by cheers and outrageous teasing. Melinda felt her cheeks redden at the jokes and refused to make eye contact with anyone.

Pulling her closely, Javier held up his hand and said to Juan playfully, "Ok, you young puppy keep your remarks to yourself or I'll make you."

"Now, Now boys, lets all move to the dining room for the noon time meal", said Senora de Soto happily.

Moving together by two's, the family all moved to take their seats at the elegantly set table.

Javier held out Melinda's chair and waited for her take her seat. Once she was seated he took the seat next to her and reassured her by taking her hand and squeezing it slightly under the table.

She smiled her gratitude and busied herself with placing her napkin on her lap.

Realizing that an awkward silence had fallen over the gathering Jean Claude spoke up, suggesting that they all go on a tour of the city. Offering them a tour of the historical sites he said addressing Melinda, "If you would like my Cherié, I could show you the places where your ancestors and mine lived during the horrible expulsion period."

"Oh yes I'd love to see the sites", she eagerly agreed.

"Then it is settled, we'll leave shortly after we've finished here", he said before signaling the servants to come forth with the many dishes they'd prepared. "Today", continued Jean Claude, "We will dine as our ancestors did."

"Oh, and how is that cousin", asked Melinda's father.

"Ah, you are curious no, today we eat Rosefish and Summer wheat bread, baked to perfection", declared Jean Claude with pride.

"Rosefish", asked Senora de Soto with skepticism.

"Wi, Rosefish is a favorite of our people, it is a tradition that newly wed couples eat a meal of Rosefish to ensure prosperity, Mrs.

De Soto." Patting her hand he continued by saying, "Trust me you will enjoy it."

"Taking a bite, Jean Claude chewed slowly while closing his eyes in delight. Swallowing, he declared that it was delicious by saying in his native tongue, "de bon gout."

Dish after delectable dish was served until Melinda felt as if she couldn't eat another bite. Noticing that all the ladies had eaten their fill, Jean Claude's wife folded her napkin and suggested that they ready themselves for the afternoon outing.

Following her lead Melinda stood and moved to leave the room but not before Javier placed a soft kiss on the back of her hand sending chills up and down her spine.

Noticing the shiver of anticipation that ran through her, Javier stood and excused himself on the pretense of helping his wife to their chamber.

This brought on more cheers and catcalls from his male relatives.

Laughing he lifted Melinda in his arms and made haste to their chamber.

Embarrassed Melinda squealed with delight and hid her burning cheeks in the front of his shirt. "Oh Javier how will we ever live this down?"

"We are husband and wife now sweetheart, what we do is natural."

"Yes, but that is the problem, they all know what we're doing."

Teasingly he answered with, "Well, maybe if you wouldn't cry out your pleasure so loudly they'd not have a clue."

Mortified she said, "Oh no am I so loud that you think they can hear us?"

Chuckling he assured her that he was only joking and was sure that what went on in their bed chamber could not be overheard by those passing in the halls.

"I am only joking corazon, I'm sure that no one can hear us, the walls are sound. But I do so enjoy those little purring sounds you make."

"What little purring sounds", she asked in curiosity.

Truly enjoying this Javier pushed open the door to their chamber and said, "You know the little sounds you make when I kiss you here, and here", he said while kissing her just below the earlobe.

Putting her feet to the floor he proceeded to kiss the soft spot just below her earlobe.

"And here", he said as he moved lower to the area between her shoulder and neck.

Just as expected she purred and then opened her eyes and tried to move away.

"Oh no, I'm not through with you yet mi amor", he murmured as he continued to move lower while unbuttoning her gown.

Melinda soon let her eyes drift close and let her head fall back into the crook of her neck as the feelings of heat began to spiral through her.

Javier smiled to himself and concentrated on removing her clothes before it was time to leave for the tour.

Wearing only her stockings and garters Melinda melted in his arms as he lifted her and carried her to their bed.

Laying her upon the covers he followed her down upon the mattress and moved to lift one dainty leg.

"I vow to make you howl with pleasure today madame."

Far beyond caring, Melinda simply gave in to the pleasure she was experiencing and lost herself to the infinite care with which he loved her so completely.

Javier trailed kisses up and down her legs and ankles until she thought she'd go mad. She wound her hands into his hair and brought him up to her, she had to feel the touch of his lips on hers or she wouldn't survive.

Javier kissed her over and over again sending her nearly over the edge and just when she thought that she could stand this sweet torture no more he moved downwards again. Javier assaulted her senses in every way that he could imagine. He kissed her flat stomach pausing for what seemed forever at her navel.

When she would have stifled a moan he redoubled his efforts and said, "Oh no Melinda I want you purring."

He moved lower still and kissed the tops of desire-flushed thighs until she couldn't contain the sounds erupting from deep within.

"Yes that's it my love, purr for me", he urged.

Writhing with abandon she gasped, "Javier...I can't take anymore please, please..."

"Please what my dear", he asked as he continued his onslaught.

Her breaths were coming in short pants and she was nearly insane with her need for release. Somehow she managed to give the answer he sought and said, "You...I need you, Javier."

Losing himself to the desire that he saw in her eyes Javier abandoned all thoughts of taunting his new wife and made love to her as if time itself was at an end.

Together they fell over the cliff of rapture and slowly floated back down to reality. Melinda knew in that moment that she'd love this man forever and looking into his eyes told him so.

"I Love you for all time Augustos Javier de Soto."

"And I You, Melinda de Soto", he answered with another lingering kiss.

Hating to break the spell their lovemaking had woven he said reluctantly, "Come we must dress for the outing."

"Oh, do we have to go out", she asked as she wrapped her legs around his waist once more.

Running his tongue along his bottom lip Javier decided that they had a little more time before getting dressed.

Soon they were lost to the feelings assuaging their senses, and loved each other once more. This time it was Melinda who took control of the direction of their lovemaking.

She delighted in the sounds of the deep moans coming from his chest as she moved to straddle his hips and rain kisses down his abdomen. Feeling the excitement ripple through him she lowered her head and loved him as he had her only a few moments ago. She chuckled as he nearly came off the bed, and suddenly found herself beneath him riding the waves of ecstasy.

Chapter Thirty-two

Laura Lee smiled into the darkness of her bedchamber at the deviousness of her plan. Earlier when her mother in law, Mrs. Camille, had gone to have tea with friends, she'd arisen and written a note to Sheriff Comeaux. She'd given the servant instructions to deliver the note to no one but the sheriff and now sat back with glee in anticipation of his answer.

She had no doubt that he would help her with this plan because he hated the negras as much as she did.

Since that Scandalous Mr. Lincoln had set them all free there had been nothing but trouble in these parts.

Families of wealth that she'd known all her life had suffered greatly because of the lost of their property. It was unfair that because some felt that the negras should enjoy the same rights as freely born whites that they could confiscate all they'd built in the south. She hated the fact that the south had lost the war and everything had changed because of that defeat.

She had written Sheriff Comeaux because his family had been one of those whose wealth had been lost because of the new laws prohibiting slavery.

It galled her that many whites were now embracing the negras and accepting them into their circles. She had been raised to believe that they were only good for one thing, to serve their betters. The races were supposed to be separate just as the bible said. While she shuddered at what others were doing in the community, it was nothing compared to what she felt over what her own husband had done. Her Negra loving husband was the worst of all. He had accepted them into his life and claimed them as his children. How dare he bring shame to her by consorting with the children of his dead negra mistress? Well she would make him pay for bringing shame upon her. She would make them all, pay!

The ship glided slowly and peacefully into the port of New Orleans with all members of the wedding party and their families standing at the rails of the deck.

Javier stood with his arm wrapped snuggly around Melinda's waist gently nuzzling her neck.

Melinda stood in the circle of his embrace and watched, as the ship seemed to float into port and wished for the hundredth time that she tried to dispel the feelings of unease that had plagued her since their departure from Canada.

Noticing the frown creasing her forehead Javier said softly, "All will be well Melinda, stop worrying corazon."

Turning to face him she laughed up into his eyes and said, "You know me so well Javier, Ok I will try, but please, please watch your back."

"I promise to be watchful my love but I assure you we de Soto's are a powerful family. None would dare to say aught against us for fear of financial ruin", he said confidently.

"Oh Javier if only it were as simple as you suggest."

"Sweetheart, listen to me, everything will work out for the best."

Gathering her in his arms tightly he kissed her until her senses were reeling and said, "Welcome home Senora de Soto." Leaving the ship Melinda took one last look at the vessel that had served as her honeymoon chambers for the last few weeks.

The family had only been home one week when Javier's mother waltzed into the dinning room one evening to announce her intentions to have a ball.

"It will be the wedding ball of all wedding balls", said an excited Senora de Soto.

"Madre are you sure that this is wise", asked a concerned Javier.

"Yes my son, we must show our friends and associates that we accept Melinda, and that she is a welcomed addition to this family."

Senor de Soto leant his voice to his wife's argument citing that everyone must be informed that she was now their daughter. "I agree with your Mother, Javier, we must let them see a united front."

And so it was decided that a ball would be given to honor the newly weds.

Melinda felt as if she were a princess newly crowned queen, as the de Soto family friends and business associates, were introduced to her. While she had felt apprehensive about the ball given by her mother in law to announce her eldest son's marriage, Melinda, now glowed with excitement as one by one the crème of the crop filed past.

Senor Alejandro Cintron, a partner in the family shipping business, kissed her hand and complimented Javier on his choice of brides. In a loud clear voice he exclaimed, "You have done well Augustos, very well indeed, she is very beautiful." Turning to face Melinda once again he said before moving on, "Once again, mujer bonita, it is a pleasure to make your acquaintance."

Next in line was the Gonzalez family. Many heads turned to watch to see if sparks would fly once these introductions were made. Everyone gathered this evening, except maybe Melinda knew of the failed attempts of this family to unite itself with the de Soto's by marriage.

Melinda felt the atmosphere change and wondered at Javier's suddenly tense posture. She turned to greet the newcomers and sucked in her breath at the hatred she glanced in the eyes of the beautiful young woman standing before her. Instantly she knew that there had once been a relationship between Javier and this woman. Stiffening her spine she smiled her most beauteous, breathtaking smile. Extending her hand to the young woman in friendship Melinda welcomed her to her home. "Hello, welcome to our home, I have not had the pleasure of meeting you, my name is Melinda."

Thrown off guard for a moment Pamela simply stared at Javier's new bride. After what seemed like an hour she finally managed to return the greeting. Narrowing her eyes she said cunningly, "Hola, yo me llamo Pamela Gonzalez."

Realizing that Pamela was trying to rattle his new bride, Javier came to Melinda's rescue by saying, "Pamela how wonderful to see you again." Kissing her hand he says for the benefit of the crowd now gathered in the foyer, "Melinda this is Pamela, she is very much like a little sister to me, I am sure that the two of you will get along splendidly." "Pamela you must come over for a visit, I'm sure I will enjoy hearing about all of Javier's childhood antics", added Melinda.

Turning to greet more of their neighbors Melinda effectively dismissed Pamela without a second thought. The crowd began to disperse once it was realized that no fireworks would be displayed between the two women this evening. Senora de Soto breathed a sigh of relief when Pamela moved off towards the ballroom, and said softly to her husband, "Praise God for small miracles." "Pequenos milagros, indeed", replied Senor de Soto.

Chapter Thirty-three

Laura Lee Savoie bristled with anger as she moved to greet the newlyweds on her husband's arm. She could barely contain her hatred of Melinda as she stopped in front of the couple to exchange greetings.

Just whom did the little Negra think she was anyway? Laura Lee couldn't believe that all these good, upstanding citizens condoned this blasphemy of a marriage.

Baring her teeth in what looked more like a snarl than a smile, she moved to stand in front of Senor and Senora de Soto. Clasping Senora de Soto's hand she said in a whisper, "I know how you must feel my dear, but this too shall pass."

Melinda sucked in her breath at the comment made by Mrs. Savoie and stiffened her spine for what was to come next.

Senor de Soto, determined to ensure that all went well, asked, "Why, whatever could you mean by such a statement Madame? This is a celebration."

Noticing the sudden change in the atmosphere, Jean Pierre turned to look at Laura Lee and raised a questioning eyebrow. Seeing his steely gaze, Laura Lee took it as a fair warning of not to cause a scene and politely excused herself without greeting the newlyweds.

Javier kissed her earlobe lightly and said for her ears only, "Pay her no attention corazon, people like her mean nothing. It is a pity however that she is Beatrice's mother."

Saddened, Melinda turned glistening eyes towards Roberto and Beatrice and received a re-assuring smile from the two of them. Turning back she was just in time to greet a Mr. Thomas Higgins. Mr. Higgins, it seemed was a solicitor who handled any legalities the family might incur in the shipping industry. Smiling he said, "A pleasure to make your acquaintance Senora, if you should ever need my services, know that I am available."

Nearly colliding with the young lady, Pamela Gonzales. Laura Lee discovered that here was someone else who hated Melinda de Soto as much as she. She heard the young woman murmur softly to herself of the need to dispose of Javier's new wife, and smiled a secret smile.

Excitement bubbled everywhere. It was once again time for the Twelfth Night celebration. Melinda had been prodded and poked as she stood for fittings. Her gown for the ball, which began the Mardi Gras season, had been designed by one of New Orleans' most sought after modesties.

Melinda now stood in front of the mahogany, oval shaped, full sized mirror and was pleased beyond measure at what she saw.

Her gown was made of a gold tissue overskirt with tiny rows of buttons covering the back of the gown. The overskirt was split in the middle to reveal a ruffled white lacy underskirt. Her waist was cinched in snuggly for a perfect fit by a bejeweled topaz belt with a diamond buckle.

Entering the chamber Melinda's maid exclaimed aloud, "Oh Senora Melinda you will be the most beautiful woman on the queen's court tonight."

"I don't know about the most beautiful, but I certainly feel that way", added Melinda.

She took her seat as the maid draped the matching topaz and diamond studded necklace around her slender neck. Next came the earrings, bracelet, and small tiara. Javier entered just as the maid finished placing the tiara atop Melinda's head. Taking in his wife's appearance he said aloud, "I am the luckiest man alive to have such a beautiful wife as you." Picking up her dainty hand he placed a feather like kiss upon it's back and motioned for the maid to leave them.

Pulling her to her feet, Javier savored the feel of her body against his. Dipping his head to capture her lips he moans deeply as she wraps her arms around his neck and opens her luscious mouth to deepen their kiss.

Finally stepping away slightly he commented, "I will be the envy of every warm blooded male at the ball."

Blushing, Melinda absentmindedly pats her hair in place and answers, "Surely you exaggerate when you say that every male will envy you."

"Oh no, I'm being completely honest. In fact many will be hard pressed not to downright knock me over the head and run off with you."

Laughing gaily, Melinda marvels at how loved and cherished Javier makes her feel. Lifting her hand to gently cup his jaw line she says, "I'd never allow anyone to run away with me, my love."

"That's good to know. Now let us go downstairs and meet everyone else", he replied.

Picking up her gold velvet, trimmed in ostrich feathered mask, she places her hand in his and descended the stairs on her husband's arm. "Yes let us go down before they send someone up to fetch us."

"Si, I can almost here Papa sending up a servant to see what could possibly be detaining us."

They were still laughing as they entered the parlor where the rest of the family had gathered pending their departure. Looking up as they entered Senor de Soto comments on their arrival by saying, "Well now that you two have arrived we can all be transported to the ball."

Coming forward, Maria Antonia stretches her hands forth to Melinda and compliments her beauty. "Oh Melinda you are absolutely gorgeous in the gold tissue, isn't she Mama."

"Si, Melinda you're simply breathtaking tonight", answered her mother.

"Thank you, all of you, for your support in this matter", said a suddenly sentimental Melinda.

"Nonsense, you are a part of this family, an no one will be permitted to exclude you", stated Senor de Soto.

"Si, to exclude you is to exclude us all", added Roberto.

Smiling her gratitude through a flood of tears that threatened to spill any minute Melinda simply shook her head in acknowledgement to the family's statements. Feeling Javier give her hand a slight squeeze she let her mind reflect briefly on the incident to which she'd eluded.

Several of the members from the Krewe de Hispaniola had arrived a week ago to inform the de Soto family that this year they would all be invited to the annual Twelfth Night Ball except she and Javier.

The family had been outraged over the decision made by the leadership of the Krewe and disclosed their displeasure most vocally.

Senor de Soto had even threatened that not one family member would attend the festivities planned by the group the entire season. However nothing had worked as well as the threat to withdraw all monetary support. Senor de Soto had demanded a full refund of the family's yearly membership dues.

Later that week the King of the Krewe had responded by apologizing profusely for the offense. Swearing that he had known nothing of what had transpired over the previous week, he made it known that all members of the family were welcomed at all of this year's activities.

Senor de Soto however had one more card up his sleeve and demanded that Melinda and Javier serve as members of the royal court. After turning all shades from red to purple, the King had finally agreed to his demands, and here they all stood; ready to go to the first ball of the season.

Chapter Thirty-four

Melinda and Javier had just danced the last of the protocol dances performed by the Krewe members only, when Pamela Gonzalez intentionally stepped on one of Melinda's feet.

"Perdoneme, Senora." Turning back to her companion she comments loud enough to be overheard, "The illustrious members who buy their positions."

All surrounding the couple laughed heartily at the comment and Javier felt Melinda's step falter. Bracing her by placing his hand near the small of her back, he whispered encouraging words. "Pay no attention to Pamela, she is a mean spirited, vindictive, unfulfilled young woman, who cannot hold a candle to you."

"If only all that you said were true", responded Melinda.

"What do you mean if only what I said was the truth, of course all I said was accurate", admonished Javier.

"No, it cannot possibly be true, she is much more beautiful than I, and…"

279

"Never are you to sell yourself short to one such as she Melinda." Tipping her chin upwards he said again, "Never, do you hear me."

"Yes, but..."

"No buts, she cannot hold a candle to your charm and beauty", Javier said within the hearing of Pamela and her companions.

Gasping with rage Pamela retorts, "That may be your opinion Javier but not everyone here shares your appreciation for the shall we say, La Negrita."

Arriving on the scene Senor de Soto says with deadly calm, "I'm sure your father would not find your slander against mi familia at all beneficial or acceptable senorita Gonzalez."

No one who heard the barely veiled threat could be mistaken about what he meant. It was common knowledge that the de Sotos owned more that 40% of interests in the Gonzalez manufacturing business.

Before anyone else could comment it was announced that all Black coats and their ladies could now enter the dance floor.

Vacating the floor for those not of the royal court, Javier escorted Melinda to the dais without another glance in Pamela's direction.

Many who had heard the exchange secretly snickered behind their masks at the set down Senor de Soto had issued to the snotty Gonzalez daughter. It seemed that she'd snubbed one too many families on her supposed climb to the top. Pamela Gonzalez had mistakenly thought she could snare one of the elder de Soto sons, but to her bitter surprise it seemed they were now out of reach.

Looking on the couple with menace, she silently vowed to make them regret not choosing to join their families through marriage. She made a mental note to send off a note to a co-conspirator in the morning. Soon Melinda de Soto would not be a problem.

Feeling much better she turned piercing cold black eyes to her escort and laughed at something he'd just said.

Laura Lee sat and reread the note she'd received this morning. She was being asked to contact Sheriff Comeaux and set up a date and time for a meeting. Smiling wickedly, she scribbled out a hasty note and sent old Benjamin off to deliver it without delay.

Only yesterday she and Jean Pierre had argued again over his preoccupation with his dead mistress' illegitimate children. Oh what a delight it would be to finally have at least one of them out of her life. After the first one was disposed of she was sure that the second one would be too occupied with the search to bother them again.

Completing her toilette she decided to go out for an afternoon drive, maybe she'd even stop by Mrs. Olson's place for an afternoon treat.

Arriving at Mrs. Olson's place Laura Lee stepped down from the carriage and entered the establishment more cheerful than she'd felt in over six months.

Looking up she spotted her dear friend Mrs. Olson, who called out a greeting, "Hello, Laura Lee how wonderful to see you again."

Taking her hands in hers Mrs. Savoie replied, "Well I was out and about and decided to drop by for some of that delectable Apple Pie you bake."

"Oh, you're in luck and guess who else is here, Abigail Owens", crooned Mrs. Olson.

"An afternoon spent with good company and good food, what else could a lady ask for", answered Laura Lee.

Chapter Thirty-five

Leaping from the bed, Melinda dashed for the chamber pot. Emptying the contents of her stomach, she clung to the sides of the porcelain pot. Javier reached her side quickly and held her hair away from her face.

"I'm here sweetheart", he said while handing her a glass of water to wash out her mouth. "I think we should have the doctor look you over corazon."

Shaking her head wearily Melinda disagrees, "No…No doctor."

"But sweetheart you have done this for a whole week straight, parts of you are tender to the touch, and you nearly fainted yesterday", argued Javier.

Rising slowly with his assistance Melinda said softly, "Please Javier no doctor."

"But what if something is seriously wrong?"

"Nothing is wrong Javier, I am simply going to have our child", she said nonchalantly as she lay back down upon the bed.

"Our what?", shouted Javier?

"Shhh, you're going to wake the dead."

"But you...you said you were to have our child, that means I'm going to be a father."

"Yes I do believe that is the case Javier, now please stop shaking the bed."

Jumping down quickly Javier asks excitedly, "Are you sure that you are with child?"

Fighting the morning sickness Melinda answers sharply, "Yes I'm sure now please just leave me alone."

"Oh this is wonderful", chimed an exhilarated Javier, "No beyond wonderful, this is magnificent." Looking over at Melinda however his happy mood soon turned to a more subdued, concerned one. Moving back towards the bed he gently cradled her head in his hands and asked, "Sweetheart what can I do to make it better?"

Unable to speak for fear of vomiting again, Melinda simply waved a limp hand in what she hoped was a sign of refusal.

Javier however refused to take no for an answer and said, "Maybe some more water, to rinse out your mouth?"

Jumping down from the bed once more he inadvertently caused Melinda's stomach to roll again sending her scrambling to get to the chamber pot.

Forgetting the water he rushed over to her side and held her while the dry heaves racked her body over and over again.

Finally after what seemed like hours to Javier, the spasms stopped and he carried Melinda to their bed and laid her gently upon the coverlet.

"Surely there must be something to help with this? I will go to get Beatrice, she will know what to do."

Uncaring whether he left or stayed, Melinda burrowed deeper into the covers, and prayed for the sickness to leave her.

Melinda groaned as she heard the excited gaggle of the women in the family as they moved to her bedchamber door.

Entering the room the women all rushed to the bedside to offer congratulations and advice on what would help.

Melinda, who was beyond caring at this moment, simply groaned her thanks and clutched her stomach to keep it from heaving wildly.

Javier's grandmother came forward then and sent Graciela to the kitchen in search of galletas or Spanish crackers to soothe Melinda's stomach.

"Gracie, ve a la cocina a conserguirme las galletas para el estomago de Melinda."

"Si Abuela", Graciella answered as she left the room. Wetting a small washcloth, Senora de Soto gently washed Melinda's flushed face. Instructing Melinda to lie still until she had something in her stomach.

"You must lie still until you have eaten something, mija."

Shaking her head as if to disagree Melinda adds, "No I can't eat anything."

"Si, you can, in fact you must", insisted her mother-in-law.

Coming to stand closer to her sister's bed Beatrice said softly, "Listen to her Melinda she knows best."

"But my stomach feels as if it will reject all sustenance, I don't think I can eat a thing", argued Melinda.

"Listen my dear, you must settle the acids in your stomach before rising from the bed", interjected Javier's grandmother.

Returning from her errand Graciella strolled towards the bed and handed over the small round crackers.

Opening the small oval tin, Senora de Soto hands one over to Melinda and waits for her to eat it before handing her another.

"Bien, bien, now after a few seconds you will be able to rise without sickness."

Surprised that her stomach didn't reject the strangely rounded, thin, crispy wafers. Melinda smiled slightly as she sat up and expressed her gratitude to the rest of the de Soto women.

"Thanks, all of you, for your help, while I would have liked to make an official announcement, I guess it just wasn't meant to be."

Patting her hand gingerly grandma de Soto said, "Oh nonsense, we are family."

"Yes, and family takes care of its own", added Graciela.

Suddenly Melinda burst into tears and for the life of her couldn't understand why she was in such turmoil.

Dashing her hand over her eyes she says while throwing her hands up, "I don't know why I'm crying, one minute crying the next laughing, I'm just a mess."

"Oh Melinda all of us have experienced what is happening to you", said Beatrice as she came to sit on the edge of the bed.

"You mean this is supposed to happen, that it is a part of pregnancy", asked a skeptical Melinda. Rushing onward she says, "I wasn't near Suzanna at the beginning, so I don't know what is normal and what isn't."

"Si, Yes we have all been there mija, it is a part of becoming a mother." Taking a seat next to the bed Senora de Soto went on to talk about all the joys of being enceinte for the first time.

"Enjoy every moment mija, for there is only one first pregnancy."

Rising from her perch at the end of the bed, the senior Mrs. De Soto gathered her flock of women and left Melinda to the ministrations of her maid.

"Come ladies, let us leave Melinda to her maid", looking at Melinda she said lovingly, "Rest, take your time coming down this morning."

Melinda nodded her assent and slowly rose to allow the maid to assist her into her bathing tub.

After bathing and choosing a gown for the day, Melinda decided to take another short nap before going down to meet the rest of the family. Snuggling under the down coverlet, she smiled knowingly and hugged her still flat stomach. Lifting her eyes heavenward she briefly whispered the news of her pregnancy to her mother and promptly fell asleep. At that moment she felt as if she was the most highly favored woman on earth.

Chapter Thirty-six

Sheriff Comeaux swallowed past the huge knot threatening to choke him, as he watched the beautiful young woman pace back and forth until finally she stilled.

Coming to stand before him she let her fingers trail a fiery path down his open shirt to the waistband of his unbuckled belt. Her eyes mesmerized him as she spoke of what things she wanted to befall the Negro wife of Javier de Soto.

"Yes she must suffer greatly for what she has cost me", murmured Pamela.

Feeling more aroused than ever the Sheriff took her hand in his and pressed it against his swollen appendage, and kissed her hotly.

"Yes, yes tell old Comeaux how the lil darkie will suffer", he rasped between kisses.

Realizing that his fevered actions were being caused by her words of near torture, Pamela described in vivid detail what she'd like to have happen to Melinda.

"She will be taken to the Sanitarium and remain there all her natural life."

Laughing at the cruelty of her own words, Pamela began to feel the stirrings of lust deep within her bowels.

"The doctors there will be told only that she is deranged, thinking that she is the wife of a wealthy landowner, but is in fact only his cast aside mistress."

"No one there will help her because they won't believe a word she says."

"It will be a joy to see her die a slow agonizing lonely death."

Now fevered to an almost dangerous pitch, the two conspirators tore at each other's clothing in an effort to satisfy their somewhat abnormal sexual appetites.

Pamela impaled herself upon Sheriff Comeaux before he'd had the chance to fully remove his trousers. Throwing her head back she was nearly mindless with her need for release. Never could she recall being this aroused, clutching his head to her breast she worked to drive them both over the brink.

Sheriff Comeaux lost himself to the wonderful feelings gripping him as over and over she grinded her hips painfully into his. It was as if some beautiful, untamed animal had taken possession of her body. Spurring her on to their mutual release, over and over he rasped between breaths of what she made him feel.

Finally with her nails craving deep scratches into his flesh Pamela threw her head back and shouted her release, which triggered the same response from her newly found partner in crime.

Still lying in his arms she smiled sardonically and said, "Never has it been this good, mi amigo."

Smiling with pride that such a young, beautiful woman as this one could pay him such a compliment, Sheriff Comeaux leaned over and replied, "We make a good team, do we not Senorita?"

"Si, most definitely, we are extraordinary together", agreed Pamela.

Finally, after several more hours spent in the sparsely furnished shack Sheriff Comeaux called a home, Pamela prepared to return to New Orleans.

"I will send you a note with instructions as soon as all the arrangements have been made."

Surprised that she once again was cold as ice, Sheriff Comeaux blinked and asked uncertainly, "How long before I see you again Senorita?"

Realizing that he was now under the magic she'd woven in order to convince him to help her, Pamela smiled brightly at her new puppet and lied without a moment's hesitation. "Soon, amigo, very soon indeed. It pains me now to leave your side but I must go back to finalize our plans."

Satisfied with her answer Sheriff Comeaux lifted her into her carriage before kissing her one last time.

Unable to do anything contrary to her nature, Pamela grasped his head and kissed him forcefully with all the sexual flavor she could muster.

Panting hard Sheriff Comeaux broke the kiss and said, "Make the arrangements as soon as possible and hurry back, I can hardly wait till our next visit."

With a satisfied glint shining in her cold black eyes, Pamela assured him of all he wanted to hear.

"I will count the hours until we are together again amigo, just thinking of being with you makes my heart race", she said as she brought his hand to her breast.

Kissing her once again, Sheriff Comeaux stepped down from the carriage and signaled her driver to pull off.

Once out of earshot Pamela laughed aloud at how gullible the Sheriff had proven himself to be. "How foolish of you to think that I could ever truly care for one such as you, amigo. But your adoration of me is touching, soon you will learn that it is all simply a game of control."

Licking her lips she let her mind stray to a scene she played over and over again, of she and Javier locked in a lover's embrace whispering of their love for one another.

Jean Pierre knew deep in his gut that something was wrong, but he was so pleased with Laura Lee's new change of heart, he simply shrugged off the feelings and lost himself to her charms once again.

Watching her sleep he wondered again at their reconciliation and what had caused it. He certainly couldn't remember any effort on his part to do anything that could have caused this sudden change.

He smiled silently as he remembered how she'd practically seduced him and then made love to him after all these years. Laura Lee had given all the servants the night off, sent his mother to visit Beatrice in New Orleans and greeted him wearing a sheer white night rail, as he'd come in from his day's work.

At first he'd thought that he was hallucinating, I mean Laura Lee had never done anything like this, not, even in the beginning of their marriage. Now they had been wed twenty-five years. Thinking back she had fairly knocked his socks off with her actions last night.

Rising quietly he placed another small kiss upon her cheek and turned to exit to his own chambers.

He nearly lost his footing as her arms wound around his neck and she kissed him full on the mouth.

Struggling to put a little distance between them, he pulled apart from her and said with somewhat slight embarrassment, "Laura Lee, hon, it is nearly daybreak, the servants…"

"Won't be up for another hour or two Jean Pierre, love me once again husband", she interrupted.

Taking her into his arms gently, he lay down fully upon her and lost himself in the loving of his wife.

Laura Lee's mind however strayed to the note she'd received from Rene the day before, instructing her to make peace with her husband so that the next phase of their plan could come to pass.

As her husband's hand roved over her flesh she closed her eyes and imagined that it was Rene making love to her instead of her husband. It was the only thing that made her husband's pawing bearable. Yes, for Rene she could do anything. She heard herself cry out as he kissed her breasts, "Yes, oh yes."

Moaning her pleasure as her fantasies bloomed to life within her mind, Laura Lee willingly gave herself up to her husband's fumbling hands with wild abandonment.

"Did you do as I instructed", asked an impatient Sheriff Comeaux.

"Yes, I did as you wanted my love, Jean Pierre won't suspect a thing when that bastard of Mary Harmon's disappears", answered his well sated accomplice.

"Good, more instructions will follow, now get dressed and be on your way before anyone sees you."

Hurt by his nonchalant attitude towards her after they had just been so intimate. Laura Lee picked herself up from the floor and began to replace her clothing.

She assured herself that he was just concerned with her safety and her reputation and not truly bored with her.

No, Rene loved her as much as she loved him. They would be together just as he promised as soon as this ugly mess was over.

Brightening over those thoughts, she fastened the last of her buttons and moved to stand in front of her lover saying, "You are right I must be going, we must be discreet about this until we can be together."

Rene Comeaux fought with all his might, the urge to throw up in her face. She was only a means to an end, but right now they needed her if their plans for Melinda were to succeed.

Swallowing the rising bile, he grinned down into her upturned face and said, "Yes, until we can be together we must be very careful." Seizing on the moment to rid himself of her unwanted attentions he continued on saying, "To be on the safe side we shouldn't meet like this again."

"But Rene, his caresses will be unbearable if I don't have yours to singe them away", she wailed.

"Shhhhhh, mon belle, in no time at all we will be together, but for now we must keep our distance. It is not safe. What if something were to happen to you? I would not want to live", he said in what he hoped sounded like an impassioned tone.

He kissed her then to keep her from arguing the point and almost laughed aloud with glee at the little mewling noises she was making in the back of her throat.

Breaking the kiss, he moved to stand away from her and turned her in the direction of the door. Glancing at his timepiece he realized that he was to meet Pamela in less than one hour. Hurriedly he walked her to the door and said, "Come now my love you must leave, soon your husband will be returning from Opelousas and you must convince him to have a party and to invite all the de Soto's."

"Anything for you my love, anything", she said as she sought to fuse their mouths once more.

Moving back quickly, he dodged the kiss cleanly and said in a near whisper, "No my love, not here in the open", letting his eyes move towards the carriage he added, "Anyone could see us and report back to your husband."

"Oh dear me, I hadn't thought of that", gasped a clearly ruffled Laura Lee. Looking up at her driver and straightening her bonnet she said in a loud voice, "Thank you for all your help Sheriff Comeaux, I look forward to seeing you soon."

"Good, any seeing us together will only report that we were discussing business." In a lower tone he added for good measure, "See you soon my love."

Feeling like a schoolgirl Laura Lee entered her carriage and wiped away the tiny beads of perspiration from her face as she watched him close the door and signal the driver.

Rene ran back inside to wash the stench of her from his body and to prepare for his meeting with Pamela. He thought of all the things the two of them would do together and instantly found himself painfully aroused.

Jean Pierre whistled a happy tune as he entered the estate. Looking around he smiled at the subtle changes that had taken place since he and Laura Lee had "fixed" their relationship.

He pulled up short as he entered the parlor and found his mother and his wife sitting on a settee with their heads close together making some sort of plans.

Clearing his throat, he announces his presence and inquires as to what they were doing.

"Ahem, what are you two ladies up to, may I ask?"

Rising Laura Lee moved to welcome him with a warm embrace and a kiss on the cheek. "Darling how wonderful of you to return so soon." Inwardly she thanked her lucky stars that she'd arrived a scant half-hour earlier. She had immediately gone to her chamber to wash quickly and change her gown. She had come in search of her mother in law and found her only five minutes before Jean Pierre's return.

"I found myself missing the two of you so much that I decided to wrap things up earlier than usual and return to have dinner with my two favorite ladies." "Oh hosh posh", proclaimed his mother. "It's your lovely wife you really missed."

Kissing her cheek he said sincerely, "Now maman you know that I missed you to."

Watching the two of them interact Laura Lee almost felt uncertain about what she and Rene were planning to do to Melinda and the de Soto's. However thinking of how things would be once she and Rene were finally able to be husband and wife she quickly shook off all such sentiments and walked over to the liquor cabinet.

"Would you like for me to pour you something to drink Jean Pierre?"

Smiling at her attentiveness he said simply "A drafter of *Taffia*, please my dear."

"And you mother Savoie, what would you like", asked Laura Lee in the sickeningly sweetest voice she could muster.

"Why, Laura Lee, you are just full of surprises today", answered a startled Mrs. Savoie." Moving she added, "Can't ever remember you serving drinks this way."

"Please mama Savoie, I most certainly have poured and served drinks right here in this parlor to be exact, you make it sound as if I'm unattentive and uncaring."

"By no means that Laura Lee, but I can't remember you ever pouring for me."

Not wishing for an argument to brew Jean Pierre intervened by suggesting they all go out to Mrs. Olson's for dinner.

"I have a wonderful idea, lets go out to Mrs. Olson's this evening, I hear she's making apple pie for desert."

"Splendid idea son, let's go up and get changed Laura Lee, nobody bakes like Olson."

Not to be out done Laura Lee agreed wholeheartedly, "Yes lets change into something more appealing and go out to dinner with the most handsome of all gentlemen around."

Drinking his glass of rum, Jean Pierre once again shook his head in wonder at this new attitude of Laura Lee's. He closed his eyes and thanked the good Lord for this new miracle he'd wrought.

Laura Lee was now the perfect wife, attentive, compassionate, his lover, everything, all in one lovely package. If he weren't careful he'd fall madly in love with his wife, not that, that was such a bad idea. He decided however, to remain cautious just a tad bit longer. Although he couldn't put his finger on it, something just didn't seem quite right with all of this.

Chapter Thirty-seven

Melinda and Javier accepted all the well wishes given them by the family as they sat in the parlor.

Senor de Soto stood and raised his glass while toasting them on the soon to be birth of their child.

"To my son and si, my daughter, God has smiled on this family once again with this gift of a new baby, May you have all the joys of parenting that Maria and I have had."

"Gracias papa, we look forward to the birth of our child and are pleased to know that you are looking forward to being grandparent's once again", Javier said as he leveled both of his parents with looks of pure gratitude.

Dabbing her eyes with her handkerchief Senora de Soto says, between tears, "We truly want you to know that we are pleased beyond measure at this news."

"Madre, all is forgotten, I know in my heart of hearts that you will love this grandchild", said a tearful Melinda.

Embracing one another, soon all the women of the room were crying, laughing, and talking at the same time. The men all promptly followed Senor de Soto out of the room and into his study.

"They will go on for hours all laughing, crying, and talking at once", said Juanito as he shook his head in wonder.

"When a woman is happy my son, she often cries and laughs at the same time", offered his father.

"Yes, and they will all talk at the same time and sound like gaggling geese", added Julio.

Bursting into laughter, the three married de Soto men gave the yet unmarried youngsters looks that said, One day soon, one day soon.

Wiping away tears of mirth, Senor de Soto placed his hands of each of his younger son's shoulders and offered them some advice.

"Take it from me, never, ever, call them gaggling geese, within their hearing."

Adding to their torment Roberto added, "Not if you value your sanity, don't ever characterize them in such a manner."

Spying the look of pure dismay on their faces, Javier burst into laughter once again while offering the two youngsters more advice.

"Women my dear boys, can be very puzzling at times, however never, ever point that out to them."

"Why", they asked in unison, causing the older three to burst into laughter once again.

"Let me try", offered Roberto. "You see wives are much more complicated than mistresses, and one must know how to deal with a wife on a very different level." Since his back was to the door he had no way of knowing that his wife had entered and was paying rapid attention to what he was saying.

His father however tried to warn him by saying, "I think that is all the advice the youngsters need for one night Berto."

Cutting him off Roberto went on to say; "One must learn to unweave all the complicated patterns of a wife's brain while one only has to satisfy a mistress' need for baubles and gowns and such."

"And just how would you know about satisfying mistresses Roberto", asked a piqued Beatrice.

Choking on the contents of his glass that he just sampled Roberto whirled around to face his wife while wiping his mouth with the back of his hand.

After managing to get the spasms of his diaphragm under control, he offered the lamest excuse any of the men in the room had ever heard. His father and older brother fought back outright laughter as he stumbled through his explanation. "Sweetheart, of course I am not speaking from experience, but I do have friends who are still unmarried. Sometimes they share their experiences with me through idle talk."

"Well the next time they offer to share their little experiences, kindly inform them that you have no need for such advice."

Taking her hand in his, he turned it over to kiss the palm and said, "Of course mi amor, you are right."

Switching the subject quickly he asked, "Now what is it that brought you in search of me?"

Beatrice marveled at her reaction to her husband's charm. She felt her pulse leap as his beautiful lips touched her palm. Now looking into his smoldering eyes she had to give herself a mental shake in order to break the spell he was casting.

After several moments she managed to say, "Oh dear me, Mama de Soto sent me to let you gentlemen know that the women will be retiring to the upstairs nursery."

"Gracias daughter for coming to inform us, we will find a way to endure being apart from our beautiful wives," quipped her father in law.

Fanning him away playfully, Beatrice says, "Father de Soto you say the most heartfelt things. I will be sure to inform Madre of your comments."

Laughing softly he suggested that Roberto escort his wife back to meet the rest of the ladies. "Walk with your wife to the nursery Berto, we will await your return here in my study."

"Si, Padre, I will return shortly", responded Roberto as he lead Beatrice from the room by linking her arm through his.

Once at the door to the nursery Roberto took Beatrice in his arms and kissed her sensually before leading her into the nursery.

Spying the heated glances passing from one to the other Maria de Soto chuckled and commented on Roberto's devotion to his wife. "Roberto, your concern for Beatrice is inspiring but she will be fine with the rest of us. We are simply discussing plans to redecorate for the new addition. Go and join the rest of the men, I will send someone to notify you of when we retire to our bedchambers." The comment promptly sent all of the women into a fit giggling and left him feeling rather doltish.

"Si mama...I'll just go back down to join papa and the others. Good night ladies", responded Roberto as he went through the door.

Once back in the study he let go of a pent up breath he'd been holding. He then assured the other males that he had wiped all traces from his wife's brain, of the conversation she'd walked in upon.

"Si, Papa I am sure that what she heard is now the furthest thing from her mind."

"I certainly hope that you have made her forget or we will all be in for a tongue lashing from our women," added his uncertain father.

Laughing the twins drove the nails in deeper by throwing back his words, "Yes and we know how difficult it can be to soothe a complex wife's mind, as opposed to our mistress' simple uncomplicated minds."

Clinking his glass against his brother's, Juan wiped away tears of mirth and said, "Excellente hermano, excellent brother."

"Bastante, enough", said his father. "Let's talk of more important matters."

Taking their seats around the fireplace, the men sat and talked of all the political changes recently occurring.

"What", asked a livid Senora de Soto.

"Yes, what do you mean, they were speaking of mistresses and wives", asked Graciela.

"Well, like I said I had just entered the room when I heard Roberto say something about how hard it was to reason with a wife as opposed to a mistress."

"Surely you misunderstood Beatrice, why would they possibly be discussing something like that", asked Melinda innocently.

"Oh I assure you that Beatrice heard just what she says", said Senora de Soto hotly.

"Well maybe we should prove them right for a change", added Graciela with a mischievous grin.

"Si mija, you may just have something there", agreed her mother.

Spying the wicked gleam in her mother in law's eyes, Beatrice couldn't help but join in and make a few plans of her own to teach her husband a lesson he wouldn't soon forget.

Laughing the ladies all went their separate ways and once again made a pact to teach their husbands not to compare them with kept ladies.

Entering their bedchamber, Javier was surprised to find Melinda already asleep. He had been sure he'd made it quite plain to her that tonight they would spend time pleasuring each other.

Sweeping a glance towards the bed, he let his shoulders slump disappointedly and padded to the dressing room.

Melinda waited until he'd shut the door to let go of the breath she'd been holding. Pulling the covers up to her chin she scratched as the long flannel gown brushed against her legs. After all, it would be worth a little discomfort this evening to teach Javier a little lesson about respect. Snuggling deeper she smiled to herself and drifted off to sleep before he returned.

Roberto was so furious he was sorely tempted to awaken his sleeping wife. He ached with his need for her and now he'd come into their chamber only to find her asleep.

Sighing deeply he entered the dressing room and began to disrobe, once again shaking his head in disgust over his situation. Spying the pitcher of water on the washstand he wet a cloth and washed his face hoping to cool his ardor.

Beatrice nearly laughed aloud as she heard him swear under his breath about sleeping wives and raging passions.

Upon hearing him re-enter the bedchamber she forced herself to breath steady even breaths, and hoped that he'd fall for the ruse.

Graciela's husband as well as her father also found sleeping wives as they entered their chambers for the evening. Neither man could believe their bad luck. Senor de Soto was certain that he'd whispered several sensuous things to his wife before retiring to his study with his sons. There was no way she could have gotten her signals crossed.

Looking at the bed once again, he swept a hand through his silver and black locks and crossed to the dressing chamber.

Maria smiled in the darkened chamber as her husband walked dejectedly into the dressing room. For a minute she'd thought that he would awaken her but breathed a sigh of relief when he'd simply gone to change. She wondered briefly how the other women were faring, knowing that it would be harder on the newly weds she whispered and extra prayer for them. Fluffing her pillow one last time she snuggled deeper into the covers and drifted off into a peaceful sleep.

Melinda entered the breakfast room cheerfully on Javier's arm and greeted all the other family members already assembled.

"Good Morning everyone."

Murmurs of "morning", rung around the table, and while the women were all cheerful and happily rested the men it seemed were all in a rather grumpy mood.

With all intentions of pouring salt on the wound, Senora de Soto said, "Oh I slept wonderfully last night, in fact I didn't even notice that Juan had retired until this morning."

"Oh I know what you mean madre, must have been all those plans we made last night, I too was asleep the moment my head hit the pillow", added Graciela.

Laughing Beatrice replied, "Imagine that, I too fell asleep almost as soon as I was changed and bathed."

"You know, I thought it was just the baby making me so tired, but I was asleep so fast that I didn't hear Javier enter last night either", said Melinda innocently.

Suddenly the twins burst into laughter and soon the women joined in the melodious chorus much to the other men's chagrin.

"And just what is so amusing", asked a slightly agitated Senor de Soto.

"Surely Padre you know", supplied a laughing Julio.

"Well my son why don't you explain it, so that I will be certain to understand", replied his now angered father.

"No my son", interjected his mother, "I will explain it."

All of the men with the exception of the twins sat and listened with dumbfounded expressions as Senora de Soto explained what had just occurred.

Turning to face his wife Roberto said, "So, I didn't make you forget the conversation about mistresses huh?"

"No sweetheart, you didn't. Never again try to seduce me in such a manner for such a purpose", answered Beatrice.

"Si, it was wrong of me to try and manipulate you in such a manner, please forgive me mi amor", pleaded a sincere Roberto.

"Forgiven, now if you will excuse us I must speak with my husband alone for a short while", she said as she stood.

Making eye contact with her, Roberto read the message in her eyes immediately and grasped her hand while heading upstairs to their chamber.

Rising, Senor de Soto declared that he too would like to speak with his wife alone. Taking her husband's hand Maria rose with all the dignity of a woman of her standing and walked out of the room on his arm. Whispering softly her husband said simply, "Lets go to my study, I don't think we'll make it up the stairs." Behind them they could hear several chairs scraping against the floor hastily and laughter from the twins, no doubt at their expense.

Chapter Thirty-eight

Rene Comeaux unwound his limbs from Pamela's and marveled at his feelings for this magnificent young woman. Who would have thought that he could have ever come to care for someone as he cared for her? All his life he'd been taught that women were only good for satisfying a man's needs especially non-white women. Now here he was perfectly content to lie beside Pamela and simply hold her in his arms.

"Well my beauty, what's the next move we make", he asked as soon as his breathing steadied.

Turning to face him, Pamela was pleased to see that she had him right where she wanted him, in the palm of her treacherous hand.

She smiled her most disarming smile and answered, "You my love will contact the authorities at the hospital and tell them of our plight."

"So, I am to tell them that she is a deranged ex-mistress who believes that she is actually the wife of her keeper."

"Si, amor. Tell them that she became this way upon learning that her lover was setting her aside and taking a wife", answered Pamela.

Just seeing the wicked gleam in her eyes was exciting him and Rene moved closer, so that he could run his hands over her lithe, olive skinned flesh.

"When...when will we be able to transport her to her new home", he asked between pants as she let her fingers wander in a tantalizing pattern over the tops of his thighs.

"I will work those details out soon, but I think that it would be marvelous to have her disappear during the Savoie woman's Ball celebration", purred Pamela seductively.

Rene nearly leapt off of the bed as she made this last statement while clutching his manhood in her heated palm.

With the conversation forgotten he delved into the art of making love to the woman of his dreams.

Pamela too found that she was amazingly excited with his ministrations and resolved to see him yet again. Somehow she'd finally found someone to stoke a fire within her although it hadn't been for lack of trying. There had been a long list of lovers, none had come close to satisfying her as completely as Rene Comeaux. Yes she would keep him around a little longer.

Turning her attention back to Rene she straddled his hips and took complete control, sending her lover nearly over the edge with her slow deliberate movements. The emotions playing over his face excited her to a fevered pitched, causing her to spiral out of control as her movements sped up to a frantic pace. Clawing and gasping she screamed her release and collapsed on top of his chest, completely drained.

After several more times of making love with her co-conspirator, Pamela stood at the door of her carriage and gave Rene his last minute instructions.

"Don't forget to see the Savoie woman in a couple of days amor, she must invite them all to her ball."

"I won't forget, although it sickens me to have to touch her, but I understand that we need her", he said dispassionately.

Cupping his chin she placed a small kiss upon his lips and said, "Good, I will contact you soon."

"Soon", he agreed as he stepped away from the carriage door. Signaling the driver he watched as the carriage rounded the bend on it's way back to New Orleans. Smiling his mind conjured up glimpses of the ways they'd pleasured each other. He would use those pictures to get through the awful moments he'd have to spend in Laura Lee's company. Bile rose in his throat at the simple thought of what he had to do in the coming week.

Going back inside he sat down to compose a quick note to Laura Lee filling it with unspoken innuendo's, to convince her of his undying devotion to her and her cause.

Laura Lee couldn't wait to for the chance to be alone so that she could read the note. A little over a half-hour ago one of the maids had delivered the still sealed note. Looking down at her name she'd immediately recognized Rene's handwriting.

Smiling over her cup of coffee, she asked her husband of his plans for the day. "So where is it that you will be off to today Jean Pierre?"

Swallowing a bite of his croissant, Jean Pierre said softly, "Today I promised Mother to ride down to Sunset to visit Aunt Marjorie."

Brightening she said, "What a wonderful thing to do Jean Pierre."

"So you don't mind my spending the day with Mother", he asked a little confounded by her seemingly jovial attitude.

"Of course I don't mind, Jean Pierre, whatever could you be thinking? You two have a marvelous time, I simply must get around to planning the Mardi Gras Ball."

"Oh yes, the Ball of all Ball's you say. Well as soon as Maman comes down we'll be off"; he answered while coming around to kiss her hand affectionately.

Fluttering her long blond lashes Laura Lee smiled coyly and whispered that she'd think of him throughout the day and would anticipate his return. "Yes well, have a good day with mother Savoie, I'll be counting the moments until you return. I'll think of you as you're away."

Pulling her to her feet he placed another wet kiss upon her closed mouth and whispered little endearments that he hadn't bothered with since Beatrice had been conceived.

Spying the two as she entered the room, Mrs. Camille cleared her throat and said teasingly, "Ahem, now, now none of that while I'm present."

Laughing lightly Jean Pierre embraced his mother and placed a light kiss on her upturned cheek, while helping her into a seat at the breakfast table.

Taking his own seat he called out to his mother, "Don't forget to eat heartily Maman, we'll be needing our strength for the trip."

"Oh Jean Pierre, I'm not fragile in the least, I'll survive a short jaunt down to Marge's place."

Turning to one of the servants, he instructed her to place blankets in the carriage as well as refreshments.

Facing her daughter in law Mrs. Savoie says, "I certainly hope you don't mind my borrowing Jean Pierre today, Laura Lee?"

"Not at all Mother Savoie, I must see to the planning of the Ball anyway."

"So you're going to go through with it", asked an astonished Mrs. Camille.

"Why yes, what better way to make amends for..., she said averting her eyes from their view."

Reaching out to cup her hand, her mother in law tries to comfort her as tears well up and threaten to spill forth. "Now, now dear all will work out just fine, don't you worry."

"Yes, but what if they won't come for fear that it's just a trick of some sort", she asked tearfully.

"How about I add a note of my own to go along with yours, my dear", asked Jean Pierre.

"Yes, that's an excellent idea, and I'll do the same", suggested Mrs. Camille.

"Oh would you really do that for me", asked Laura Lee hopefully.

"Yes, in fact I'll go to my study and do it before we set out today", he said while excusing himself from the table.

Next Laura Lee instructed one of the serving women to retrieve writing materials for her mother in law.

Waving, Laura Lee watched as her husband and his mother drove away for the day. Excitement bubbled deep within her as she anticipated seeing Rene.

Taking the stairs nearly two at a time she raced to her bedchamber to change into a riding outfit. Calling for the footman to bring around her personal carriage and set out to meet the Sheriff.

"Well did he agree to the party", asked an anxious Sheriff Comeaux.

"Ball, and he did more than that, in fact he added a note of his own to help convince them all to attend."

"Now just how did you manage that small miracle", he asked with a sinister grin.

"Why Rene Comeaux, surely you know that a husband cannot abide his wife's tears."

Giving a bark of laughter he whirled her around the room to some imaginary music only the two of them heard. Bending her at the waist he leaned down to bestow a kiss on the exposed flesh spilling from her generous neckline.

They spent the afternoon, sitting and talking of what was to come. Finally, and only after he could put it off no longer, did he make love to her.

"Jean Pierre do you suppose that Laura Lee is alright", asked his mother quietly as they drove along.

"I too am wondering about her behavior Maman, I can only pray that all is well."

Clutching his hand she continued to express her concerns by adding, "She just changed so quickly, I mean practically overnight, you don't thing she's had some sort of break down do you?"

"Honestly Maman, I don't know what to think. While I have absolutely come to adore her these last months I can only pray that all is well."

"Only God knows, only God", whispered his mother.

Looking out of the windows of the carriage they both grew quiet and soon Jean Pierre sat and watched as his mother dozed. Thinking over the concerns she'd just spoken of he sent another prayer up to Heaven that things would be fine with Laura Lee.

Laura Lee sighed contently as the memories of her time spent with Rene flowed through her mind. Looking out of her bedroom window she spied the carriage winding it's way down the lane towards the house. Taking a deep breath she assured herself that this wouldn't be for much longer, soon she'd be able to rid herself of this undesirous union and live happily with the love of her life.

With her spirits brightening at those very thoughts, she made her way downstairs to greet her husband and mother in law.

Standing beside the door, she greeted her husband with a sound kiss as he entered and followed with a warm hug for Mrs. Camille.

"Welcome home you two, how was your trip down to Aunt Marjorie's", she asked as she handed them each a warm mug of apple cider.

"Here take these mugs and get near the fire", she instructed them as she assisted her mother in law out of her wool cape and gloves.

"God Bless you Laura Lee, how thoughtful of you to prepare for our return this way.

"I happened to spy you all driving up to the house and knew that you'd be needing something to warm you", answered Laura Lee.

"Well either way my dear it was very thoughtful of you and much appreciated", Jean Pierre said as he kissed her cheek lovingly.

Turning back to face her mother in law, she informed her that a hot bath had just been drawn to take the chill out of her bones. "And Mother Savoie, if you'll just follow Edna upstairs, we've prepared a nice hot bath for you." Continuing on she added, "Simply let me know if you wish for a small repast and I'll send a servant up with a tray."

"Dear, dear Laura Lee, so thoughtful you are", crooned Mrs. Camille.

"Nonsense Mrs. Camille. Now go along and get out of those traveling clothes and into something more comfortable."

"Yes I'll do just that", glancing at her son she says, "Thanks for today son."

Kissing the back of her hand, he assured her that it was a son's duty to see to his mother's needs.

"No need to thank me Maman, you're my responsibility, besides it's a joy to spend time with you."

Looking upon the two of them with adoration, Mrs. Camille informs them that she will remain in her bedchamber for the evening and wished them a good night.

After watching her mother in law disappear upstairs Laura Lee turned and purred seductively, "Well any suggestions on how we should spend our evening."

"I suppose we could have an evening snack alone in our chamber", he suggested. "What a marvelous idea, you go on up and get into the bath awaiting you and I will give the servants their instructions for the evening."

"Then I shall see you shortly my love", Jean Pierre said as he kissed her deeply before going to their bedchamber.

Chapter Thirty-nine

"Oh Melinda can you believe this, an invitation from Maman and Papa?", exclaimed Beatrice.

"Does it really say we're all invited?"

"Yes, and here is a note addressed to you in Maman's handwriting."

Taking the note Melinda eyed it warily as if half expecting it to incinerate before her very eyes.

Opening the note she read and then re-read the contents again to make sure that she hadn't missed something. Laughing she sits down on the mattress and says, "This…this is unbelievable, she wants Javier and I to be the guests of honor at her ball."

"I know isn't it marvelous. I knew that father would bring her around."

"This is all so out of the blue, I,…, I mean to receive an invitation to her annual ball, I just don't know what to think Beatrice."

"Think yes Mel, simply think yes", said a smiling Beatrice.

The two dissolved into a round of giggling so much so that they were unaware that their husband's had entered the room.

"And just what is so funny", asked Roberto loudly.

Rising Beatrice greeted him with a kiss before answering; "You'll never believe what came in the post today.

Melinda rose to her tiptoes and placed a kiss on Javier's lips. With their faces only inches apart she greeted him lovingly, "I have missed you husband, it's about time you returned."

Hugging her close to him, he nipped her earlobe and said, "Why don't we go to our chamber and you can show me how much you missed me."

"Um, sounds good but", she said as she pushed away from him, "Dinner will be served in less than half an hour."

Laughing, Roberto can't resist the urge to tease his brother by saying to Beatrice, "Marvelous idea to skip dinner sweetheart."

Winking at Javier, he took her by the hand and led her out of the room before she could answer.

Out in the hallway, Beatrice stopped and questioned his behavior. "And just what was all that about?"

"Just teasing Javier a little mi amor, come lets go down to dinner, I'm starved."

Tapping him on the shoulder she giggled and said, "How terrible of you to tease him so, Berto."

Laughing they descended the stairs and entered the Dining Room to await the arrival of the others.

"So we have been invited to Bristol for your Parent's Annual Ball, no", asked Senora de Soto.

"Yes, Mother de Soto, she extends the invitation to everyone", answered Beatrice as she let her eyes briefly linger on Melinda.

"Well if agreed by everyone, she said pointedly, we'll all attend this Ball as requested."

Clasping her hands with delight, Beatrice thanked her mother in law and hugged Melinda, "It will be wonderful, Maman gives the best Balls in Bristol."

Laughing, Melinda says while wiping tears of mirth from her eyes, "Your mother gives the only Balls in Bristol."

The rest of the family joined in on the laughter and soon the men were excusing themselves and heading to the study for an evening drink.

"What do you think of this invitation mijo", asked Senor de Soto of Javier.

"It is a mystery to me, I would never have believed that Mrs. Savoie would have had such a change of heart."

"Yes, but didn't Beatrice mention that her father also sent a note", asked Roberto.

"Si, Melinda to, had a note from him as well as the elder Mrs. Savoie", answered Javier.

"Do you believe the note from Mrs. Savoie to be sincere", asked his father.

"I would have to believe that the added weight of the other two notes make her request legitimate", answered Javier.

"Well then gentlemen, I suggest we prepare ourselves to attend the Savoie's Ball", supplied Senor de Soto as he lit his cherry wood pipe.

"Oh Melinda say you'll attend", urged Beatrice.

Going on to add more to her plea she added, "After all Papa wouldn't have included his own note if he wasn't sure about Maman."

"Yes but it just all comes as such a shock that she'd have a change of heart so quickly", questioned Melinda.

"I too question this change of heart Beatrice", added Senora de Soto.

"But surely you know that Papa would never do anything to harm Melinda, he loves her, his own flesh...flesh and blood", she reiterated as she glanced Melinda's way.

Placing a hand on her sleeve Melinda reassured her that she was sure of her father's feelings for her.

"I'm sorry Bea, of course I know that Father would never harm me. It's just a shock coming from your mother."

Breathing a sigh of relief Beatrice said quietly, "I understand, but I can not help but be ecstatic over her change of heart."

Sympathizing with the gleam of hope shining in her daughter in law's eyes, Senora de Soto patted her hand softly and said, "I understand clearly mija."

Standing, she stood in front of the fireplace and proclaimed, "In light of the invitations we received this week, we will attend the ball and request that the rest of you accompany your father and I to Bristol."

Smiling her thanks, Beatrice stood and went to hug her mother in law while saying, "Thank you mother de Soto, for your support."

"Melinda", called her mother in law, "will you also attend with us, as a family united?"

"Si, madre, I will attend the ball", Melinda answered as she looked towards Beatrice.

Coming over to take her hands, Beatrice reveals her deep feelings of gratitude, "Thank you Melinda, honestly thank you. I will send our reply to Maman if you don't mind mother de Soto."

"Of course I do not mind, send the reply letting her know that we will all attend, every one of us", replied Senora de Soto.

Chapter Forty

Melinda laughed into Javier's face as he twirled her around the dance floor. So far the Ball had been absolutely everything one could hope for in such an event. Dinner had been served in the elegant dining room, where guests had eaten on gold trimmed china and matching gold flatware.

Duck swimming in a sherry and orange glaze sauce had been served over deliciously curried rice. Maquechou and sweet potato crunch had also been served along with fried cabbage and turtle soup.

Champagne flowed readily throughout the evening and if Melinda had to admit it, she was delighted to have been welcomed into the Savoie home for this Annual Event.

"Tell me what you are thinking about", asked Javier.

"Can you believe that we are dancing in the Ballroom of Savoie Mansion", she asked breathlessly.

"I agree it does seem rather strange that we were accepted so openly, but I believe that the gesture has been made with sincerity", replied Javier.

Laura Lee seethed from across the room, swearing to herself that she would soon wipe the grating smile off of Melinda's simpering face.

"Smile my love or all will know your true feelings towards the de Soto woman", whispered Sheriff Comeaux.

"Yes, you are right my love", she returned before adding, "After all I wouldn't want any to be able to point to me when the little negra disappears."

"Keep your voice down, and don't make statements like that with so many around", he warned.

Waving him off, she replied through pouting lips, "You worry too much Rene, look around you, they have all obliged themselves of my private stock of taffia amongst other spirits."

"Yes but we must still be careful not to set tongues wagging. Go back and dance with your husband. Be careful to stay near him the rest of the evening."

Looking at him speculatively, she raised an eyebrow and asked, "Will it happen tonight then?"

Not caring to continue the conversation, Sheriff Comeaux simply picked up her hand and kissed it briefly before moving on.

Before she had time to realize that he'd moved away without answering her question, her husband came to stand next to her saying, "This was a fine idea Laura Lee, a fine idea."

"Why thank you for saying so Jean Pierre", she responded nervously wondering if he'd witnessed Rene kissing her hand.

"Come", he said, "Lets dance to your success my dear."

Leading her out to the dance floor he twirled her round and round until she was as giddy as a young school girl.

With her cheeks flushed and her breaths coming in gasps she suggested that they get refreshments after the third dance.

"Lets…lets get something to drink."

Leading her off the dance floor, he stopped to grab two glasses of rum punch from a tray and guided her to one of the wicker chairs.

Coming to stand before her parents, Beatrice glowed with pleasure as she said, "Maman, everything is absolutely wonderful."

"Thank you Bea", turning her attention to Roberto she asked, "Are you also enjoying your self son?"

"Si, yes Mrs. Savoie, everything is wonderful", answered her son in law.

Waving over his parents Roberto added, "I haven't seen Madre and Padre dance so in years."

Señor and Senora strode over to take their seats on the wicker furniture. Fanning herself Mrs. De Soto said while taking her seat, "The Ball is absolutely marvelous Mrs. Savoie."

"Oh please, do call me Laura Lee, after all we are family."

"Si, Laura Lee, you have done an outstanding job, I cannot remember having a more enjoyable evening", answered Senora de Soto.

Javier and Melinda made their way to where the rest of the family stood drinking refreshments and chattering gaily.

"Thank you for including us in the celebration Mrs. Savoie, we are having a wonderful time", said Melinda as she stood facing their host.

"Well I'm glad you are enjoying yourselves", answered Laura Lee.

Placing his hand at her elbow Javier said, "Yes we have enjoyed this evening immensely, but now we must depart."

"But I have not had the chance of twirling this beauty around the dance floor, the host always gets at least one dance", quipped Mr. Savoie.

Laura Lee nearly bit off her tongue to keep from objecting to this suggestion. Turning quickly to hide the look of disgust on her face she quickly said, "Oh I think I see an old friend that I simply must speak with before she leaves, please enjoy yourselves." Moving away from the group she took several deep breaths to calm herself.

Making her way outside she stood and seethed silently at the thought of Jean Pierre twirling around the ballroom with Melinda Harmon. So lost in her thoughts was she, that she didn't hear the Sheriff walk up behind her. Clearing his throat a second time he said calmly, "Get back inside and act as if all is normal."

Turning quickly Laura Lee argued that she could not endure the knowing glances from the townspeople. "I can not do it Rene, I just can't, they all know that she's his bastard mixed breed of a daughter."

"Listen to me my love, all must seem as normal as possible or all of our planning will go awry", he stated smoothly.

Shaking her head no, she made as if to object but was quickly silenced as he held up a hand and said, "Now, listen to me, You must not be suspected of having anything to with her disappearance my dear. Go back in there and dance with your husband as if you've not a care in the world."

"Rene, I", her words stuck in her throat as he pulled her into the shadows and kissed her until her head spun.

Still reeling from the kiss bestowed upon her by her lover, Laura Lee found herself making her way back into the house. Making her way towards Javier, she told herself that soon it would all be over. Conjuring up a smile, she placed her hand on his sleeve and said, "Why don't we join them on the dance floor my son, afterall they can't have all the fun?"

Surprised at her request, Javier turned and politely accepted the invitation. Soon they were whirling round and round while conversing happily. Sheriff Comeaux motioned slightly with his head and several men left the ballroom and disappeared into the night.

When the music stopped, Javier took Melinda's hand and faced the Savoie's saying, "We have an announcement to make, if you would permit us."

"An announcement you say, what sort of announcement", asked Laura Lee.

Smiling Javier said, "One that will undoubtedly please many here tonight."

Suddenly Jean Pierre had Melinda in his arms congratulating her while Laura Lee stood watching puzzled at his behavior.

It was only when she heard the statement, "A grandpa once again you say", did she understand what the reason for Jean Pierre's sickening behavior.

Cold fury now ran through her veins as she watched Javier receive congratulations from those who had been close enough to overhear what had been said.

She felt as if she'd incinerate on the spot so strong was the anger coursing within her blood stream. Digging her nails into her palms she managed a tightlipped smile and said, "Congratulations, it is truly a blessing to have children with the one you love."

Jean Pierre flinched at the pinched statement made by his wife. He sighed deeply and lifted hesitant eyes to her face. The smile she wore confused him, he was certain that there would be a look of pure fury on her face.

Laura Lee moved away quickly and spoke quietly with the musicians. Motioning for her husband and the de Soto's to join her she waited until they were all near her side and whispered in her husband's ear to make a formal announcement.

Jean Pierre raised his hand for silence and brought forth Javier and Melinda. Once he had everyone's attention, shared the couple's good news with all of their guests.

Cheers and toasts followed the announcement and as the music started up again, Melinda found herself dancing with none other than Sheriff Comeaux.

Chapter Forty-one

"Congratulations Melinda, yeah looks like you doin mighty fine with your new husband", said the Sheriff.

Blushing deeply Melinda marveled at the courtesy in which he displayed as he spoke to her. She couldn't once remember him speaking with her, during her stay here in Bristol. Now he was not only holding polite conversation with her but dancing with her as well. Finding her wits, she replied to his comment by saying politely, "Thank You and yes we are doing wonderfully."

Hatred, pure unadulterated hatred consumed Laura Lee as she watched Rene dance with Melinda. How she wished that she could claw the young woman's eyes out at this moment. She consoled herself with the knowledge that soon and very soon, maybe even tonight, Melinda would only be an unpleasant memory of the past.

Smiling, she took a glass of wine from a passing waiter's tray and returned her attention to playing the perfect hostess.

Oblivious to Mrs. Savoie's true thoughts, Melinda continued dancing with the Sheriff while conversing lightly as he asked about the length of their stay amongst other things. As the dance ended Melinda found herself being secretly dashed out of the Ballroom by her husband. Giggling like two school kids they made their way to stable and secured their carriage. Laughing Melinda asked, "And just what will our hostess think of our hasty departure when she notices that we've left?"

"Merely that we wish some time alone amor", answered Javier as he branded her with a scorching kiss.

Breathless Melinda responds, "But Javier we are the honored guests."

Laughing at her reaction to his enticing kiss, Javier assures her that all will understand their reasons for secretly leaving and will write off their absence as nothing out of the norm for newly weds.

Moving into his arms and onto his lap, Melinda initiates the next searing kiss but is nearly thrown onto the floor as the carriage suddenly lurches to the left.

Settling her onto the seat Javier sticks his head out of the window only to come face to face with the barrel of a rifle. "Please, please anything you want, just don't harm us", he pled.

"Oh God what is it Javier", asked a terrified Melinda from inside the coach. Keeping Melinda safely inside the carriage he peers out into the darkness again.

Laughing the leader moves into view and Javier loses all hope as he spies the white sheets covering the men's faces. "Well boy what you got inside dat dere carriage, and how much you offerin", asked the Leader carrying one of the many torches lighting the dark sky.

Swallowing the lump of fear in his throat while praying they didn't get a glimpse of Melinda, Javier answered as calmly as he could manage. "My wife who is with child is inside please take all that I have", he said while handing over his money pouch.

Peeking inside the pouch, the leader whistles and says, "Look like we done hit the jackpot fellas." Turning back to face Javier he says, "Don't usually do this but feeling a little generous tonight besides we only burns out negras."

Javier was grateful that the group's raucous laughter drowned out Melinda's outraged gasp. Praising God for his mercy Javier sat down and slowly let out the pent up breath he'd been holding as they pulled away.

When he was finally able to move again, he reached for Melinda and held her close as the tears fell unchecked down their cheeks. They cried together, both for the injustices of the world, and out of pure joy that they had come to no harm this night. Javier placed his hand over Melinda's as she slowly caressed her abdomen where their baby nestled safely.

The driver descended from the carriage as they pulled into view of the house and immediately sought help from the de Soto servants. "Hurry the Master and Mistress nearly came to harm tonight", he yelled.

Javier accepted the help of Benito as they helped him down and turned to assist Melinda himself.

"What happened Senor", asked an anxious Benito.

"The Klan stopped us a mile away, please send extra servants to escort Mama, Papa and the others home safely", instructed Javier.

"Si Senor, I will send them out at once", declared Benito as he barked orders to the nearby servants.

Sheriff Comeaux and the others laughed as they reached his dilapidated farm. "Like taking candy from a baby eh fellas."

"Yes suh candy from a baby", agreed the deputy.

"Ok boys na listen here, first one talks bout what we done tonight loses his tongue", states the Sheriff. Moving on towards the house he calls for his cohorts to join him in celebration. "Come on boys lets celebrate."

"Hear, hear", they echoed as they followed him in, one by one until all six of them were settled near the hearth with a bottle of whiskey in each fist.

Raising his hand for silence, the Sheriff waited for the men to quieten down before speaking of their plans. "Listen up well my friends, we must make sure that the word is spread that the Klan is once again returned to the Bristol." "Then and only then will our plan succeed, remember all are to believe that the little negra has been taken by the Klan."

The deputy then turned glazed eyes to the Sheriff and asked, "But what do we do wit hur afta wards, seems we letting hur off easy, sendin her up north."

"Yeah, seems dumb to let her go afta goin to all dis trouble ta catch hur", replied one of the other men.

"Well that's why I'm the one in charge. See the son wants to get rid of her quietly, don't even want his parents to know the truth", answered the Sheriff quickly.

"Boy dem rich fore'iners got some peculiar ways bout em", added the deputy before taking a long swallow of the fiery golden liguid.

"Yep, but longs dey pay when it's time, I gots no qualms", answered one of the others.

"Here, here let's drink to that", called out the Sheriff.

The de Soto's gathered around the fireplace discussing the events of tonight. With his brow furrowed with concern Senor de Soto says, "This Klan business concerns me greatly, I just praise God that they didn't get a glimpse of Melinda."

Crying Melinda throws herself once again into her husband's arms and declares, "I want to go home, I don't want to remain here another moment."

"Shhh, sweetheart, we'll be much safer returning in the morning."

"Yes, we should all go right up and rest for the journey on tomorrow", added Senora de Soto.

"But how am I to sleep, I keep thinking of what could have happened out there", wailed Melinda.

Signaling the butler forward, Senora de Soto instructs him to bring Melinda a glass of sherry to calm her fears. "Come mija sit near the fire and enjoy a glass of sherry with me. It will help to calm us."

"Yes, a marvelous idea", added Javier as he led Melinda to the settee.

"Si, lets all have a glass", chimed in Graciela.

Before anyone could respond to her comment however a loud pounding sounded at the front entrance.

"Who could that be at this hour of the night", asked a worried Maria.

Benito rushed in to announce that the Sheriff was there to speak with the family.

"But who could have notified the Sheriff of what happened to Javier and Melinda", asked Beatrice.

"I'm sure we'll find out shortly", replied Roberto.

Extending his hand, the Sheriff greeted Senor de Soto with concern deeply etched into every line of his face.

"I understand that someone here had a run in with the Klan tonight, can anyone tell me what happened?"

"Yes", said Javier as he stepped forward, "My wife and I were on our way home when we were stopped by a group of men whose features were covered by white hoods."

"Jesus", swore the Sheriff. "I was afraid that the rumors were true. The Klan hasn't been here for quite some time, can't phantom why they'd return now"?

"But what puzzles me Sheriff is that they didn't harm them in any way just lifted him of his money purse and rode away laughing", supplied Roberto.

"Well, I hate to be the bearer of bad news to Ms. Melinda but these infidels did more than just rob you tonight." Taking her hand he said, "I'm sorry to tell you this ma'am but Old Ms. Nell and her family were burned out tonight."

Melinda let go of a bloodcurdling scream that brought all the servants within earshot to the great room. "No, Oh God No, not Ms. Nell, No."

Javier rushed to her side and caught her up just as blackness engulfed her.

Melinda stood stiffly with Javier's arm around her waist as the priest droned on at the graves of Ms. Nell and her family. She listened as he said spoke the familiar words, "Ashes to ashes and dust to dust. From dust you came and to dust you must return." On and on he went while the community paid their final respects to one of their oldest living residents.

Javier felt Melinda's knees buckling and lifted her in his arms and began to walk towards the waiting carriage.

Protesting weakly she said, "No I must see this to the end."

"Melinda there is nothing else that you can do, hush now you must get some rest."

"Yes you are right, I must take care of the baby", she said as tears escaped down her cheeks. Burying her face in the front of his coat, she cried herself to sleep as he held her on his lap. Sleeping through the entire carriage ride back to town Melinda didn't even notice when Javier carried her out of the coach and into the house.

Settling her into bed, he swore as he noticed the dark circles under her eyes. Moving quietly out of the bedroom he headed to his father's study to see if anymore had been discovered about the horrible events that had thrown this small community into sheer panic.

Chapter Forty-two

Tomorrow they were returning to New Orleans, but before that Melinda decided to visit the gravesites of her Mother, and Old Nell. Taking care to dress warmly she exited the small home she'd once shared with her Mother and began the walk to the cemetery. She breathed in the clean air and let her mind wander back to the argument she'd had with Javier before leaving his parent's home that morning.

"Absolutely not", Javier had yelled as she told him of her need to go to the gravesite alone. "I will not have you place yourself in danger by going out alone."

"Oh come now Javier, it's been two weeks since that horrible night, and besides I'm going out in broad daylight, who would dare to accost me at this hour"?

"Melinda, I don't care what time of day it is, you will not go out alone, without protection. Anything could happen to you and the baby."

"Ah so that's it, the baby, you're worried that something will happen to the baby."

"Now that's unfair and you know it Melinda, my concern for your well being is just as important", stressed a slightly annoyed Javier.

"Well, there is no need to keep me under lock and key. This is where I was reared Javier, I will be fine."

"Melinda I disagree with this totally, just wait until I return from my meeting, and I will spend the afternoon doing whatever it is that you wish."

"But Javier I don't need,..."

Cutting in angrily he yells, "No! No buts, you will do as you're told in this matter."

Swallowing and angry retort, Melinda bowed her head and sat stiffly as he pressed a kiss to her cheek.

Melinda had sat there for over an hour debating over whether to obey his command or to do as she wished. She was afterall an adult, not some little child.

Picking up her bonnet, she left the sanctuary of the de Soto home and headed out towards her old home. There was so much she needed to share with her mother…

Leaving the small home now she decided to take the short cut through the woods to the cemetery. The time she would save getting there would allow her to reach her destination and then return home ahead of Javier.

There it was again, another snapping of a twig. She was sure of it now, someone was following her, and they were very close from the sound of it. Turning she scanned the woods in every direction. Seeing no one she decided to try a different approach.

"Ok, I don't know who you are but I know you're following me, probably at the direction of Senor de Soto. "Come on out, you've been discovered", she called.

So frightened was she at what she saw that no sound emerged from her opened mouth. There must have been ten of them standing all around her dressed in white hoods and robes. Only dimly aware now of her surroundings, she fainted as the leader began to advance upon her.

"Well this was downright easy", said one of the disappointed members. "Thought that at least she'd a given us a fight", he added.

"Yeah well let's just get this over with", said the leader quietly. Turning to the deputy he said, "And make sure that you're not seen by anyone, get her to the cabin, and wait for more instructions."

"Sho thing Sheriff, we'll be waitin at your place."

"You fool, no names remember", hissed the Sheriff.

"Sorry, but I don see no harm, I mean the lil negra's out cold", added the contrite man.

"Yeah well don't forget no more", replied the Sheriff. Turning to one of the other men he continued, "You know where I'll be for the next few days, make sure all goes well until we come for her."

Her head felt as if it were splitting in two. Groaning she tried opening her eyes. The pain she experienced as the bright light pierced her pupils was enough to send her back down into the awaiting blackness. Trying to still her spinning head she placed her hands on either side of her temples and moaned softly, "Oh dear God, where am I?"

Hearing the young woman speak one of captors rushed to her side and asked anxiously, "You gon live gal?"

Stiffening against the pounding in her head caused by the loud voice, Melinda managed to sneek a peek at the person whom the unfamiliar voice belonged. Upon taking in the long white robe and hood, Melinda stuggled to stand before being wrestled down by the little man.

"Easy now gal, no harm gon cum to ya, long as ya do what you's told", sneered the voice from behind the terrifying mask.

Trembling with fear, Melinda managed to say quietly, "Please sir, let me go, I won't say a word to anybody."

"Don't you fret none gal, we ain't gon hurt ya, just do what we tells ya and all will be well", came the voice of yet another accomplice.

Sobbing greatly now Melinda cries, "Oh God, please help me, please don't hurt me, I'm with child."

Waiting for his reply she was thoroughly surprised as the little man stepped back, stared and threw back his head and laughed with abandon.

Unsure of why this would amuse her captors so much, Melinda tried another approach. "Please you must listen to me, my husband is Mr. Augustos Javier de Soto, he will pay for my safe return…"

She would have said more but he waved a hand to silence her before saying coldly, "But gal he's the one wanted you gone, didn't you know."

Her heart stopped beating as he made this announcement. She fought against the urge to scream. Staring half crazed her eyes settled upon the leader.

As laughter sounded around her, she fought the rising bile in the pit of her stomach, and finally heard no more of their laughter as she slipped into blessed darkness.

"Don't take much ta sen her under, do it", remarked one of the men hired by the Sheriff.

Shaking his head, the man left in charge said simply, "Nope none atall, let's get back ta our drinks gentlemen."

Moving single file back towards the table they each picked up their mugs and moved out into the front of the shack where they could remove their masks.

Try as he might he couldn't seem to concentrate on what the young investor was saying. Over and over he tried to push all thoughts of Melinda aside but couldn't.

He just couldn't forget the look on her face that morning after their argument, something about her demeanor afterwards puzzled him. Finally giving up with a groan he said apologetically, "Mr. Blake I'm sorry but could we possibly reschedule this meeting for another time, there is something else I must see to immediately."

Somewhat flustered the young man shrugged and said, "Sure, why don't we agree to meet next week? I will be traveling to Nawlins' then, and will have some free time."

"Yes sure, see my assistant on the way out", Javier said suddenly cutting him off. He'd been trying to figure out all morning why there was a nagging suspicion at the back of his mind regarding their discussion this morning.

Suddenly he knew what was wrong, grabbing his coat and hat he ran from the office downstairs to his awaiting carriage. Spying the driver standing on the corner he barked out an order to be taken home. "Eduardo, Home please."

Settling in while the driver climbed into the box up front, Javier seethed in anger at her deception.

"Oh yes Melinda, I have not a doubt that you left as soon as I was stupid enough to pull away in the carriage. My early return will undoubtedly be quite a surprise for you", he said aloud to himself through clenched teeth.

The drive back to Bristol seemed as if it would take all day. Yet the closer he got to home, the angrier he got. Oh when he got his hands on her, she'd never be so foolish as to try and pull the wool over his eyes again.

"Doesn't she know the danger she could be in, with the Klan about like this", he asked aloud.

When the carriage pulled into the drive of his parent's country home he leapt from it as if the devil himself was chasing him.

Rushing up the steps he entered the foyer and began bellowing her name. "MELINDA", come down here this instant."

Even as the words left his mouth, he felt in his spirit that she was not there to hear his summons.

Rushing down the stairs his sister in law, Beatrice skidded to a stop in front of him and asked, "What's all the yelling about? I just got the baby down for a nap."

"I'm sorry", said Javier, "I am looking for Melinda but I'm willing to bet she's not here is she Bea?"

Torn between her loyalty to Melinda and the concern she saw on his face, she shrugged her shoulders and said softly, "I don't know, I haven't seen her since you left earlier this morning."

"Yes well, just as I thought", running a hand through his glorious shoulder length black mane he continued by saying, "I have an idea of where she went, we'll return shortly."

Beatrice placed a hand on his arm and said gently, "Please try to understand why she felt she had to go alone."

Closing his eyes to the pleading he saw there, Javier said curtly, "I will take all considerations into account."

Turning swiftly on his heel, he stormed back out the door and bellowed for his horse.

Mounting in a single leap, Javier rode away from his parent's home towards the graveyard at break neck speed.

Cursing, her vowed to teach Melinda a lesson she'd never forget for making him worry like this. Swallowing a curse, he ducked just as a low hanging branch nearly unseated him.

Melissa A. Ross

Missing You

I wonder if you think of me as often as you cross my mind?

I can be doing the simplest of tasks,

And there you appear, ...,

behind me, in front of me, or beside me.

I can smell the scent you always wear.

I can feel the warmth of your breath on my neck.

It's like I close my eyes and you are really there.

Your hands reach around my waist

And you kiss me gently behind my right ear.

Your gently brush my hair aside

And run your tongue down the back of my neck.

I feel a chill of excitement run up my spine

And break the dish I was washing.

You spin me around and cup my breast inside your hand.

I breathe in deeply your scent

And it fills me with such wanting for you that

I shiver all over and explode in passion.

I open my eyes and you're gone,...

But your scent lingers everywhere.

Time has a way of making you long for someone that is not there

But knowing we will be together someday

Eases the pain of being apart from you now.

The memories we shared

Sustains the ache in my heart

And the thoughts of your body touching mine

Satisfies my longing for you.

You have loved me enough to last an Eternity

And I patiently await the Return of you

My One True Love...

Author: Araina Rigmaiden

Chapter Forty-three

Dread set in as he combed the graveyard and then rode back to her former home with no sign of her in sight. He stopped off at some of the black families and asked if any had seen her. When none reported seeing her, he knew something horrible had happened to her.

He searched for her until dark set in. Dismounting at the family home he sent Benito to find the Sheriff, as well as to notify Mr. Savoie.

Roberto held Beatrice as she sobbed quietly into the front of his chest. Laying a hand at the back of her head he listened as Javier told the Sheriff that he feared Melinda had been taken. "Well, are you sure she was taken, don't think she left now do you, Mr. De Soto", asked the Sheriff.

Outraged at such a question Javier said angrily, "Of course she was taken, why would she leave?"

"Just want to make sure we have a crime here, You two weren't fighting or nothing were you", asked Rene Comeaux.

Hesitating Javier acknowledged that yes they'd had a disagreement, but not anything that would cause his wife to run off.

"We did have a slight disagreement but nothing that would cause her to run away, Sheriff."

"No insult intended but, I've found that sometimes them mulattos are a little high strung if you know what I mean", the Sheriff said cautiously.

He flinched as Javier took a menacing step in his direction. With fury bursting to flames within his midnight eyes, Javier rasped, "Melinda did not leave of her own accord."

Stepping quickly between his brother and the Sheriff, Roberto spoke up saying, "Sheriff Comeaux please contact us as soon as you hear something", gesturing further he went on to say, "Come I'll show you the way out."

As they reached the door, Roberto shook the Sheriff's hand and said, "Once again thank you for coming out, and please let us know immediately if you discover anything at all."

Clasping his hand in a firm shake, the Sheriff assured him that he would do all he could to find out what happened to Melinda Harmon.

Before Roberto could correct him, he turned and sauntered off towards his horse and rode off back towards town. Muttering to himself Roberto mumbled, "de Soto, her last name is,...de Soto."

The family had been recalled to Bristol as they were told of Melinda's disappearance. It had been nearly two weeks and still there'd been no sign of her.

They all sat now in gloomy silence as the Sheriff finished by saying, "I'm sorry to say, but we've found no trace of her since the day she disappeared.

"But how could this be", wailed Mrs. De Soto. "How could she have just disappeared Sheriff Comeaux", she asked as the tears streamed down her face unchecked. "Well we don't believe that she was taken by the Klan or else we would have found her body", answered the Sheriff. For two weeks now he had been trying to convince Javier that Melinda had simply run away, and now as he looked at Senor de Soto, he pressed on with his belief.

Holding her closely in his arms Senor de Soto tried to soothe his wife while whispering words of love and little endearments. Looking at Javier he said sadly, "Son we must face the truth, she is not coming back to you, for whatever reason I now begin to believe she left on her own."

"NO!" Screamed Javier with fury dripping from his every fiber of his being. "Never will I believe that she left me, never, do you hear me, never." Storming from the room, he left the house and mounted his horse. He rode heedless of the fact that the rain was soaking him thoroughly. He tried to fight the tears of despair that had been fighting for release for more than two weeks now. Biting his lip he cursed as finally he lost the battle.

Crying earnestly now, he let the tears fall as they may. Riding into the drive of the tiny home that had once belonged to Melinda and her mother he entered and collapsed onto the small iron bed. There he sobbed his heart out for what had once been. Looking up at the portrait of her he had recently commissioned, he said as his voice cracked, "I will never believe that you left me, amor, never." "Our kind of love never dies, I will never stop looking for you."

It had been a month since she'd been taken in the woods. Melinda felt the tiny life within her stir. Hugging her knees she prayed yet again that today, someone would discover what had actually happened to her.

She tried to keep a glimmer of hope alive as she told herself that her captors had lied. Javier would never pay them to take her away and have her committed. He would never play her as falsely as her tormentors had suggested.

"Well glad ta see ya up, time for your bath Ms. Harmon", taunted the stern faced heavyset nurse.

Trembling Melinda said with the look of a trapped hare, "Please not today, the baby…"

Chuckling the nurse said, "Don't worry none bout the youngun, I'm told babies like water, sides old Doc, don't think it'll harm ya none."

Melinda shuddered as she realized she'd get no help from this vessel of evil. Melinda stiffened her spine and resolved not to give the horrible woman a moment's pleasure by seeing her squirm.

It seemed unthinkable that someone could get so much joy from watching others suffer. But her experience for the last month, here at the State Hospital for the mentally ill, had taught her differently.

There were those whose sole purpose in life was to make other people miserable.

Looking around at her roommates, her eyes swept over those who were truly mentally ill, to those who were as sane as she, but had somehow ended up in this pit of suffering.

Casting a furtive glance towards the nurse, she gathered her clothing and walked slowly towards the bathing room. She tried not to dwell on what would happen once she entered the bathing house. She fought off the dread that tried to cease her as she visualized the dousing of ice-cold water she would receive. Melinda was terrified that these dousings would cause some harm to her baby. She thanked God that she didn't have to sit in the spinning chair anymore. After old Doctor Gray had discovered she was really and truly pregnant he'd ordered that the spinning chair treatments be stopped until delivery. But he hadn't seen a reason not to use the cold water therapy, and so it was continued.

The thought was that these treatments helped to calm those patients suffering from mental delusions such as young Mary Harmon. The doctor had shaken his head and walked away only two days ago when he'd called her Mary and she'd once again informed him that her name was Melinda. She'd heard him say to the nurse that, "As soon as she delivered the baby she needs to be placed in the spinning apparatus, maybe then she'll remember her name." Feeling it would be better to remain silent until she could figure out what to do. Melinda decided that until then she'd keep her mouth closed and refuse to say another word.

Feeling the nurse nudging her into the room, she snapped out of her revelry and began to undress. Steeling herself against crying out, she stepped into the chamber and sucked in her breath as the cold water washed over her.

Sputtering, she prayed for God to deliver her from this madness. She bit down on her lips until they were bloodied. She refused to cry out and give the nurse something to smile about.

Returning back to the large room she shared with ten other patients during the daylight hours, she walked over to the window and prayed over and over again for deliverance. She looked around at the metal bars across the windows and doors. The small narrows cots without feather mattresses, and the other misfortunate souls scattered about the dayroom. The nights however were the worst, then she was locked into a dank, dark room with one other patient. So frightened was she to fall asleep at night locked in with one truly insane such as Annie Bell, that she stayed up as long as she could manage until exhaustion claimed her.

Once she had awakened to find Annie Bell standing over her with her hands around her throat. Struggling for breath she had lashed out and clawed at her assailant's face. Miraculously one of the orderlies had been doing bed check and had shone the light into the room. He'd then called for help and wrestled Annie Bell to the floor and away from Melinda. Since the incident they kept Annie Bell pretty much sedated but somehow Melinda just couldn't stop thinking that they'd somehow forget and that Annie Bell would finish what she'd started. Melinda managed to learn that Annie Bell had once been a sharecropper's wife, but that he'd been hung when the landowner's wife had claimed he'd tried to rape her. She learned that Annie Bell had witnessed the hanging and then had been turned out along with her four children. Soon after leaving, Annie Bell had been forced to abandon her three remaining children to strangers when she could no longer care for them.

It was said that the fourth had died from starvation and that Annie Bell had fed her surviving children it's remains to keep them alive. Soon after, the authorities had taken her into custody and brought her here to the Mental hospital in north Louisiana. In her weakened mental state, she had confused Melinda with her old mistress and sought to avenge her husband's death. Melinda would never forget the fear she felt when she woke up struggling for air, and couldn't move the ironclad hands around her neck.

Clutching her rosary beads tightly against her bosom, she prayed and finally let the tears of despair fall unbidden down her cheeks. After the tears dried up she snuggled into a nap knowing that as night approached sleep would not come again until the wee hours of the morning if at all.

Hours turned to days and days to months until finally the day came for her baby to be born. During the time she had spent here she'd watched as some of her roommates had left with their families while new ones had taken their places, and still no one had come for her.

At first she hadn't believed her captors lies of Javier wanting her out of the way? But now after so many months here in this hellhole, and no one coming to get her, she struggled with the doubts ebbing slowly into her mind.

Her sanity was on the verge of deserting her as she thought of her circumstances.

In the beginning she had held out hope that someone would come for her. She had foolishly written them letters telling them of her whereabouts, only to hear nothing from any of them.

How could she have believed all of their lies of love and being a family? The thought had never occurred to her that not one letter had been sent, as soon as it was discovered that she was writing to the very person who'd had her committed.

Chapter Forty-four

Entering the Ballroom, Benito announced the arrival of the Gonzalez family. "Senor y Senora Luis Gonzalez con Senorita Pamela Gonzalez".

All eyes turned as the family entered the ballroom. Invitations had gone out over a month now announcing the marriage of Juan de Soto, the eldest of the twins.

Many began whispering behind their hands, alluding to the rumors that Pamela would soon be the wife of the eldest de Soto son, Javier.

Clasping the hands of Senora Gonzalez, Maria says politely, "Bienvinida, Xiomada, and thank you for coming."

"We are honored to attend dear Maria", replied Mrs. Gonzalez.

While the welcome for Mrs. Gonzalez was warm and genuine the reception Pamela received from Senora de Soto was equally as cool.

Without batting an eye, Senora de Soto fixed her eyes just above Pamela's head and said dryly, "Wonderful to see you again Pamela." Dismissing her sharply without even a by your leave she turned her attention to the arrival of the next set of guests invited for the engagement celebration.

This set off another round of speculation, with many ruefully smiling behind their hands.

Pamela stiffened as she heard someone off to her left say with unsuppressed glee, "I told you the rumors were untrue my dear."

"Oh yes, and right again you were dear, certainly no marriage in the wings there."

Fuming at the actions of her hostess Pamela vowed to prove them all wrong, they would all be made to look like the fools they were when Javier wed her. He just needed a little more time to get over the disappearance of his first failed marriage. Spying the object of her desire she made her way over to where he was standing further down the receiving line.

Flashing a dazzling smile she said, "Hola Amor, good to see you here tonight." Returning her smile he said, "Yes, well my brother means the world to me, as you know, so of course I would be here to support him."

"Yes I know how important family is to you. How are you?" She whispered into his ear seductively. Unaware of her true intentions, and grateful of her concern for his well being, he clasped her hand into his and said, "Fine, I am doing fine."

"Know that I am here for you, if you need anything amor", she whispered again.

Seeing her as a dear friend from his childhood, he accepted the endearment and bestowing a soft kiss to the back of her slender hand, said, "Gracias Amiga, please save a dance for me."

Making certain to respond a loud enough for those standing near, she purred, "All my dances are for you, amor".

"Ahem", said Roberto as he noticed that Pamela was trying to cause comment by speaking overly long with his brother in the receiving line.

Taking the cue, Javier said while kissing her hand once again, "Yes well, until later."

Moving down the line, Pamela was pleased beyond measure at the ploy she'd just managed to pull off. Smiling she accepted a glass of champagne and moved to stand where she knew Javier would have her within his line of sight.

As soon as the guests were greeted Roberto clasped Javier's arm, while leading him outdoors and asked, "What are you thinking Javier?" Turning Javier asked nonchalantly, "Thinking? About what? Berto."

"About Pamela that's what", answered Roberto.

"What about her? I greeted her. She asked about my well being and I asked her to save a dance for me, that's all". "What's wrong with that Berto"?

"Javier you are not as dense as all that", "You know perfectly well that she was trying to make it look like the two of you were having an intimate conversation. Yet, you played along", Roberto said with anger enunciating every word.

"I did no such thing, played along?", "And just what if I did Berto? Afterall I'm free to do as I please. My wife left me remember?"

Roberto staggered at the venom present in the statement he brother had just made. Never had Javier believed Melinda had left of her own accord, now he'd just declared it.

"NO, Hermano. Surely you don't believe such nonsense? She would never have done such a thing", pointed out Roberto.

Raking his hand through his overly long midnight black tresses Javier took a calming breath and said, "I don't know what I believe anymore Berto, maybe Papa is right."

Astounded by what he was hearing, Roberto rushed forward and clasped his brother's shoulders while saying, "Listen to what you are saying Hermano. That she left, without a change of clothes, no money, and with child, your child Javier."

Breaking his hold Javier jerked away and shouted, "Bastante, enough, I don't want to hear anymore of this." Stalking away he searched the crowd until he spotted the object of his desire.

Reaching his destination, he stepped to the center of the small crowd gathered around Pamela. Taking her hand away from some young man he wasn't acquainted with, Javier said, "I thought all your dances were saved for me Amor?"

Nearly fainting with delight at this new turn of events Pamela allowed him to lead her onto the dance floor. Melting into his embrace she closed her eyes and let him lead her into a series of twirls and dips around the room.

Pamela opened her eyes to peer up into Javier's gaze reveling in the feel of elation sweeping over her. With her lips slightly parted and her cheeks prettily flushed from their dance she said, "You dance like no other amor."

"No, it is you who dances with all the grace of a queen sweetheart", returned Javier.

"Well if all our dances will be like this one, I can hardly wait", she said as she molded her body closer to his.

Feeling desire rifle through him Javier clasped her closer to him and let her feel exactly what it was she sought. He was rewarded by a low moan meant only for his ears, and bent to place a kiss on her upturned lips.

Pamela heard the startled gasps of the guests as Javier touched his lips to hers, and quickly placed her head near his shoulder in an effort to appear the shy young virgin and more so to hide the desire coursing through her blood.

Chuckling Javier whispered in her ear, "Surely you are not the shy virgin you'd have everyone to believe now are you amor"?

Feeling her stiffen in his arms he added quickly, "I hope not because it is a woman with experience I seek to grace my bed this night."

Swallowing the pain his words caused, she dropped the shy act at once and smiled brightly saying, "My body was formed specifically for your pleasure Javier, I am more woman than anyone in this room and can be any and everything you wish me to be."

Laughing loudly and not caring that he caused even more speculation, Javier kissed her once again and led her to the refreshment table at the conclusion of the dance.

Looking on, Senora de Soto bristled with anger at her son's behavior with Pamela Gonzalez. She had heard all the vicious rumors started by Pamela to make everyone believe that Javier had gotten rid of Melinda so that he could marry her.

Turning to face her husband she said, "How dare she make a spectacle of herself in my home with my son.'"?

"What? I think it wonderful that he has finally stopped wallowing in self pity, afterall, Melinda does not wish to be found, and little Camille needs a mother", answered her husband.

"But Juan, Melinda,…" she started to respond.

"Melinda is gone," he said silencing her in mid sentence. "Now lets join our guests in this next dance, and look as if you are enjoying yourself", he admonished further.

Knowing better than to argue the point and causing more comment, Maria placed a pained smile on her face and followed her husband to the center of the dance floor. She decided that while she may not be able to get through to Juan, she would do whatever it took to make Javier see Pamela for whom and what she really was.

Roberto and Beatrice looked on as Javier drank glass after glass of champagne and danced nearly every dance with Pamela. Unable to stand it anymore Beatrice turned to her husband and said, "Oh I just can't watch anymore, I'm going up to bed now Berto."

"I will escort you and then return for the toast to the future bride and groom." Placing her arm at his elbow, he walked with her to their quarters and called for her maid.

Returning to the ball, he found his brother Julio watching the scene that Javier and Pamela were causing and said sadly, "I never thought to see the day when our brother would be taken in by the likes of that one."

"Si, neither did I. It makes me what to pound some sense into him", answered Julio while clenching his fists tightly.

"Well let's put on a cheerful face for Madre and of course Juanito, this is his night", resolved Roberto.

"I'll follow your lead", came the quiet response.

Making their way to stand near their Mother and Father, the two brothers instructed everyone to get a glass of wine so that the formal toast introducing the engaged couple could be made.

Raising his glass in the air, Senor de Soto proclaimed the couple officially betrothed by saying, "Everyone please join me in expressing sincere best wishes for my son Juan Alessandro de Soto and my future daughter, Veronica Gisela Santiago.

With glasses raised and tapped against one another, the couple was toasted over and over again as each and every son of the family paid homage to Juan and his lovely bride to be.

Embracing her son and future daughter, Maria let go of the ill feelings she was experiencing and dabbed away tears of joy as he placed a kiss upon her slightly moist cheek.

"Oh mijo, I wish you all the happiness in the world."

"Gracias Mama", and turning to clasp Veronica's hand he said, "We will strive to be as happy as you and Papi for the rest of our lives."

Maria enfolded Veronica in an embrace that left no doubt in anyone's mind that she was well and truly accepted into the formidable ranks of the influential de Soto family.

Looking on, Pamela vowed to make Javier's mother welcome her into this family one day very soon. How dare she welcome one as Veronica Santiago, and shun her. Veronica was simply the daughter of one of their laborers, while she Pamela, was the daughter of just as powerful a family as theirs.

Feeling her nails digging into her palm, she looked down to see a light trickling of blood dusting her palm and moved to quickly find the powder room so that she could clean the blood away.

Maria noticed Pamela's hasty retreat and followed her out of the ballroom and down the corridor. Waiting a few seconds in the hallway she entered after making sure that no one else was around.

Turning at the sound of someone entering the room, Pamela pulled up short at the look of pure hatred on Maria's face. Taking a step backwards she said nervously, "Senora de Soto, I was just finishing up, and was about to return to the ball."

"Listen to me Pamela and listen carefully. I am aware of the rumors you have purposely been spreading about Javier and Melinda."

"Rumors? What could you possibly mean about rumors, Senora?"

"Don't try to play the innocent with me Pamela, I know exactly what type of woman you are. Let me assure you that unless you set your sights elsewhere, my son will also know all there is to know about you."

With anger rampaging through her, Pamela said menacingly, "Your son, Senora de Soto, will marry me, whether you approve or not." "I should have been the one he chose the first time, but make no mistake I will be the one he chooses this time around. "I will not lose him again, for any reason, not even to a Mother's love."

Something flashed in the young woman's eyes then that left Maria with no doubt of her part in Melinda's disappearance.

Falling back as if she'd been struck, Maria placed a hand over her mouth and stumbled out of the room.

Pamela laughed as she watched the older woman nearly run on stiff legs back into the ballroom. Following, she formulated a plan to explain Maria's behavior to her son's, whom Pamela had no doubt would question their mother's behavior.

Placing the tips of her little fingers into the corners of her eyes, she let the tears flow freely while pretending to cry gently into her lace handkerchief.

Re-entering the ballroom, she made as if to leave through the French doors on the other side of the room.

Placing herself in the path of an unsuspecting Senor de Soto, she mumbled an apology as they collided and he reached out a hand to steady her.

Noticing her tears, he motioned Javier to his side and spoke soothing words to the beautiful young woman in his arms.

Listening as their mother told them of what had just transpired between herself and Pamela, Roberto swore aloud at the audacity of Pamela to threaten their mother in her own home. Just as he and Julio were about to go and confront her, in she came crying and ran smack into their father's awaiting arms.

Maria, Roberto, and Julio looked on with disgust as they witnessed Pamela's false display of distress. Speaking quietly, Maria cautioned her sons against acting too swiftly.

Laying a hand upon Roberto's face she said gently, "No my son, she is very conniving that one. Lay no accusations against her tonight or we will be made to look like the villains."

"But Mama, surely Papi will listen to what you have to say, about your suspicions", argued Julio hotly.

"No, Mama is correct, lets leave it be for tonight, we'll discuss this on tomorrow at length, I too now believe that Pamela was responsible for Melinda's disappearance", said a once again collected Roberto.

Reaching Pamela's side Javier asked, "What is it sweetheart."

"Nothing, I'm only being silly. I am just so happy for Juanito and Veronica. I just got sentimental is all, such happiness, if only it were for everyone."

"Oh my dear, such happiness is for everyone, I have a feeling that your day will come sooner than even you could imagine", said a sympathetic Senor de Soto while looking pointedly at his eldest son.

"Javier", he said to his son, "Place this lovely creature on your arm and make her smile, do not let her out of your sight until she is happy once again."

Taking Pamela into his arms, Javier said while leading her away, "My pleasure Papa."

Pamela nearly burst into laughter at the success of her hastily thought out plan. But one thing puzzled her, she was sure that Senora de Soto would have gone straight to her son and told him of the encounter. Looking around she spied Maria speaking quietly with two of her sons. Just as she began to lift the corners of her mouth into a smile of victory, Roberto turned to peer in her direction. What she saw written in the planes of his face nearly caused her knees to buckle.

With concern lacing his voice, Javier stopped and asked, "Que Paso, amor"?

"Nothing, please, please take me home Javier, I don't wish to stay any longer."

"Si, come, you go and retrieve your wrapper from the footman and I will get the carriage", he instructed.

A now worried Pamela, moved to do as instructed by Javier and congratulated herself on all that she'd accomplished this evening. The gossipmongers filled nearly every nook and cranny of the ballroom tonight, and she'd made sure that they had plenty to speak of for many upcoming months.

Javier would have no choice but to marry her. Once it was known that he'd bedded the "virgin" daughter of his father's business partner and that she was with child. Her father would demand a wedding after her personal physician announced that she was enciente. Now all she had to do was convince Javier to let her stay all night with him in his rooms at the Paladdio.

Chapter Forty-five

Pamela smiled up into Javier's face as he helped her into the carriage. As he stepped into the carriage she cried delicately into her handkerchief causing him to abandon the seat across from her instead for the place on the seat next to her.

She sighed as he took her into his arms and began to croon softly to her. "Shhhhhh, amor, please no more crying."

"I'm sorry", she sniffed, "It's just that it always seems to be someone else finding happiness and never me", she said as she went into another round of crying.

Knowing only one way to stop a woman's tears, Javier took her into his arms and placed feather light kisses over her closed eyes, her flushed cheeks and finally on her enticingly, sexy, full lips.

Something in the back of his mind tried to surface, but at the touch of their lips, all good sense went flying out the window of the carriage. It had been so long since he'd held a woman, Javier was instantly lost to the sensations coursing through him and deepened the kiss.

Pamela melted into his embrace and clung to him as if her life depended upon this kiss, this moment. Oh the feelings of exhilaration, for so long she had dreamt of what it would feel like to be intimate with this man.

Pamela wound her arms around his neck pulling him closer and kissed him with all the fervor she was feeling.

Javier pulled her onto his lap and began caressing her breasts while never breaking the lava molten kiss. Settling her perfect little bottom onto his lap, Javier groaned aloud as she wiggled expertly sending waves of pleasure washing over them.

As he felt her hand slide down between them he pulled up short and broke off the kiss.

Grabbing her hand he said, "No, Pamela, we must stop. I know what I said earlier but I could never take advantage of you this way."

"Please amor, please show me that I...", she said without finishing. Placing her hand over her mouth she turned to look out of the window, hoping that she could convince him to do as she wished.

Placing his hands on her shoulders, Javier asked with concern, "Show you what Pamela?"

"Nothing, I understand fully. Thank you for all you did tonight." She said all of this with a tear choked voice, as she kept her back to him.

"Sweetheart, please tell me, what is bothering you, maybe I can help."

Turning to face him with her tear stained cheeks Pamela said sadly, "You believe the rumors also, that's why you stopped."

With confusion written on his face Javier asked, "What rumors Pamela."

"The rumors that I am a courtesan who devours men."

Embarrassed that she had spoken aloud the sentiments that he and his brothers had held, Javier stumbled over an appropriate response.

"Pamela, I…No one…that is,…, why don't you tell me the truth."

Oh this was too easy Pamela thought as she ran her tongue over her bottom lip. Taking a deep breath she told him of how she'd been approached by one claiming he loved her. How he'd promised marriage and then left her after he'd taken her virginity. She claimed he'd then told all of his friends of their relationship and then as she had turned down their proposals they had viciously lied while claiming that she had slept with them also.

"It is true that I am no longer a virgin but I have only been with one other, the one whom I thought loved me as much as I loved him", she said once again losing her composure.

"Pamela", he said gently, "I didn't stop for that reason."

When she looked up hopefully, he quickly went on to say, "I stopped because I don't want to hurt you, by taking advantage of you in this way."

"No, I don't believe you", she said with trembling lips.

Desiring to banish her tears, he then moved closer and said, "Then let me show you what you do to me." Kissing her deeply he slid his hand up her thigh. When his desire to take her in the carriage nearly overwhelmed him, he finally pulled away and said between breaths, "Dios, Pamela we must stop or I will spend the night loving every inch of you."

Looking into his passion laden eyes, she said boldly while pressing her breasts into his chest, "Then by all means don't stop,

Javier." Fighting the urge to take her on the seat of his carriage, Javier called out new instructions to his driver while taking her into his arms once more.

Javier trembled at the feel of her body against his in the tight confines of the carriage. He groaned and let his head fall back as she cupped him in her hand expertly.

Pamela caressed him as she rained kisses at the opening of his shirt. Seeking to inflame him to the point that he wouldn't change his mind she picked up his hand and kissed his fingers lovingly by placing them in the warmth of her mouth one by one.

"Ummmm, Pamela", he rasped, "Stop or we'll never make it to my rooms."

"I'm just so frightened that you will change your mind and send me away, I..."

Bringing her back for another searing kiss, Javier whispered against her mouth, "The truth is I may never let you go."

Seeking to make sure that he never let her go after tonight, Pamela deepened the kiss while allowing her hands to roam freely over ever curve of his body.

Pulling apart as the carriage stopped Javier helped Pamela straighten her hair and bodice as they prepared to alight from the carriage.

Helping her down, Javier clasped her elbow and escorted her past the concierge's desk and up the stairs to his apartments.

Unable to keep his hands off her, he pressed her back against the wall and gave her a searing kiss that nearly made her knees buckle. "Pamela, what have you done to me?" He asked huskily as he pulled her further down the corridor to his door.

Breathless with anticipation, Pamela hurried after him and gave a small cry of delight when her lifted her in his arms and carried her over the threshold into his lush apartment.

Closing the door with his booted heel, Javier caught her bottom lip between his teeth and tugged gently. Losing herself to the delightful feelings of rapture, Pamela hugged him closer and said, "Oh, amor, you set me on fire."

"Oh no sweetheart this is only a spark, when I'm done with you tonight, you will feel as if you've been consumed", he answered.

A ripple of excitement ran through her at the steamy promise, and the absolute look of desire in his eyes. Running her tongue over her suddenly dry lips she said simply, "Make me burn, Amor, make me burn."

Chapter Forty-six

Melinda sighed as she looked out of the window and wondered who would deliver her baby. Old Doctor Gray had died just last week and she had no idea who the new physician would be. She knew in her heart of hearts that there would be something wrong because of all her ill treatment these long months. Looking at her reflection in the window she nearly cried out at what she saw. Gone was the glow that had once shown in her cheeks, even her hair was now a dull shade of dark auburn. She was so thin that if she'd not been pregnant, she had no doubt that one could count every one of her ribs.

Thinking of her circumstances, she prayed for God to take away all the hate she'd built up inside at those she had once loved. How could they make her and her unborn child suffer such atrocities?

Standing, she suddenly doubled over as a sharp pain stole over her and her water broke. Struggling to stand she called out for the guard, "Help me, please my baby's coming."

Panting she laid down on the narrow cot in the infirmary, where all the black patients were taken. She clutched the sides of the cot as wave after wave of pain hit her. She listened as the nurse spoke with someone about her condition.

Finally turning to her the nurse said, "Doctor will be here shortly."

"Oh God", Melinda screamed as another pain rippled through her frail, nearly gaunt body.

"No, don't bear down yet missy, not til you're told", admonished the unfeeling creature.

"Oh dear Lord help me", cried and anguished Melinda as another contraction hit her.

"Too late now ta be talking to the Almighty, should have followed his commandments about not wallowing in sin with Men you're not married to", said the nurse with a gleam of pleasure lighting her cold blue eyes.

Wise not to rise to the bait of arguing with the woman, Melinda stuck her tongue in her cheek and prayed silently for a miracle. On an on the pains went until Melinda felt she'd lose not only her life, but that of her unborn child as well. Surely this was too long. Gathering her courage, she called out weakly for the nurse, "Help me please, help me."

"Now listen gal the Doc's getting cleaned up, be here real soon, hush all your caterwalling", came the cold unfeeling reply.

Moaning as another contraction rippled through her body, Melinda fought against the urge to push. Through the fog of pain she heard the voices of the nurse and the man she assumed was the doctor. Shock made her gasp aloud as she noticed that not only was he ancient looking, but he was also white.

Shaking her head from side to side she said, "No must be a mistake."

"Nope, no mistake gal, new colored Doc ain't made it in yet." With the grin of a sly fox he continued on with; "Sides, won't be the first time I delivered a little mixed breed and won't be the last I'm sure. Naw, no indeed. Well open up gal, so's I can take a look see."

Forcing herself to comply, Melinda spread her thighs for the Doctor to do his examination but stiffened as yet another pain gripped her distended abdomen.

"Now just hold on a minute gal, don't push yet, got a little ways to go, but not too long", he said as he concluded his non too gentle examination of the young lady.

Washing his hands he asked, "This yo first one gal"?

Panting between contractions Melinda answered, "Yes, yes it is."

"Sho don't talk like the rest of them darkies, where you from gal"?

"Doc you wanted up front", suddenly came the voice of the nurse, whom Melinda was sure had been listening to every word.

Smiling coldly at Melinda she said, "Busy night here at the hospital."

Turning away, Melinda tried to push aside her sweat drenched matted hair and faced the wall. For her efforts she was rewarded with a rusty laugh from the nurse, and later silence as the nurse exited the room.

"What", shouted Roberto at Javier's announcement.

"My son, surely you are not serious", asked Senora de Soto incredulously.

"Si Mama, Pamela is pregnant, with my child, answered a somber Javier."

"But how can you be sure, everyone…"

"No Mama, this child is mine and I will marry Pamela", he said effectively silencing her apparent objection.

When his mother would have voiced further concerns his father held up a hand and said, "Javier has the right to make his own decisions Maria." Turning to his son he added, "You have my support in this matter Javier, as well as the support of all of your family", he said while ensnaring them with his gaze.

"No Papa, I'm sorry but I will never support this decision, Pamela is a conniving witch who is not to be trusted", shouted Roberto as he stood to face his father and brother.

"I stand with Berto on this, I will never accept Pamela as my sister.", chimed in Julio.

Trying to be a voice of reason Senora de Soto placed her hand upon Javier's arm as she pleaded with him to reconsider. "Please my son think this over carefully, what about Melinda."

Snatching his arm away Javier answered coldly, "Melinda is no longer a part of my life. Pamela and I will be married before our child is born."

With this said he stalked from the room leaving his father glaring at his wife and sons. When he was nearly out of earshot he heard his father say, "Well I for one am more in agreement with this marriage than the first."

Rising from the table, Beatrice walked slowly out of the room before bursting into tears and running up to her room.

Cursing, Roberto ran after her, but not before turning to his father and saying, "Papi, Pamela is not as she seems. She is not the innocent she has led everyone to believe. Nor do I believe she is capable of being pregnant."

"What could you mean by this", gasped his father.

"I don't have time to discuss this now, I must see to Beatrice, but I will return after she is settled.

After what seemed like ages, the doctor returned and ordered Melinda to open up again for another exam. Clucking his tongue he said to her, "Well that didn't take long a'tall did it, you sho this be the first one gal"?

A pain like no other prevented her from answering, as she clutched the sides of the bed and screamed, "Ohhhhhhhhhh."

"Alright, alright, start pushing gal.", "Push when the pains hit, and breathe deep when's they don't", instructed the old doctor. Feeling for the baby's position he once again instructed Melinda to push as he felt her abdomen tighten, "Yes that's it, push hard gal, almost done."

Pushing with all her might, Melinda tucked her chin into her chest and cried out as the baby gushed forth from her body into the waiting hands of the old doctor.

Bursting into tears, she cried loudly until she heard the doctor ask the nurse what was to be done with the little boy. "What's to be done with him, can't keep him here with all these loonies?"

"Arrangements have already been made he leaves for a good home at first light", replied the nurse.

"Well I guess it'll be alright for her ta nurse him till then, just make sho someone's here wit her at all times", answered the doctor before returning to the baby.

Fighting the terrible darkness that threatened to claim her, Melinda began trying to sit up. She had to get out of here and take her baby to safety.

Looking up the doctor admonished, "Lie down gal, you ain't supposed ta be up."

Shaking her head, she defies him by throwing her legs over the side of the bed, "No, you can't take my baby."

"Gal you can't raise it here. Maybe when you done wit treatment you can have another, Good Lord knows yall ain't got no trouble breeding."

Entering, the nurse yells, "Get back into bed gal or I'll tie you to it."

Beyond caring, Melinda continued trying to rise while crying, "No, you can't have my baby, I want my baby." "Now you listen to me gal, get back in that bed or you'll regret it, sides the child's father will be here to collect him in the morning."

Reeling from this new revelation, Melinda hesitated just long enough for the nurse and two orderlies to force her back down upon the bed and restrain her hands and feet.

Yelling nearly incoherently, Melinda begins to scream at the top of her lungs and crying hysterically until she felt them pricking her arm with something sharp. While floating somewhere between the here and there, she heard the doctor say quietly, "Guess the birthing was too much for her fragile condition. Well, no never mind, got another negra gal just give birth few days ago, she can feed this one for one night I reckon."

With a lone tear falling from her eye she began drifting into the waiting darkness. She welcomed the numbness stealing over her and finally slept.

Chapter Forty-seven

They were trying to push her over the edge into a world of madness. But she would not lose her hold on reality. Melinda shuddered as a chill passed through her, as she was being spun round and round in the spinning chair. Her clothes and hair were plastered to her slender body from the dousing of the cold shower she'd received this morning.

Forcing her mind to remain blank, she closed her eyes and whispered a fervent prayer to God. "Please God", she prayed, "Help me, help me." Lying still as a corpse she recited the "Our Father Prayer", over and over in her mind.

Finally she heard the voice of the nurse tell the orderly to stop the apparatus. "Stop the chair, I believe she's had enough for one day. Sides a New Doc will be arriving this morning."

"That right", replied the orderly.

"Yes, new colored Doc finally due to arrive", she said with a sneer.

Grasping Melinda by the arm, she forced her to stand and walk back towards her room while saying, "Come on Gal lets go, ain't got all day".

With her head still spinning wildly, Melinda fought to stand unassisted. Forcing one foot in front of the other, she made the torturous walk back to the room.

Collapsing onto her bed, she curled herself into a ball and cried soundlessly as she once again prayed for God to rescue her from this living nightmare.

"Oh God, please let someone find me." The first thing she would do is contact her brother and inform him of what happened. One thing she was sure about was that her brother didn't know what Javier had done to her.

"Please Lord, keep my son safe until I can once again find him and hold him in my arms. She turned as she heard the key turning in the door.

The nurse entered and informed her that it was time to meet with the new Colored Doctor. "C'mon gal new doc wants to meet with you. And you listen to me, you better behave or I'll strap you into that chair you love so much."

When Melinda realized that they were not headed for the Doctor's chambers she asked, "Where are you taking me"?

"Well we gotta clean you up a bit, afore you see's the doc", answered the nurse.

Confused, Melinda stumbled and screamed as the nurse grabbed a fistful of her mangled hair.

"Get up gal, I'm a warning ya, make trouble and I swear, I'll make you pay", hissed the nurse.

"You're hurting me", whimpered Melinda as she stood to her feet. "Shush gal, let's go, they waitin for ya", quipped the nurse. Arriving at their destination, she gave Melinda a hard shove propelling her forward into a small room where a Barber stood with cutting shears.

Shaking her head, Melinda tried to back away but stopped as she felt the orderlies take her arms into their hands and lead her towards the chair.

"No, Please don't do this, I'll do whatever it is you want", pleaded Melinda.

"Quiet down girl, nobody gonna hurt ya, just gonna tidy ya up a bit", the Barber said softly.

"If we have to we'll strap you in, now sit still and let him do what needs to be done", instructed the nurse.

Melinda sat mutely as her tangled mass of auburn curls began to fall unto the floor. She retreated to that safe harbor deep within her consciousness and imagined herself far away singing softly to her son.

She imagined him smiling up at her as she crooned softly to him. So real was the vision that she was shocked and nearly leapt out of the chair when the Barber informed her that he was almost done.

"What's the matter with you gal, I'm just letting you know we almost done", admonished the Barber.

"Sorry, I'm sorry", stammered Melinda.

"Alright, we all done", he replied as he motioned for the nurse to come forward.

"Well, well, well, you look almost decent gal", the nurse remarked as the orderlies laughed.

Grabbing Melinda by the arm once more, she ushered her back towards the sleeping quarters.

"I thought that I was to see the doctor", Melinda inquired.

"You'll see the doctor soon enough and just so's you don't forget, I'll be right there in the room, so don't try nothing foolish", reminded the nurse.

Pamela smiled up at Javier as he kissed the bridge of her nose. "Buenos Dias amor, good morning love", she said as she gazed upon her face with tenderness.

"Good morning", he said as he looked upon Pamela and his young infant son, who was sleeping soundly in his small crib next to his mother's bedside.

He marveled at the small child who had arrived nearly three months early. He remembered the fervent prayers he'd prayed when he was brought the news that Pamela had gone into labor while off visiting an ailing relative. They had not thought the child would live, but it seemed as if God had heard the prayers and answered. It was a miracle that the child had survived and now he even seemed to be thriving under his mother's care.

"How are you feeling today my love", he asked.

"Well enough to leave my chambers, the doctor says that I can leave my chamber for a brief visit downstairs today", replied Pamela.

"In that case", he said while extending his arm, "Let's take a stroll to the parlor."

"My pleasure", whispered Pamela huskily as she left her small son in the care of his nurse.

As an after thought she turned and quickly said to the nurse, "Be sure to inform me immediately when my son awakes."

"Si, senorita Gonzalez, I will notify you immediately."

Pamela bristled at the woman's reminder of her unwed status. Gasping she turned to stare down the silly woman but was reminded of Javier's presence as he said suddenly, "Gracias, Senora, gracias.

Once downstairs Pamela decided to prick Javier's conscience when a little barb of her own, "Oh Javier everyone knows that we are unwed, and have a bastard child."

"Never, ever call my son a bastard", said Javier angrily.

Frightened by his outburst and the unspoken threat she read in his eyes, Pamela tried another tactic.

Bursting into tears she wailed, "Oh Javier how do we fix this."

Gathering her in his arms he said softly, "Soon we will be able to marry soon. The lawyers are nearly done with all the paperwork."

Sniffing loudly she wipes away more tears before turning to face him. After taking several breaths to compose herself she stated passionately, "I know that you are doing what needs to be done to make our son legitimate but, it seems to be taking longer than usual."

"Si, it has taken some time but we had to make sure that all was done legally, so that none could challenge our union", supplied Javier.

"Oh Javier, I'm sorry for being so emotional these days, I know that you are doing what is best for all of us, I trust you implicitly", she replied as she walked back into the safe cocoon of his arms. She fought the urge to make love to him, she knew that it was too soon after the birth of their son's birth. Changing the direction of her thoughts, she asked after the well being of his parents.

"So how is your mother, is she reconciled to our union"?

Sighing, Javier took a seat next to her and said sadly, "No, Mama can not bring herself to call you daughter yet. I simply don't understand her actions towards you or her wild accusations against you."

"Neither can I amor, how I wish that I could change her mind, our son needs the love of his entire family, I want him to know that he is loved", Pamela said in a tear choked plea.

Kissing her softly, Javier reassured her that his family would come around once they got a chance to visit little Augusto. "Shhhh, I'm sure that once the doctor says it is safe for them to visit him they will love him upon sight as much as I do."

"You are right amor, I will stop worrying, I know that you will make me your wife as soon as it is possible", answered Pamela as she laid her head upon his shoulder.

She let him caress her neck and smooth away the hair from her face as they sat in front of the fire.

They sat that way for what seemed hours, while Javier seemed content to do so for the rest of the afternoon. Pamela itched to be away, just this morning she had received a threatening note from Sheriff Comeaux. In the note he'd threatened to make public his association with her. As soon as she read the note she made plans to dispose of him without ever having to do the nasty little deed herself.

She nearly shouted with joy when the nurse entered to inform her that her son was awake and ready to be fed.

"Our time together never seems to be enough amor", she said as she began to rise.

"One moment spent in your presence is more than any man could ask for sweetheart", replied Javier as he kissed her goodbye.

"I will return on tomorrow to see how you are getting along. Please kiss my son for me and tell him that I Love him with all my heart."

Walking to the foot of the stairs, she said before turning and going up to her sleeping chambers, "I will count the moments until we are together again my love."

Javier watched her walk up the stairs with all the grace of a royal and wondered again how he could have been so lucky as to lose one child only to be blessed almost immediately with the birth of another. He tried never to think of the child he'd created with Melinda, the child that he would never get to know. Only God knew if the child had survived to be born. He convinced himself that he'd been given another chance with the birth of this new son.

It did not matter, he told himself, that he didn't love the mother of his son as he should. He told himself that in time he would grow to feel some genuine affection for her. He believed that in time he would grow to love her as much as she loved him. But he knew beyond a shadow of a doubt that even if he lived to be a hundred years old, he'd never love anyone the way he'd loved Melinda.

Swearing, he stalked off in the direction of the shipping yard upset and angry that he couldn't keep the thoughts of her at bay. Why? He wondered was she so much in his thoughts these days. Whether awake or asleep, she was always with him.

He often awoke to find himself wringing with sweat, his heart pounding and the blood rushing through his veins, knowing that he had just made love to her in his dreams.

Chapter Forty-eight

"Berto, are you sure about this information you were given by your investigator", asked Senora de Soto anxiously.

"Si, Mama, it is just as we thought Pamela did not give birth to this baby as she claims", replied Roberto.

"Dios, she is more of a snake than we thought, what do we do now Berto", asked Julio.

Rising to pace back and forth in front of the fireplace Roberto ran a hand through his hair and said, "Well for starters we try to find the one who did birth him."

"But my son, it will be nearly impossible to gain this information, and for certain Pamela will not help us with this", his mother shouted.

Placing his hand on his mother's shoulder, Julio squeezed slightly while saying, "We will find a way to prove it Mama, don't worry."

"But how can I not worry when we still don't know what happened to Melinda, and I know that Pamela caused her disappearance."

"My investigator is also looking into this also", Roberto said trying to reassure her.

"Dear God, how could she harm such an innocent person as Melinda", she cried out.

Turning to face the fire, she didn't see the look that passed between her two sons. Clearing his throat, Roberto made his way to his mother's side and took her hand into his. Seeing the serious look upon his face and noticing that Julio was also now standing within close proximity of her chair, she was suddenly alarmed.

"No, tell me that Melinda is still alive and so is my grandchild", she wailed before letting the tears flow down her cheeks.

"Shhhh, Mama listen carefully", said Julio.

"We believe that this child Pamela is claiming as hers and Javier's may actually be Melinda and Javier's child", supplied Roberto.

"What"? "How can this be", asked Senora de Soto.

Moving to close the door to the room, Roberto turned back to face his mother and said, "I now know that Pamela arranged for this trip in order to conceal the fact that she wasn't really pregnant and to further claim that she'd had the baby early."

When she continued to stare at him, he went on to say, "Remember I once said that Pamela was unable to have children, well last night I got the information I needed to confirm my suspicions."

"But how Berto", she queried. Dropping his voice to nearly a whisper Roberto said softly, "My ex-mistress is now the mistress of her physician, I had her question him while…"

"Say no more my son", she said cutting him off. "Use whatever methods necessary to accomplish this task. Never must Pamela be allowed to marry into this family, Never", she finished this last sentence with ice dripping from every word.

Laura sat fuming at the information she'd just received. Rene was seeing someone else. All these long months he had assured her that they would be together once the task of Melinda was taken care of. Now he always seemed to be too busy to see her or he was always being called away to Orleans on some flimsy excuse or another. She wasn't sure what had tipped her off but something told her to have him watched, and today she had gotten the information she sought.

"How dare he try and make a fool out of me, how dare he string me along like this", she said with her voice rising to a crescendo. Picking up one of the vases that adorned her dressing table she flung it against the wall and collapsed onto the fainting couch with her face buried in her hands.

With tears streaming from her eyes, she made a promise to make him pay for his lies, and most especially his unfaithfulness.

How could she have been such a fool to trust a man again, after all Jean Pierre had put her through with his lust for that negra servant, Mary Harmon.

"I vow to make you rue this day Rene! With my dying breath, I will make you regret the day you sought to use me", she said with a demented gleam shining in the depths of her eyes.

She now knew what had to be done but for the life of her she didn't want to face it. Rising slowly, she went to her dressing table and picked up the witch hazel, dabbed some on a soft cloth and dabbed it around her eyes.

Melissa A. Ross

Pinching her cheeks, she then put her hair back into the neat bun it was twisted into. After making sure that all was in order, she opened her bedchamber door and called for her maid.

"Celia, please call the housekeeper it seems that I have dropped one of the vases."

"Yes ma'am, I'll call her right away", came the reply from the servant.

Watching her head down the stairs Laura Lee swept the room with a parting glance and made her way to her husband's study.

Chapter Forty-nine

Melinda could hear the doctor's voice as he spoke kindly to the patient in his office. Sitting in the hallway she kept her head down so that her face would be hidden from view.

She cocked her head to the side and listened carefully to what he was saying. Something about his voice was vaguely familiar, but she could not fathom why.

Hearing the door open, she averted her eyes so as not to make eye contact, and stood when directed to do so by the nurse.

"Stand up gal, your turn."

When she hesitated, she heard the doctor say softly, "It's ok dear, come, no one will hurt you."

· Without looking up, she allowed the gentle hands to lead her into the office. She nearly giggled with relief when she heard the doctor instruct the nurse to remain outside for their visit.

"It's ok nurse, we will simply sit and talk, I'll be sure to call you if you're needed."

"But Doctor, I,…" the nurse interjected.

"No, I meet with all my patients alone, and I assure you that I've had lots of practice."

Infuriated by his uppity attitude the nurse said malignantly, "I'll leave, but not cause you say so, but cause I got other things to do." With another glance in Melinda's direction she added crudely, "Remember to mind your p's and q's gal."

Turning she exited the room, leaving Melinda alone to speak with the Doctor. Melinda's heart beat with trepidation over what the doctor would say when she told him who she was. Would he even believe her or would he simply believe what was in her records. Chewing her bottom lip, she pondered over what she would say to her new doctor. So caught up was she in her musings she jumped when he told her to have a seat and immediately got an apology from the kind man.

"Have a seat,…, Oh, I'm sorry, I didn't mean to startle you, Mary."

Looking up for the first time, the breath was sucked out of her at the sight of him. Standing abruptly she clutched her head in her hands and crumpled at the startled doctor's feet.

Rushing to get his bottle of smelling salts, he ran to her side and turned her over. Placing the bottle under her nose he examined her more closely to make sure that his eyes were not deceiving him. Gone was the vitality and the long beautiful auburn locks, gone were the soft rounded curves, and the glow in her cheeks but he would have known her anywhere.

Sure her locks were shorn closely to her head and she was thin as a rail, but here before him was the woman who had haunted his dreams for the last 2 years.

Watching her eyes flutter open, he instructed her to take it slow. "Just lie still for a moment, and yes you are not mistaken, it is me, Michael.

Crying softly, Melinda began to thank God for rescuing her at long last. "Oh thank God, thank you God."

"Shhhhh, it's alright now", he crooned. Crying earnestly now Melinda lost herself to the torrent that burst forth.

They sat with her head cradled against his heart for quite some time. Neither moved nor spoke until all the sobs wracking her body ceased. Finally when her tears turned to an almost hysterical sounding laughter, he spoke gentle words of reassurance.

"Everything is going to be alright now Melinda. Trust me to take care of things."

"I prayed for so long for someone to find me", she said once again on the verge of tears.

"I know, I know, we prayed also to find you. Hoping that you would be ok when we did", rushing on he added, "Your brother was nearly mad with grief when you left."

"I didn't leave, they sent me away, they planned this", she answered.

"What do you mean they sent you away", he asked with alarm.

"I heard them talking, they said that the de Soto's arranged for me to be sent away so that Javier could marry into the influential Gonzalez family."

"My God, Jean Charles will kill them when he finds this out! And your father, My God the man was nearly beside himself when you couldn't be found."

"My father", she shouted, "Was a willing participant in all of this."

"What? No, Melinda I was there when he came to tell Jean Charles and Ana of your disappearance", he replied.

"But, but I heard them say that the Savoie's as well as the de Soto's wanted me out of the way." When she saw him shaking his head in denial she said quickly, "No Michael, I heard them talking, I pretended to be asleep and listened while they discussed what was to be done with me."

"Who, Melinda? Who were these people", he asked quietly.

"I don't know Michael. They kept me blindfolded, but I will never forget their voices, never!"

"Well, first things first, we must get you out of here and get word to Jean Charles that you are safe", responded Dr. Jones.

"You mean they'll just let me go, just like that", she asked uncertainly.

"Melinda I'm a doctor remember, and I know who you really are, no matter what the records say. Besides, I doubt it will take Jean Charles long to get here", he said while enfolding her in his arms once more.

Helping her back into the chair, he walked to the door and called for the nearest orderly to find the administrator in charge of the clinic.

"You there, find the administrator at once", he instructed before closing the door once more.

"What do you mean Pamela is not as she seems", asked an angry Javier.

"Hermano, you know as well as I, that there is something strange about the birth of this child", answered Julio. Shaking his head no, Javier said, "Hermanito, I appreciate your concern, but I have made up my mind. I will marry Pamela."

"Mijo, listen to what we are saying", his father pled. "Pamela is not the mother of your son", his mother added quickly.

"Not his mother, what could you possibly mean by this Madre", asked a confused Javier.

"Sientate mijo, sit down my son", instructed his father before turning to look at Roberto.

After his brother was seated, Roberto stood before him and dived into giving Javier the information they'd uncovered.

"First and foremost I think that you should know that Pamela was involved in Melinda's disappearance".

Standing Javier shouted, "What madness is this Berto! Do you hate Pamela so much that you would accuse her of something so horrible as this?"

"Mijo we have the proof", inserted his father while clutching Maria's hand in desperation.

After receiving a disbelieving glance from his brother, Julio spoke up saying, "It's true Hermano, Pamela planned all of this, she is even now working with someone to make sure that Melinda does not return."

Seating himself once again, Javier looked up at Roberto and said, "How do you know this Berto? Do not give me a false hope that Melinda could still be alive and that our child could be as well."

427

Looking at each other with a new found hope, Senora de Soto stepped forward and took her son's hands into hers before saying, "We believe that the son Pamela is claiming to have given birth to, is actually the son of Melinda and yourself."

When he would have risen, Roberto placed a hand on his shoulder and squeezed softly. With tears glistening in his eyes, Javier struggled to digest the information and finally managed to say, "Dear God, can this really be true?"

Fighting to speak against the lump in her own throat Senora de Sota said gently, "Si, Mijo it is true." Cradling his head to her, she cried with him as a torrent of tears rocked him.

When he was finally able to compose himself, Javier turned to Roberto and demanded, "Tell me everything Berto." Catching the quick glance shared between his family members, he said enunciating every word, "NO! Berto, all, I want to know all!"

Chapter Fifty

Laura Lee made her way to the small cabin she and Rene used for their trysts. Making sure to keep in the shadows, she pulled up short as she spied Rene kissing a young woman passionately.

As the woman got into the carriage she watched as Rene fell all over himself bidding her goodbye. She watched the sickening farewell with a burning hatred and knew that she would never be the same again.

Watching the carriage pull away, she waited until she saw Rene removing his pants and began washing up. Slipping into the cabin she heard him humming happily and once again felt the waves of hatred wash over her.

Busy removing his pants to wash away the evidence of he and Pamela's lovemaking, Rene didn't hear Laura Lee as she entered the house with the drawn pistol.

Moving closer, Laura Lee aimed the gun and leveled it at his back. At the sound of the click, Rene spun around to face the intruder and pulled up short at the sight that greeted him.

429

Laughing nervously he said, "Laura Lee, darling you had me there for a minute, thought some outlaw had come to settle a score." Turning his back to her, he did a quick scan of the room to see where his shotgun was and finally spotted it on the kitchen table. Taking a step towards the kitchen he stopped dead in his tracks as Laura Lee said, "Stay where you are Rene, or I'll blow a hole right through your back."

Facing her again, he swallowed the lump in his throat and replied, "Now Laura Lee, what's this all about? I was just on my way to see ya,…,"

Cutting him off in mid-sentence she asked sarcastically, "For what reason? Seems to me you were already busy Rene."

"Oh that, listen that was just to ensure that you and I are free to marry soon", he said stalling for time.

"Marry?, Ha ha ha I'm already married Rene. What could I possibly want with two unfaithful husbands?" The coldness of the statement and the wild glint in her eye sent a shiver up his spine.

Feeling the sweat bead up on his forehead, he tried another approach by suggesting they talk things over.

"Let me explain Laura Lee, she's part of the plan to help us get rid of Jean Pierre."

"And just how is she going to accomplish this deed Rene", asked Laura Lee.

"We haven't worked all the details out yet, but sweetheart, it will be soon I promise", he said with a shaky laugh.

Leveling the gun now Laura Lee shakes her head and says, "No, no more lies Rene, you never loved me. You just used me to help you and that young woman get rid of the Harmon chit."

Rising he pleads, "Darling everything I've done, I've done for you, for us."

"You disgust me Rene, How could I have ever thought that you could really care for me", she asked.

"Laura Lee, honey, I do love you, that young lady is nobody, she…"

"Silence!", she commanded cutting him off. "Enough of your lies and your scheming!"

Jumping up, he dove for the gun and pulled up short as the shot reverberated off the walls. Looking down at his stomach, he watched as a crimson flood began staining the front of his shirt. Suddenly a burning sensation started from somewhere deep within and he fell to the floor writhing in agony. Laura watched in muted silence as he lay there clawing at his stomach and trying to form words. Numb with shock she listened as he finally managed to ask.

"La, Laura, whhhhy"?

Trembling and unable to speak after what she'd done, she felt the gun fall from her hands. Taking a step towards him on legs that felt as if they were made of wet paper, she stretched forth a hand to steady herself.

Suddenly, she became aware of someone screaming. Searching the room frantically she turned her head this way and that trying to locate to whom the voice belonged.

Finally her subconscious mind won the battle and she felt herself sliding towards the floor. Falling, she fell next to the outstretched body of the man whom she had loved beyond all reason. She turned her head slowly and looked straight into his dying eyes, glimpsing the pain, agony, and desperation etched so deeply in the planes of his face. Unable to block out his wide-eyed stare she succumbed to the blessed darkness and retreated to that safe place within where no one could ever harm her again.

Roberto, Julio, and Javier heard the shot as it rang out and slowly made their way towards the house. They had been holed up in the bushes when Laura Lee had approached the cabin.

Roberto and Julio restrained Javier as the three of them watched Pamela enter the dwelling and fall into the arms of the Sheriff.

They had watched in disgusted silence as Pamela had eagerly stripped down to her silk stockings and made love to Rene with wild abandonment.

The three stood silently, each lost to his own thoughts as she drove away in the hired carriage after kissing the Sheriff passionately several times. Just as they were about to come out of hiding, the Savoie woman had come upon the scene. Wanting to wait and discover her purpose for being here, they hid in the bushes and listened at the opened window.

Galvanized into action by the ringing out of the shot, the three ran around to the front of the cabin. Entering the small dwelling they searched for the shooter. Unsure of who was holding the weapon they carefully padded their way towards the kitchen. Upon entering they stood in shock at what greeted them. Bending, Roberto went first to the Sheriff, who was bleeding profusely from the large gaping wound in his stomach.

"Dear God", he proclaimed as he searched for some small sign of life from the injured man.

Javier moved to the woman, he examined her for wounds and when he found none, said, "She collapsed with shock no doubt." Motioning for Julio's help he added quickly, "Come let's see if we can revive her. Berto secure the weapons, we wouldn't want anymore surprises."

"Si, afterall there is nothing to be done for the Sheriff. He is beyond help now, May God have mercy on his soul", replied Roberto as he moved to gather all the weapons.

"Don't you think we should notify the authorities, Javier", asked Julio, eager to be away from the grisly scene.

Understanding his youngest brother's need to be away Javier nodded and said, "Si, you are right hermanito. Go, bring back the authorities, as well as Senor Savoie."

Leaving the confinement of the small cabin, Julio stumbled to his horse and rode at breakneck speed towards Bristol.

Stopping twice along the way, he emptied his stomach of it's contents and cursed his weakness. Wiping his mouth with the back of his closed fist, he staggered back into the saddle and rode on towards town. Fighting the urge to once again stop and give in to the heaves racking his body, he clenched his teeth and forced himself to ride on. Forcing himself to think of something other than what he'd just seen, Julio began remembering happier times when the family had celebrated various milestones. Losing himself to those happy memories, he made his way first to the Sheriff's office and then to the Savoie place.

Chapter fifty-one

Jean Charles wept with joy as Melinda walked into his arms. He'd thought her dead. He sat and listened with disbelief as the investigator informed him of her being discovered in a mental institution.

"Mellie, I thought you dead, oh God I thought never to see you again", he cried as he held her within the cocoon of his embrace. Melinda stood in the safety of his arms and cried along with him for several moments until Jean Pierre discreetly cleared his throat and said, "Now, now Jean Charles, you're not the only one who missed her."

Turning, Melinda stopped dead in her tracks and began backing away from him into the corner.

Alarmed, Jean Charles asked, "Melinda, what is it darling?"

Reaching, Jean Pierre took a step in her direction but halted when she shouted, "No stay where you are, don't come near me."

"Mon Fille, I simply wish to greet you, I have been so worried", he explained trying to calm whatever anxieties she was feeling.

"No, I'm not your daughter, a father wouldn't do as you've done", she answered.

"Melinda, just what is it do you feel papa has done", asked Jean Charles."

Speaking up for the first time, Michael stepped forward with an explanation into Melinda's puzzling behavior.

"Melinda believes that you, Mr. Savoie, played a role in her disappearance and commitment into this hospital."

"Never!", gasped an outraged Jean Pierre. "Daughter, I'd never do something so despicable, never!"

"Melinda Papa is telling the truth, we have searched together for you since you disappeared", argued Jean Charles.

"But I heard them, I,...", said a confused Melinda before stopping to stare at them quizzically.

"Why don't we all sit down and discuss this", suggested Dr. Jones.

When all parties were seated, Michael said, "Melinda recalls hearing her captors speak of the Savoie and de Soto families wish to be rid of her."

"But that's not true", interjected Jean Pierre. "Melinda listen to me, when you went missing, we were worried out of our minds. Javier went without sleep or food for days on end, searching for you, bebe."

"But, I heard them say that Javier had paid them to take me away so that he could marry into the Gonzalez family", supplied Melinda.

"Dear God, That's it, that's it. Roberto was correct in his belief that the Gonzalez girl was involved", said Mr. Savoie suddenly.

"What do you mean about Roberto, papa", asked Jean Charles.

"A few weeks ago the young man came to me with suspicions that this young woman, the Gonzalez daughter had worked with someone in Bristol to arrange for Melinda to be taken away and disposed of in some way. Now based upon what Melinda just said, there can be no doubt", answered his father excitedly.

"But why would she do such a thing", asked Dr. Jones while squeezing Melinda's hand gently.

"Roberto claimed that this young lady was obsessed with marrying his brother and would go to any lengths to accomplish the deed. He even believes she faked a pregnancy, and somehow acquired a baby boy to…"

"What", shouted Melinda. "You say she has a baby boy".

"Yes, it seems that he was born 3 months ago."

Turning to face Michael, Melinda asked with hope shining in her eyes, "Do you think it could be him?"

"Anything is possible Melinda, but we just can't be sure", he responded.

Watching the two, Jean Charles asked, "Melinda, Are you thinking that this is your son?"

"Yes, yes I am. My son was taken away at birth and the nurse said that his father would be here to take him away the following morning", she answered with tears wetting her eyelashes.

"What kind of twisted monster could do such a thing", asked her anguished father. Taking her hand into his, her brother turned to her and said, "Melinda listen, I know that you have your doubts but, I'm not so sure that Javier was involved in this in any way." Rushing on he said, "Mellie, Javier was so beside himself with grief when you disappeared that we all feared for his sanity." Listening quietly to all he said, hope leapt alive within her breast. What if her beloved had not sent her away? What if someone else had planned this and,..., oh the joy she felt at these thoughts. Seeing the hope alighting her features, her brother continued by saying, "Melinda, I believe that we should notify your husband's family that we've found you and that you are safe. I believe with all my heart that Javier is innocent of this dastardly deed." Suddenly another thought surfaced and looking into her brother's eyes Melinda asked simply, "And what about Javier, you've talked about Roberto, but what about my husband, what does he believe?" Jean Charles glanced nervously towards his father and Michael before attempting to answer the question posed by his sister. "Melinda, Javier is,..., that is, he believes you left him."

Pains of despair rippled through her at this statement causing her to suck in a shocked breath. Clutching her heart, she asked in a strangled voice, "But how could he believe such a thing of me?"

"Pretty much the same way you could believe that he had anything to do with what's happened to you", responded her brother. Realizing the logic of his well intended words, Melinda straightened and said, "Then I guess we must be going, I have a husband and a son awaiting my return."

Pleased that they had finally gotten through to her, Jean Pierre took a tentative step forward and was rewarded with a hug from his daughter. When their reunion was over he looked over at Michael and extended his hand saying, "I'll never be able to thank you enough for what you've done today Dr. Jones."

"No thanks necessary, Melinda's welfare means the world to me", answered Michael. Melinda asked her father and brother to leave the room so that she could have a private moment with Michael. After shaking hands with the young man, they exited to wait as she asked. Watching them close the door, she turned and said, "I will never be able to repay you for all you've done Michael. You've given me back my life."

"Well as I said, no thanks are necessary", he said dryly.

"Michael, I,...,", she stumbled trying to say the right thing. Cutting her off, he raised a hand and said, "No, some things are just not meant to be. No matter how much we may wish them, Melinda."

Crossing to where he stood, before he knew what she was about, Melinda molded herself against his small frame and kissed him sweetly. Michael, who had been caught unawares slowly crushed her to him and kissed her back, savoring the feel of her in his arms.

Breaking the kiss, Melinda stepped out of his embrace and said, "You will always hold a special place in my heart Michael, please try and find happiness. You deserve to love and be loved in return. My heart is, and always has belonged to Javier." Then before he could respond she slipped out of the door and into the hallway where her father and brother were waiting. Upon seeing her they stood and together helped her leave behind a place they never wanted to see again. Michael stood at the window and watched as the only woman he'd ever loved walked out of the building and out of his life forever. He nearly called out as she stumbled against the brightness of daylight momentarily blinding her. Watching as she was helped into the carriage he placed his hand against the window as she looked up in his direction once more. Michael knew that if he lived forever he wouldn't care for anyone else as much as he did Melinda. Whispering his undying love he said to the empty room, "Never, will there be another, Melinda." Taking out the handkerchief that she'd left behind when he'd first found her, he placed it next to his nose and breathed in the scent of her while saying, "I will love you with my dying breath." Turning away from the window he walked slowly back to his desk, letting the tears fall unchecked.

Chapter Fifty-two

The deputy looked at the grisly scene before him in utter dismay. Running a hand through his salt and pepper hair, he looked from one brother to the other, then in Laura Lee's direction before saying, "Well I reckon we ain't gon git no help from her."

Stepping forward Roberto said, "No, I'm not sure she is even still in this world."

"Si, as my brother told you, we heard the shot ring out and came in as quickly as we could. We found her lying beside him on the floor", said Javier as he spoke up quickly.

Looking again at the silent, staring, Laura Lee, the Deputy asked if anyone had gone to notify Mr. Savoie of the incident. "Anybody go to tell her husband?"

"Yes, but he is away on business. However, his mother has sent over servants to get Mrs. Savoie and take her home."

Moving to look out of the window, Roberto confirmed what Javier had just told the deputy as he said, "The servants have arrived. I will help them to put her in the carriage if that is alright with you, Senor?"

Gesturing towards the silent Laura Lee, Deputy Boudreaux said, "Can't see why not, she can't help us none." "This sho some kind of mystery, yep indeed, just can't figure out who shot the Sheriff, and why?"

Looking from one to the other the de Soto brothers kept quiet about their suspicions. Afterall it would do no good to tip their hand before they knew the whole story.

"Well, if you have no further need of us Senor, we will see to Mrs. Savoie and then be on our way back to Orleans", suggested Roberto.

Waving them off the deputy said, "Sure, nuthin else to be done, Sheriff dead and no body kin tell us what happened."

"Yes well, we will be in touch", said Javier as he walked towards the door. Tipping his hat he added, "Let us know if you discover anything new."

"Yep, will do", murmured the deputy before turning back to stare down at the dead Sheriff.

Pushing his hat up with his hand slightly he scratched his head as they heard him say, "Knew you'd get yoself inta sumptin like dis one day, just knowed it."

Once Mrs. Savoie was loaded into the carriage, the three men mounted their own horses and rode beside the conveyance as it made it's way towards the mansion.

When they were out of earshot of the deputy and his men, Julio turned quizzical eyes on his brothers and asked, "Why didn't you tell the deputy that Mrs. Savoie was the shooter?"

"Because we don't know that for sure. Maybe he had the gun and there was a struggle of some sort", suggested Javier.

"Yes but,…" he managed before interrupted by Roberto.

"We don't know what happened for certain and I for one am not willing to pull the Savoie's through a scandal of this sort."

"Neither am I", agreed Javier.

"Until we know more, I feel that it is best if we keep our suspicions to ourselves", Roberto said as he leveled Julio with a glare that bespoke, the matter is settled.

Upon arriving at the mansion, the young men dismounted and strode towards the house. They were let in by the manservant and shown immediately into the study. Mrs. Camille arrived soon afterwards more shaken than either of them had ever seen her.

Wrigging her hands she said, "Oh dear what am I to do? Jean Pierre is out of town, and I'm afraid for Laura Lee's sanity."

Rising, Javier strode to her side and tried to give her some reassurance. "If it is alright with you Madame, I would like to send over several servants from our place to assist you until your son returns."

"That would be wonderful, but can you tell me what happened? Why is she like this", asked an anxious Mrs. Savoie.

"We are unsure of what happened exactly, we only know that the Sheriff was shot to death and your daughter in law was present", answered Roberto.

Pulling her shawl snuggly around her shoulders, she said with fright threatening to overcome her, "Dear God, dead you say, and Laura Lee was there in the same room?"

"Yes ma'am, we found her lying beside him in an unconscious state", supplied Julio.

At this news Mrs. Savoie sat down heavily and cried out, "Oh Lord have mercy upon us, have mercy. Oh Mary mother of God pray for us, praaaaaay for us."

Concern etched Roberto's features as he came forward and asked, "Mrs. Savoie would you feel better if we had someone send for the doctor and have your daughter in law moved to a place where she could be helped?"

"But I don't know what to do, Jean Pierre always takes care of everything, why did he have to go out of town", wailed a helpless Mrs. Savoie.

"Shhhhhhhhh, all will be fine", Javier said as he sought to calm her fears. Speaking on he said, "We will handle all the details and send a servant to locate your son with the details of what has transpired."

"Thank You, she said weakly, before asking, "How can I ever thank you gentlemen for what you've done today?"

"There's no need madame, afterall we are,…, we are family", Javier said as he swallowed past the sudden lump in his throat.

Chapter fifty-three

Benito went in search of Senor and Senora de Soto as soon as he was notified of the return of Javier, Juilo and Roberto. Rising they went to greet them so that they could find out what news if any there was about Melinda.

Stepping forward Senora de Soto went straight into Javier's arms and asked with great anticipation, "Well, anything mijo, what have you discovered?"

Untangling her arms from around his neck Javier said, "Papa, Mama, let's go into the study, where we can discuss things in private."

Feeling that the news was not good, Senora de Soto's step faltered, and she cried out as she nearly fell to the floor. So upset was she that she had to be steadied by her husband who said, while wrapping his arms around her, "Calm your fears, Maria, I'm sure that things are not as bad as you fear", "Come let's do as our son wishes."

Entering the study they all took their seats and waited for Javier to speak. Taking a deep breath he looked his parents straight in the eye and said, "I must go through with the wedding to Pamela."

"What", shouted his father. "Que Pasa Mijo, I thought that you were going to Bristol to prove that Pamela was involved in your wife and child's disappearance?"

"Javier, listen to me, there must be some other way to get the information you seek, please my son don't do this thing", pled his mother.

A frustrated Javier swept his hand through his hair and said, "No this is the only way, I must marry her if I'm to ever find Melinda and the baby alive."

As his mother burst into tears, Roberto spoke up by saying, "Mama, in this Javier is correct, we will never find them without Pamela."

"But I don't understand, I thought that you had information about Pamela and that Sheriff, in Bristol", pointed out their father.

"The Sheriff is dead, Papa", Javier informed them with his shoulders slumped in fatique.

"Dead, what happened?, And please don't tell me he died at your hands, mijo", his father stated hesitantly.

"Papa how could you suggest such a thing", asked Julio from the corner of the room.

"No it's ok hermanito." Turning back to face his parents he said "I did not kill the Sheriff, we are unsure of exactly how he was shot."

At their puzzled expressions, Roberto spoke up by saying, "We heard the shot ring out, and when we ran in to investigate, we found him lying on the floor with Mrs. Savoie, lying next to him."

"Mrs. Savoie, your mother in law", they asked in unison. Rushing on Senora de Soto asks, "Dear God what was she doing there, what could she possibly have to do with all this"?

Looking uneasily from one to the other, Roberto took a deep breath and foraged ahead with their supposition of how all the pieces fit the puzzle.

"We are unsure of just why Mrs. Savoie was there, we don't believe that she was involved in Melinda's disappearance. Rather that she and the Sheriff were having an affair and that she somehow discovered that he was also involved with Pamela", explained Roberto.

"So you believe that she was involved with the Sheriff and then went to confront him because of this", asked his mother with astonishment. "Si mama, we heard them arguing, then a scuffle ensued, and next we heard a shot, and ran in, but it was too late, and now Mrs. Savoie is unable to tell us what happened", offered Julio.

"This just gets more unsavory by the moment", replied his father as he walked over to pour himself a snifter of taffia.

Suddenly their mother gasped and looked to Roberto as she asked, "Oh son what will you tell Beatrice?"

"Honestly I haven't thought that far ahead Mama. How can you tell someone that their mother may have shot her lover and then lost her senses", answered Roberto as he stopped his pacing just long enough to down the contents of his glass in one swallow.

"So with the Sheriff dead, you have no choice but to go through with this farce of a marriage, eh son", asked Senor de Soto.

"Si, Papa, as much as the idea sickens me, I must do this, if I'm ever to find Melinda", Javier said with disgust threatening to suffocate him.

With a resolve that came from the very depths of her soul, Senora de Soto declared, "You have my support in this Javier, and I will do whatever I must to help you in anyway I can."

Taking her in his arms and bestowing a loving kiss upon her cheek Javier expressed his gratitude, "Gracias Mama, I knew that I could count on you."

"And me also Mijo, know that you can count on me also", his father added.

After a few more drinks were downed and plans were made Roberto resolved to go in search of Beatrice and divulge the information about her mother.

Chapter fifty-four

"Father, wake up something's happened", urged Melinda as the carriage made it's way towards the Savoie Mansion. Blinking sleep from his tired eyes, Jean Pierre asked, "I wonder what could possibly being going on? All the lights in the entire house are on." Then a frightening thought surfaced as he said, "Dear Lord, please let mother be alright." Then, calling instructions to the driver, he sat back and rode out the final half mile up the driveway.

As soon as the carriage stopped he bade Jean Charles to see after his sister as he raced up the steps to the front entrance. Once there he stepped quickly through the entrance and began calling out for Laura Lee. Hearing the ruckus, Mrs. Camille hurried to meet her son, calling out she said, "Jean Pierre, is that you son?"

Relief flooded through him like water running through a ravine, and taking an unsteady step forward he said, "Yes, yes it's me Maman. I was so worried when I saw all the lights." Suddenly he grew quiet and listened as an animal like keening wafted through the house. Turning disbelieving eyes towards his mother he began to shake his head in denial, "No, no that can't be Laura Lee."

"Oh son, I'm so sorry, she,..." his mother said before bursting into tears.

Stuffing his fist into his mouth to keep all sound in, he rasped, "No God, no, not Laura Lee."

Exiting the bedroom old Doc Miller cleared his throat and said as he came face to face with Jean Pierre, "Mr. Savoie, I'm glad you've returned, I need to discuss Mrs. Savoie's condition with you." Before he could reply a loud piercing scream sounded from within and the doctor ran back inside with Jean Pierre close upon his heels. As an after thought he turned quickly and said to his mother, "Go get some rest Mamman, I will see to Laura Lee."

"Good night son", came her distraught reply as she walked with leaden feet towards her own sleeping chambers.

The sight of Laura Lee curdled Jean Pierre's blood within his veins. She was restrained with bonds on her hands and feet, and there was a crazed look in her eyes. Upon spying him she began to scream obscenities such as like he'd never heard. Attempting to somehow calm her, he stepped forward and in as gentle a voice as he could muster, "Laura Lee darling it's me Jean Pierre, don't you recognize me?"

In return all that echoed was a mad sounding laughter that sent chills up and down his spine. Looking to the doctor for some sort of solution he asked, "What can we do for her?"

"At this point Mr. Savoie the best thing would be to put her in a place where they specialize in helping people with mind disorders such as hers", answered Doc Miller.

Taking a seat upon the chair closest to her bed he looked at the woman there writhing indecently and speaking of obscenities he'd never imagined. Finally after a long mental battle, he sighed and said to the doctor, "Alright, I'll send her to a place where she can get help." The doctor then moved to inject something into Laura Lee's arm, which he claimed would help to calm her enough, so she could fall asleep.

Melinda and Jean Charles had been shown to their father's study and there they waited for him to return. Jean Charles sat with his arm around Melinda's shoulders as every scream from Mrs. Savoie sent her cowering within herself. Speaking in soothing tones he tried to calm her fears by saying, "It's alright Mel, I'm here now. Everything will be alright."

"She's mad, Jean, mad, just like Annie Bell", wailed Melinda before hiding her face in his chest.

"Shhhhh, those days are over for you, sweetheart. No one will hurt you, look at me", he said while coaxing her to look up at him, No one.

Lifting her head slowly, she began to let the warmth of security penetrate and flow through her body. "You're right Jean Charles, I'm safe here, I'm safe."

"Yes, you're safe, remember that feeling Mel", he reiterated. Pulling away he stood and walked over to the sidebar and poured an amber liquid into a snifter. Walking over, he handed it to Melinda and ordered her to drink. "Here drink this slowly, it will help." When she would have refused he said more forcefully this time, "Drink it Mel, it will help to calm you."

Taking the glass she took a small sip and let the warmth seep through her. After several more, she was feeling quite a bit more relaxed and sat there speaking to her brother of what was to come in the near future.

"What do you think will happen when he sees me Jean", she asked shyly.

"Well I for one would be beside myself with happiness, don't worry little sister, Javier will welcome you home with open arms."

Tearing up as she thought of her small son she said, "I pray that this baby is my son, otherwise I,...,"

"Hey this child is your child, you must believe that it is so, Cherié", crooned Jean Charles.

"Yes, I believe that it is just as you say", she said smiling brilliantly.

Jean Pierre entered the study as she stood smiling at her brother and allowed her happiness to take away some of the gloom that he was feeling.

Turning as he came in, Melinda went to him to offer some small measure of comfort by saying, "I'm so sorry father, what can you tell us about what's happened?"

"Thank you daughter", he said before continuing with, "It seems as if Laura Lee has had some sort of mental breakdown."

"But what could have caused such a thing", asked Jean Charles.

"It seems as if the Sheriff was murdered and that somehow Laura Lee was found unconscious at the site, God only knows why", answered Jean Pierre as he shook his head in disbelief.

"Sheriff Comeaux is dead, but how, when", asked Melinda in a loud voice.

"He's been dead now a couple of days, it appears he was shot through the stomach and died at the scene", confirmed her father.

"Now the question is, how does Mrs. Savoie fit into what occurred", remarked Jean Charles with a raised eyebrow.

"What are you thinking son", asked Jean Pierre in a voice tinged slightly with anger at his son's obvious assumption. Deciding not to open a new can of worms, Jean Charles changed directions quickly and stated the obvious.

459

"Nothing more than that maybe what she saw at the murder site has caused her to retreat to a safe place deep inside herself."

"Yes, that seems to be what the Doctor Miller believes as well", he said, surprised in the change of direction of his son's thought pattern. Jean Pierre had been sure that his son had been implicating Laura Lee in the murder. Now it seemed as if he'd had a change of mind. He couldn't be sure of just what Jean Charles was thinking. He hoped and prayed however, that his son would not openly accuse his wife somehow.

"What can you do for her father", asked Melinda in a voice filled with compassion.

Sighing deeply he said, "Ironically Dr. Miller just suggested sending her to same facility we just rescued you from dear."

"Dear Lord, I wouldn't wish this on anyone, there has to be something else you could do father", she answered.

Shaking his head sadly he said, "I wish there was sweetheart, but the doctor feels that it would be in everyone's best interest if she were with people who know about these types of disorders."

Noticing the dark smudges beneath Melinda's eyes, he remembered how far and fast they'd traveled and just how far they still had to go. "Listen I will handle this situation. My son, I will now need to depend upon you to deliver Melinda to her husband."

"That goes without saying father, we will rest for a couple of days and then set out for Orleans", answered Jean Charles.

"Well let me ring for a servant so that you can be shown to a room", said Jean Pierre.

Placing her hand upon Jean Pierre's arm Melinda said, "Father I wish to spend the night in my own home, please understand."

Acknowledging that he understood, Jean Pierre said sincerely, "I understand perfectly, my dear. Go with Jean Charles, I will come around tomorrow." Placing a kiss upon the top of her head, he then looked to his son and said, "I will send servants with you to ensure your safety."

"Thank you father", and extending a hand to Melinda he said, "Come along Mel, lets go get some rest."

Jean Pierre watched as they got into the carriage and rode off towards the small home that Melinda and Mary had once shared.

461

Looking up towards heaven he whispered, "She's home now Mary, once again she's home my love."

Turning away from the window, he walked back towards his desk and composed a note for the doctor's at the hospital. The note addressed to the administrator asked for admittance for his wife, Laura Lee Savoie, suffering from some sort of mental collapse.

After he signed the note, he moved his chair away from the desk and walked slowly out of the room and up the stairs to his own sleeping chamber.

Chapter Fifty-five

Pamela smiled into the mirror at her reflection and thought for the thousandth time that things could not be more perfect. Today was her wedding day. Finally all of her life's dreams were coming true. Javier had come by a week ago and demanded that they marry right away. It had been a mad scramble to arrange everything but all was in readiness. All the arrangements had been made and the quests were now arriving. Looking at her reflection she said to the maid, "Bring me the pearls and string them through my hair, Gisela."

"Si, senorita, they will match your gown perfectly", replied the maid as she moved to do Pamela's bidding.

Pamela dusted the bridge of her nose and applied a small amount of lip paint to her mouth. Turning as the door opened, she greeted her mother by asking, "Have the de Soto's arrived yet Madre?"

Unmoved by her daughter's concern for only herself, for such as had always been the case, Mrs. Gonzalez said, "Yes they have just arrived and been seated in the parlor until the ceremony."

"Make sure they are afforded every comfort Madre, no indulgence is to be denied my future in laws", remarked Pamela.

"As you wish Pamela, is all in readiness for the ceremony", asked her mother.

"Yes, all is perfect, just as it should be", answered Pamela with the smug smile upon her features that nearly always drove her mother to slap her face. Giving in to the urge, to wipe the smile from her conceited daughter's face she asked, "And how about the baby? Has he been fed and put down for a nap?"

Turning hateful eyes towards her mother, Pamela screeched, "The baby has been seen to. This is my day! The day I am to marry the man I have loved all my life."

"Pamela calm yourself, I only meant to,…,"

"You meant to take some of the focus off of me and place it on the child", Pamela interrupted.

"But Pamela, he is your child, yours and Javier's. You should be more concerned for his welfare", argued her mother.

Rising to stand before her mother Pamela said through clinched teeth, "Don't you dare speak to me about the child's needs! You've certainly never cared about mine."

A knock sounded at the door preventing Mrs. Gonzalez from answering, as Pamela called out, "Come in."

Maria entered the bedchamber and greeted Pamela, "You are beautiful child, my son will be pleased.

Glowing at the compliment Pamela said, "Gracias,..., Madre."

She'd decided to throw in the "Madre" just to see if she could get some satisfaction from seeing Senora de Soto's discomfort. Pamela knew that Javier's mother was against the marriage but had had no choice in the matter, as her son had threatened to marry with or without the family's support.

However, today was not the day. Lifting her chin, Maria looked her square in the eye and said, "Bienvinidos a la familia, mija." She smiled brightly to hide the fact that the rising bile was threatening to spill forth at any moment.

Pamela, momentarily thrown off by her seemingly good natured attitude was farther startled as Maria gathered her in an embrace and bestowed each cheek with a motherly kiss.

Maria almost laughed aloud at the look of pure wonderment on Pamela's face. In fact she had to cover up the laughter bubbling inside with a cough. Placing a delicately gloved hand over her mouth she coughed gently before saying, "The weather lately has been a little unsettle, but who's to complain." "Today I gain another daughter. Are you ready to go down now Pamela, my son awaits anxiously." Totally mesmerized by her soon to be mother in law, Pamela answered breathlessly, "Si, I have been ready for this moment all my life."

Stretching forth a hand, Senora de Soto gestured towards Senor Gonzalez and said, "Then take your father's arm and walk down to your future."

Filing out into the hallway, Senora de Soto, followed by Pamela and her mother, paused to place Pamela's veil over her face. With a parting wish for her happiness, Maria descended the stariwell next to Senora Gonzalez and took her seat next to her husband.

Benito stared in shock at the young woman standing before him in the entranceway. Crossing himself he said, "Dios Mio, Senora de Soto, you've returned." Swaying unsteadily, he had to be helped by Jean Charles to remain on his feet. Reaching out a hand Jean Charles said, "It's ok Benito, come show us inside and notify the de Soto's that we are here". Benito unable to move until this moment said excitedly, "You must stop him, Senor Savoie, you must, before it is too late."

"Slow down Benito, too late for what", asked a confused Jean Charles.

"The wedding, he is to marry the Gonzalez girl today, in fact they are all there at this very moment."

Fighting a wave of nausea Melinda shouted, "No, I can't let this happen."

"Where are they Benito", asked Jean Charles.

"Come, come I'll show you the way", answered Benito as he jumped inside the waiting carriage.

Javier sucked in breaths of air to calm himself as Pamela glided down the aisle towards him. Dear God to be married to one such as she was almost unimaginable. But if he was ever to be reunited with his one true love, he had to go through with this unholy union. He watched as she moved closer and closer towards him and had to force himself not to recoil visibly when her father placed her hand on the bend of his elbow.

"Who gives this daughter to this son in Holy Matrimony", asked the Priest.

"I do", answered Senor Gonzalez.

Javier watched as if in a trance as her father then lifted her veil and placed a fatherly kiss on her upturned cheek. He forced a smile as Senor Gonzalez then shook his hand and said, "I give my daughter into your hands for safekeeping the rest of her natural days."

Swallowing deeply, Javier said, "Gracias Senor, I will strive to never disappoint you."

Turning to face the priest Javier listened as he droned on and on about the sanctity of marriage and was transported back in time to another marriage. A marriage, which had been one of great joy and fulfillment. Javier was so deep in his thoughts that he didn't hear the priest instruct him to repeat his vows. He was suddenly brought out of his thoughts when Roberto nudged him gently. "I'm sorry, could you repeat the request", he stammered.

"I understand my son, she is very beautiful, no", remarked the unknowing priest.

"Si, padre, I apologize once more", "I'm ready now to get on with the ceremony", said Javier.

"Ok my son, then place the ring on her left finger, and repeat after me", replied the priest. Javier took the ring from Roberto and placed it on Pamela's cold hand, but just as he opened his mouth to speak, a loud shriek sounded in the room. Turning to view the source of the scream, he stood rooted to the spot as the young woman made her way up the aisle.

"No, you can't do this", shouted Melinda.

"Dear God" shouted Senor de Soto as he reached to revive his wife who had fallen in a dead faint.

Shouts of disbelief bounced from every corner of the room as they looked from Melinda to Javier. Javier stood in shock as he tried rationalize what was happening. Melinda was alive and standing in the very room before him, but how? Then out of nowhere he heard another voice, one so filled with malice and hatred that he shuddered. Turning he faced Pamela in all of her rage and listened as she screamed, "No, go back, never will I allow you to take him away again." Before anyone could imagine what was happening she ran to attack Melinda. Reaching her before anyone else, she knocked her to the floor began clawing at her face.

In a voice as demented as could be imagined she repeated the phrase, "He's mine, he's mine,...,"

Fighting off the unstable young woman, Melinda tried to cover her face with her arms and cried out as Pamela's talons dug into her flesh.

Finally able to move, several men ran to pull Pamela off of Melinda.

Jean Charles was the first to reach the two women, and dragged Pamela away from his sister by her hair. Roberto and Julio then assisted him by restraining her arms and legs.

Javier didn't stop however, until he had Melinda in his arms. "Is it really you, Melinda", he asked as he held her closely. Crying earnestly, she answered, "Yes, it's me, I'm home Javier."

Running his hands up and down her arms and body he said, in between kisses, "Never will I let you out of my sight again, mi amor, never."

"My love, am I really still your love Javier", she asked skeptically.

"Forever Melinda, I will love you forever, never have I stopped loving you and never will I stop loving you", he declared loud enough for everyone in the room to hear.

Wrapping her arms around his neck she cried tears of joy and sorrow all at the same time. She whispered a prayer of thanks to God for answering her prayers, for bringing her home safely to her loved ones. When she was finally able to speak she asked, "Where is my son?"

Gasps were heard throughout the room. Stepping forward, Senora Gonzalez said quietly, "He is upstairs with the nurse, I will have him brought down to you."

"You traitor! I'll make you pay for this!", screeched Pamela as she renewed her efforts to once again attack Melinda. Twisting her arm up high behind her back, Julio recoiled and almost let go as he saw desire burst into flame and dilate her pupils.

"Dear God, you're sicker than any of us knows", he said disgustedly. "Come brother, let us remove her to a more secure place", he added as together they dragged Pamela out of the room.

"No, I will go up to him, please take me to him", answered Melinda.

"Please, come with me", gestured Senora Gonzalez as she led Melinda and Javier upstairs to the nursery. No one moved as they left the room, with the buzz of conversation swelling to a crescendo. Once upstairs she lead them to the nursery and upon opening the door, dismissed the nurse from her duties. "You are no longer needed Senora, you may return to your home, I will see to it that you are paid for your services."

Senor Gonzalez, who'd, watched all of this in mute silence suddenly clutched at his chest and fell to the floor writhing in pain. Jean Charles rushed to his side and ordered someone to find a physician.

Senora de Soto awoke to this new development and nearly swooned again, had it not been for Juan saying, "Don't you dare faint again, Maria, or I will leave you to your own devices."

Taking their mother by the hand, Graciela and Maria Antonia, walked her slowly towards the foyer where she could compose herself. "Oh, I can't believe it, our prayers, they've been answered", she said once out to the room. Graciela answered with tear steaked cheeks, "Si, Mama, Melinda has come back, she's been found."

The three cried for several moments before composing themselves and determining how they best be of help in the surprising turn of events.

"Well I will go and direct the servants and help to disperse all the guests. Dear Lord, has anyone informed Xiomada, of her husband's condition", asked Senora de Soto suddenly.

"Si Mama, Father sent someone to inform her immediately", answered Maria Antonia.

"Praise God for that. Well, come we must take charge of things until Xiomada is able", said Maria as she walked back into the room. Suddenly a shout of alarm went forth as it was discovered that Pamela had managed to climb from the window into the street, to freedom.

Senor de Soto sent men to locate the Sheriff and hired some of his own men to find her, with instructions to bring her back at all costs. On and on the search with no one being able to discover her whereabouts. Then one evening as the de Soto's sat to dinner, nearly two months after Melinda's return. Benito entered the Dining Parlor to announce that senorita Gonzalez had been found. Pamela it seemed had been found wondering the streets of the small town of Houma. In her maddened state she had attempted to flee from authorities and had been struck by an oncoming carriage. She had been killed as she tried to run across the street and the horses trampled her. No one moved or said a single word for several moments, before Senor de Soto stood and said simply, "May God have mercy and give her tormented soul eternal rest."

Later that evening after Javier and Melinda retired to their sleeping chambers, and while holding thier small son in her arms, his beloved had cried until he feared she would do herself harm.

"Shhhhhh, amor, it's alright, everything is alright", he assured her.

"I wondered if I'd ever see him again, it was so horrible when they took him away", she said through her tears.

"Melinda listen, you are safe now, we are together once again, all will be well from this day forward", Javier said passionately.

"Say you love me Javier, say that you love me", she cried, holding their child gently.

"Until time itself ceases, will I love you Melinda", he declared.

Melissa A. Ross

Epilouge

The storytelling of all the accounts of she and her beloved's life had taken a visible toll on old Ms. Melinda. Always conscious of her mother's frailty, Camille very quietly ushered all of her extended family members out of the room so that her mother could rest.

Later that evening as Camille sat slumbering near her mother's bed she heard her name being whispered. Blinking sleep from her eyes she looked towards the bed and noticed a faint light surrounding her mother. Unsure of just what was happening she quickly shook her eleven brothers and sisters awake and watched as her mother began lifting her eyes towards the ceiling. They watched as she smiled brightly and said, "I knew you'd come for me when it was time." They watched in utter amazement as the light bathed their mother's features completely and seem to draw her life's essence away. They cried silent tears as they realized that the time had come for her to move on to that land of everlasting joy, and peace. They gasped collectively as they saw not one but three figures standing at the head of the bed. There before them was their dearly beloved father, their

477

grandfather, Jean Pierre, and their grandmother, Mary Harmon. They watched as their father opened his arms and the essence of their mother glided into his embrace, as the two were reunited and greeted each other lovingly. They sat silent as their grandparents then greeted their mother. "Welcome my child", Mary Harmon said to her daughter as both of her parents embraced her. The joy upon her face told them all they needed to know. Turning back to look at them Melinda said softly, "I must go now, my time here has ended, but know that I will always be with you", and pointing to her heart said, "Here, I will always be here."

They listened as their father said, "Come my love it is time to go now. Are you ready?"

"I have been ready for forty years my love", she answered simply.

"I too have been ready for your arrival for quite sometime now", he replied. With the light fading they heard their mother say to their father," Forty years is a long time, do you still love me Javier?"

Through his deep laughter they heard him say simply, "Yo te quiero para siempre, mi amor, I will love you forever, my love.

About the Author

Melissa A. Ross, a Licensed Minister, has been writing for over ten years. While she's written many things to include a Monthly Marriage Corner piece, published in the True Spiritual-Grapevine. This is her first attempt at a Historical Romance. Her favorite genre to read is Romance novels. She reads everything from Western, to Modern, and even Paranormal Romances. After years of friends and family telling her just how good her work was, the author decided to work towards publishing her first book. Love is Forever, the first of a trilogy, was a joy to write. She is now researching material for the next book, and hopes her reader's find enjoyment in the series.

Printed in the United States
719400001B